A WOMAN BURNT

A WOMAN BURNT

Imayam

Translated from Thamizh by

GJV Prasad

SIMON & SCHUSTER

London · New York · Sydney · Toronto · New Delhi

PARAMOUNT

First published in India by Simon & Schuster India, 2023

1 3 5 7 9 10 8 6 4 2

Simon & Schuster India
818, Indraprakash Building,
21, Barakhamba Road,
New Delhi 110001.

www.simonandschuster.co.in

Paperback ISBN: 978-93-92099-81-6
eBook ISBN: 978-93-92099-82-3

Typeset in India by SÜRYA, New Delhi
Printed and bound in India by Replika Press Pvt. Ltd.

CONTENTS

PART ONE

1

When she entered Revathi's room, Amaravathi's body was trembling slightly. She gritted her teeth. She glared at Revathi as if she wanted to set her on fire. With her eyes tearing up, she asked, 'Is what your father says true?' Since Revathi didn't say anything, neither no nor yes, it was clear to her that Natesan had spoken the truth. So, she became even more enraged than before.

'Are you even my daughter?' she shouted in anger.

Revathi's mind was not so much on giving an answer to Amaravathi as on figuring out who must have tattled on her to her father.

'Who is he? The whole town seems to know about it!'

Revathi did not open her mouth.

'Where is he from?' After being asked this many times, she opened her mouth, 'Burma.'

'Is he working in Burma?'

'...'

'What caste?'

'Refugee.'

'Refugee?' There was so much disdain in Amaravathi's voice. She glared at Revathi as if she were saying, 'Why couldn't you have died?' As if it had struck her just then, she asked with hatred and bitterness in her tone, 'Is refugee a caste?'

Amaravathi couldn't stand any longer. Her body was shaking in anger. So, she sat on a corner of Revathi's bed.

'Are they Thamizh folks?'

'Mmm.'

'Those who went from Tamil Nadu, and came back as refugees?'

'Mmm.'

'Then, how can he be without caste?'

'...'

'Is he a Muslim?'

'No.'

'Christian?'

'No.'

'What's his name?'

'Ravi.'

'What a lovely name,' Amaravathi looked at Revathi as if she was seeing a disgusting object. Then she asked as if she was taunting her, 'What has saar studied?'

'...'

'What does saar do?'

'He drives an autorickshaw.'

'What? He drives an autorickshaw?' She asked loudly. 'Thoo,' she hawked and spat. Even though she was uncontrollably angry now, she still spoke in a measured tone, 'It is the highest job in the country. You have caught a good groom. It is so wonderful to get such a groom. Everyone will praise you for this.'

She sat for a while without saying anything. As if she didn't even like to look at Revathi, she kept staring at the wall in front of her. Even though she didn't speak a word, her eyes were watering all the time. 'Do you know what your father was asking me for the past one hour?'

Revathi didn't open her mouth. She didn't look even once at Amaravathi. She sat still like a stone sculpture.

Amaravathi and Natesan had been married for twenty-six years. In all these years he had never spoken to her in anger, scolded her, or spoken to her disrespectfully, or shoved her around, or told her to get lost. He had done all this in one hour.

While she had been shocked by his words and action, she was even more shocked by what Revathi had said. 'How could you do this to us? How did you have the guts to do this? When did you learn to lie? Don't you have any shame?'

Revathi didn't open her mouth.

'Where did you see the guy; how did you meet saar?' She piled on the questions one after another. As she asked each question, Amaravathi used the word 'saar' to refer to him deliberately. She said it with as much disdain as possible.

She looked at the silent Revathi and said, 'This is not so uncommon in the world. Just tell that boy that my family will not agree to our relationship. The problem will be solved. Will you do it?' Amaravathi asked. Not a peep out of Revathi.

'Just tell him, "I am not that kind of girl. I can't do this. My father and mother will die if they come to hear of it." Will you say this?' Amaravathi asked. Revathi's lips didn't move at all.

'I am asking you, the mother who gave birth to you, will you tell him?' When Amaravathi asked this, it was five a.m., early in the morning. Even then, not a word escaped from Revathi's mouth.

'I have given birth to a stone,' saying this Amaravathi began to weep.

2

Whatever struck Natesan's mind when he was about to leave for school, he paused and sat down on the chair placed in the hall. He checked the time. Then he gazed at the framed photos hung on the wall in front of him. He looked at the photo of his parents, his wedding photo, and Revathi's photo. The photo taken when Revathi turned one, the photo of hers when they had ritually shaved her head, the one taken when her ears had been pierced, the photo taken when they had celebrated her reaching puberty—he looked at all her photos one after another. For some reason, he kept looking again and again, only at her photos. He sighed deeply, as if looking at the photos had induced great fatigue in him. Then he wondered whether to talk to Revathi. In his anger, he hadn't spoken to her for a week. How could the problem be resolved if he didn't talk to her? He thought that it would be good to talk to her and bring the issue to a close. So, he called Amaravathi who was making coffee in the kitchen. When she came, he said, 'Call Revathi'. Her face changed immediately.

She was confused whether to call Revathi or not, she dreaded what clash would happen as a result. So, she stood there in silence. As if he understood her hesitation, Natesan said, 'I will try to talk to her. She will respect my words.'

'Isn't it getting late for school?' Amaravathi asked softly. As he realised that she was trying to change the subject, Natesan looked towards Revathi's room and called out, 'Revathi.' Revathi couldn't hear him. So, she didn't come out. That Revathi hadn't come out even though Natesan had called her made Amaravathi even more tense. 'Call her,' he said to Amravathi who was standing there, helpless, not knowing what to do. When she realised that she couldn't say anything to change his intention, she went to Revathi's room and brought her out to the hall.

'You can go,' said Natesan to Amaravathi. She didn't leave. She looked at Natesan and Revathi in turn. She was perspiring, worrying about what he would ask and what she would say in reply. Her eyes misted over. He didn't pay any attention to her and said, 'Sit, amma.' Instead of sitting where he pointed, Revathi went and stood leaning against the wall that had the photographs. Amaravathi went to the kitchen.

'Sit down, amma,' he said again. She didn't sit. She didn't look at Natesan. She stood looking at the floor.

After checking his wristwatch, he asked. 'Is all that I have heard true?'

'…'

'Only if I know whether it is true of false will I be able to take the next step.'

'…'

'Even if it is true, it doesn't matter. Tell him nicely that my family has fixed a different match for me, that all this will become a problem. The matter will be over. After all, it is only a chatting, a conversational relationship, isn't it? And for this, why are you lying around in your room, refusing to eat or have a bath or talk to anyone?'

'...'

'If you find it difficult, you don't need to tell him. I will tell him. Only if it is said properly, will he understand.' Revathi didn't open her mouth. To see her standing withdrawn into herself, unwashed, not having eaten, with her hair uncombed, with even her clothes unchanged, caused him great irritation. Natesan was angry. He was in a rage. But he didn't show anything. In an even tone, he said, 'I trust you would not have done anything very wrong. After all, you are my daughter.'

'...'

'Do you know how much your mother is crying?'

'...'

'Do you know how angry your brother is?'

'...'

'There is no peace in the house any longer, you know?'

'...'

'I am a Headmaster. If people realise that my daughter herself is acting like this, will they have any respect for me? If you yourself don't listen to me or respect what I say, why would the teachers who work with me, the students who study with me, listen to me or respect me?'

Slowly, Natesan started to lose the patience he had displayed when he began the conversation. 'It isn't right that you keep silent. It is you who should speak, not me!'

'...'

'Tell me what's in your mind. You are my daughter. I believe you will listen to me.'

'...'

'I have asked around and I don't think the boy will suit you. He doesn't look like a good boy. I am not saying this because of any hostility.'

'...'

'There is too much of a difference between you and that boy. There will be ego problems within a week. Then, it will turn into beatings, fights and disputes. You can do whatever you want before you get married, before the thaali is tied. After that, you can't do anything even if you wish to. This is Tamil Nadu. Not a foreign country.'

'...'

'Your silence tells me that you are steadfast in your decision. You think only what you think or do is correct! Isn't it?'

'...'

Revathi did not open her mouth. Didn't even move. Didn't shift her feet or her position. She didn't look at Natesan even by mistake.

'Do I know or not when to get you married? What have I learnt in these many years of teaching? Am I a teacher who can't understand the minds of youngsters?'

'...'

'It is usual to get a maths problem wrong. Don't we check if we got the answer right or wrong? Look at it like that. When we realise we have made a mistake, we must redo the solution to the problem. Isn't that the way? How much you wept when you returned home because you got a step wrong in your Plus Two exams! Have you forgotten? The problem you tackled in your Plus Two exams wasn't a major one. Your problem now is the major one.' Having said this, Natesan remained silent for a little while. He looked angrily away from Revathi. Then he raised his voice a little.

'Will you insist your calculation is right because you did it, even when you know it is wrong? Because your heart desires something how can a wrong move be the right one?'

'...'

'I teach a hundred youngsters every day. I have taught you as well. What I am speaking of now is not addition or subtraction. It is on how to act to earn other people's respect, how to live; understand? You have studied in a good school. You have studied in a good college. You understand everything. Go. Go, have a bath, change your clothes, eat, think of going to work. I will go now. Do not bring dishonour to the names of your parents,' saying this, Natesan picked up his bag and left the house slamming the door behind him.

3

Amaravathi tried many strategies to convince Revathi. Revathi didn't listen to her or to her father and was determined to marry Ravi. She didn't agree to an arranged marriage with anyone else. When Amaravathi contemplated how to change her mind, it struck her that perhaps she should go to Ravi's house and talk to them directly. Throughout the night she lay awake thinking of how to go to his house, what to say, how to fight. In the morning, soon after Natesan left for school, she left for Ravi's home.

After crossing the Drivers' Quarters, Amaravathi arrived at Burma Nagar, and asked a number of people which was Auto Ravi's house and found it. Ravi's father, Ganapathi, mother Kokila, and elder sister Priyanka, were all in the house. Amaravathi disliked the house at the first sight itself as she entered it. The house had only two rooms. It was in a mess. The very look of the house increased her anger. As soon as she entered the house, without giving the others the opportunity to ask her who she was and what she wanted, when she announced, 'I am Revathi's mother,' all three, Ganapathi, Kokila, and Priyanka, were taken aback, their faces showing their surprise. They didn't know what to say or how to speak. They even forgot to invite her to sit down. Ganapathi and Kokila didn't open their mouths. It was Priyanka who brought a stool and said, 'Please sit down.' Looking at the stool with disgust, Amaravathi said, 'I didn't come here to sit down.'

In her anger, she forgot all that she had thought of the previous night, as to how to speak and what to say. She felt like shouting, 'Is what your son doing right?' She broke into a sweat in her rage. She found it difficult even to stand. She sat down on the stool. Thinking that the matter would be spoiled if she started off in anger, she asked a few general questions first.

Ganapathi and Kokila sat on the floor next to Amaravathi's stool. Priyanka stood a little apart.

'We were born in Burma. We stayed in a place called Tons.'

'Where is it?'

'It is in Bhamo district.'

'What were you doing there?'

'We did different jobs.'

'Were there a number of Tamilians there?'

'Around 1930, Tamilians were a majority in Rangoon.'

'Why did you come here, then?'

'In 1938, the Burmese rebelled against the British. Instead of supporting them, Tamilians supported the white men. It was because of this that we had to return to India.'

'How were you affected by it?'

'In 1960, the rule of the whites was over and Military Rule took over. The Burmese rioted saying that Tamilians who supported the white rule should no longer stay in the country. They chased us out.' Kokila said. Ganapathi, who had kept silent till then, said, 'Not Military Rule, the rule of the King.' Kokila didn't pay him any attention. Amaravathi understood immediately that Kokila wasn't one to respect her husband.

'Since the Burmese beat up Tamilians and wanted us to leave the country, all the Tamilians asked India, "Please send us a ship, please put an end to our tears." In 1963, India sent three ships.'

'You people came in that?'

'Yes.'

'How did you come to this town?'

'For refugees from Burma they had set up camps at Ponneri, Senkundram, and Thiruvallur. We were in Ponneri camp. We did business in Burma Bazaar.'

'You were in business?' Amaravathi asked in a surprised tone.

'Our parents sold the stuff we had brought from Burma on the platforms there. As time went by, they began to buy stuff from people coming by ship and selling it there. It is because people from Burma did business there that it came to be called Burma Bazaar.'

'Why did you come to this town?'

'They gave citizenship to people who had come from Burma. They allotted us land in several towns. Because we were married, we got a place in this town.'

'Where are your relatives?'

'Some are in Ponneri. One or two are still in Burma.'

Kokila seemed to be a person full of speech. She was the kind to answer all questions, both asked and unasked. It seemed that Ganapathi would talk only if she signalled with her eyes. Kokila was chubby and quite fair. When Amaravathi was thinking how to bring up Revathi's problem, Priyanka offered her some water. 'No,' said Amaravathi in one word, without any grace or consideration.

'Are you married?' She asked Priyanka. She didn't reply. It was Kokila who answered.

'She is the age. But we haven't found any boy. I have contacted people in Ponneri, Senkundram, and Thiruvallur camps. But all the boys work in Burma Bazaar. That is the problem.'

'When is your son's marriage?' Kokila didn't open her mouth to answer Amaravathi's question. Amaravathi showed the anger that she had controlled till then.

'You seem to be good people. That is why I am telling you. It is not good to spoil the mind of a family girl. Tell your son this. You also have a girl.'

'We know our status. We are living according to it.'

'Coming to our street. Coming near our home. Standing at our street corner. Are these things done by a boy who belongs to a good family?' Amaravathi asked.

'The day he began to drive an auto, he stopped listening to us.'

'If your son comes once again near our house, I will complain to the police. The issue will blow up. Tell your son.' Amaravathi spoke as if ordering them.

When Kokila, looking at her directly, said, 'Do tell your daughter as well,' Amaravathi lost control on her rage.

'Is it my daughter who roams around insolently?' She asked loudly.

'That is not what I said. I meant that if the female doesn't give encouragement, how can any male do anything?' Amaravathi didn't pay any heed to the conciliatory tone of Kokila's. She raised her voice even more, and with more anger, more rage in her voice, she said, 'What can a girl do if she is harassed day and night? Isn't the female heart full of sympathy? If the boy had been brought up correctly everything would have been right.' She said with firmness.

It looked as if Kokila was getting slightly angry. 'You have no idea how we were in Burma. We became beggars only on the day we boarded the ship for India. We regret coming to India every day,' she said.

'I haven't come to listen to your Burma story. I came to ask you if you think what your son is doing is right. He stands in front of our house with our daughter's name tattooed all over his body. He stands there having slashed his hand with a blade.' Amaravathi began to lose control over herself as she said this.

'We ourselves learnt of this only a month ago. We are fighting with him about it.'

'It is disgusting to witness your son's doings. Will he look after his job or run after a female?'

'If the female doesn't smile at him, why would a male go after her?' Kokila spoke in general terms. But it enraged Amaravathi.

'From now on, if your son comes near our house, hands slashed by a blade, or with tattoos on his body, I won't simply stand around talking. If like this, some cur arrives with your daughter's name tattooed all over his body, with his hand or leg slashed with a blade, and stands outside your house, what would you do?'

'Don't get angry,' Ganapathi said in a low voice. Kokila turned her face away. Priyanka didn't say anything.

Amaravathi got up from the stool suddenly. She said as if issuing a warning, 'I have said what I wanted to say. If now I see the guy near my house, I will beat him myself with slippers.'

Kokila didn't say anything. Ganapathi was sitting there without any movement. Priyanka was standing and looked as if she was about to cry.

'If a rowdy fellow like him comes and harasses you day and night, what would you do?' Amaravathi asked Priyanka. She stood there in silence. Her face seemed dead.

'This is the final warning. If he doesn't heed this, I will send him to jail.' She said to Priyanka and left the house immediately. Then, she could hear Kokila saying, 'If the female doesn't smile at him why would the male go after her?' Immediately, she wanted to turn back and fight with her. At the same time, she wondered what she would say if Kokila spoke even more insultingly.

'A girl who makes her mother hang her head in shame, why can't she die?' Amaravathi's eyes filled up with tears even as she said this to herself.

4

'I heard about a possible match. I'll go and enquire about it.' The very moment after Natesan left saying this, Revathi got up and left the room in haste. Because her manner made her afraid, Amaravathi, who was separating the leaves of the greens from their stems, dropped her work and ran to the kitchen. Revathi was standing with a box of matches in her hand ready to turn on the gas. As soon as she saw it, she snatched the box from Revathi's hand and threw it out of the window. Her body was trembling; 'What are you doing?' she asked.

'You should not look for a husband for me.' Revathi was standing stiff as an iron rod.

'Why should you die for it? You shouldn't die. I gave birth to you, I will die for it. You can fulfil your desire.'

As if she didn't want to look at Amaravathi, Revathi was looking at the window. She acted as if she didn't care for Amaravathi's tears. She walked swiftly out of the kitchen and went to her own room. Amaravathi continued to cry for some time in the kitchen and then went to Revathi's room and sat on her bed. She looked intently at her. She spoke in a measured tone.

'You were going to immolate yourself for someone from the streets? What a girl!' She wiped her eyes with the thalaippu, the free end of her sari.

'If what you are saying, what you were doing, were good, why would we stop you?'

'...'

'Has he studied to be a doctor, an engineer, or even a teacher? A tin-shed of a house. No relatives. He doesn't even have eight annas to call his wealth. Even the auto isn't his own. He has got it from the seth on a mortgage. Just give me one reason why he is the man for you and I will marry you to him.'

'I can't say,' Revathi muttered. She thought of why she liked Ravi. She had seen him seven or eight times in the temple. He had tattooed her name on both his arms and his chest. He would be sitting in the temple awaiting her arrival. He would pass by her house at least thirty or forty times every day. He had a stylish hairstyle, sideburns, and moustache. He was well-built. Was fair complexioned. He had good features. Every time he saw her, he would say, 'I will die if I can't have you.' That was all. What did she like in all this? She couldn't give any answer to this instantly.

'You must have seen him on the streets, in the temple, in any case only for a month or so. How much would you have interacted with him in this time? One month is enough for you to die for him?'

Revathi sat there, her head hanging down. Even though she didn't answer her, Amaravathi did not stop crying or asking her questions.

Amaravathi suspected that all this was due to the misalignment of planets. It must be so. Why would a girl who was known to be as good as gold when she was in college lose her mind in the month or two that she had spent at home? If it was because of the planets, they could arrange for expiatory prayers to make it right.

First, she cried because her daughter was about to immolate herself. Now she cried because she thought that the planets were creating havoc in her daughter's life. Her anger against Revathi lessened. She wondered, what could Revathi do if the planets were so? It struck her that she should take Revathi's horoscope to an astrologer and ask him what the matter was. She wondered where Revathi's horoscope notebook was. She went immediately to the almirah and began to search for the horoscope. She found it only after searching for more than an hour. Finding the horoscope notebook itself gave her immense happiness as if she had found a treasure of gold. She now strongly believed that whatever be the problem in the horoscope, a solution could be found. She visited her neighbours on the street, both who lived on the same side and those who lived across from her. She went to each house to enquire for a good astrologer in any nearby town.

She didn't trust her neighbours who all said Kazhutur Sundaramurthy was the man and, so, she rang up all the people she knew. Which astrologer from which town was good at reading horoscopes? This is what she asked everyone. Finally, she decided to meet Kazhutur Sundaramurthy only. She found out all the details that she might need in advance, like where Kazhutur was, the timing of the bus service, how distant it was, where she should get off, and what was the name of the street where the astrologer stayed. It was only after she had decided that she would consult the Kazhutur astrologer that she could sit down in peace.

Amaravathi couldn't focus on any housework. She kept checking the clock to see when Natesan would come back. She wondered whether to tell him or not. It was better to tell him. If there was a problem in the horoscope and they had to do some propitiation, it couldn't be done without his knowledge. He wouldn't object to anything they had to do for Revathi. It must also be on his mind that somehow something good should happen, that Revathi's mind should become alright. She looked at the clock. It was time for Natesan to come back. It was then that she remembered she had not eaten anything at midday. She asked Revathi if she would eat anything. Revathi didn't reply. So, she went to the kitchen and began to make coffee.

Natesan arrived. He hadn't even washed his face, hands, and feet. As if she had uncovered a great mystery, she told him about the horoscope notebook, about the fault in the position of the planets, and about the Kazhutur astrologer. He heard everything and had only one question, 'If her brain were alright, what could the planets do?'

'What happened where you went?' She asked.

'What will it be like when the whole town knows about your daughter's affair,' he said and went into his room and lay down.

Amaravathi fully believed that if she met the astrologer and found out which planets were in the wrong houses and propitiated them, Revathi's obstinate behaviour would change. Wherever she was, whatever she was doing, her mind was full of horoscope, fault in the planets, and adequate propitiation. When would night fall, when would it be dawn, when would she be able to go to Kazhutur, these thoughts were running in her mind all the time. Throughout the night she kept awake thinking. What could be the fault in the horoscope? What propitiation for it?

Next morning, soon after Natesan left for school, she boarded the bus to Kazhutur, the horoscope notebook in hand. It was eleven by the time she arrived at the astrologer's house. The astrologer was busy reading a horoscope for a family. He took more than an hour to read one horoscope. It irritated Amaravathi intensely. He had smeared his forehead fully with sacred ash. The lips were stained with the juice of betel leaves. He was quite stout. He looked like a doll made up of all the black colours available in the world. Only his hair was white. His voice was like a temple bell's. The time he took with them tested Amaravathi's patience. Her mind was filled with the worry about what could be wrong with Revathi's horoscope, what could be the problem. A man and a woman arrived on a motorcycle to have their horoscopes read. Having finished with the horoscope that he was reading, the astrologer called out to Amaravathi, 'Come in, amma.'

Amaravathi handed him two hundred rupees in cash, betel leaf and nuts, and the horoscope notebook. He took the horoscope notebook and read every page. Then he took a white sheet and made some calculations. Once he had finished his calculations, he began to tell her about the horoscope.

'It is a very strong horoscope. The owner of this horoscope will not cause any harm to befall the father or mother, elder brother or younger brother. Because the position of education is so strong, she must have finished her higher education. Perhaps even a doctor or an engineer. Because the position of speech is high, we can say with certainty that she will go for a government job. No fault can be found in the house of knowledge. There is nothing wrong in the seventh house either. Mars isn't malevolent also. There is no obstacle to her marriage. The man who will marry her will be at her beck and call. The husband will be of a high status, will have great opportunities. Yet, he will he ruled by her. If you want to check if she has the good fate to have children, I think there will be three. The horoscope gives scope for me to say one son and two daughters. Saturn wasn't in a malignant position at birth or later. Since Mercury is in a strong position, her nature will be to believe only what she says is right. She won't give any anxiety to her parents. She will not cause any sorrow, misery, heartache, or pain. She will have a good life.' The astrologer stopped and looked at Amaravathi as if to ask what else she wanted to know.

'When will this girl get married?' asked Amaravathi with eagerness.

'Because Mars is the eighth house, even if god were to try, her marriage won't take place for three years.'

'Will the marriage go off well?'

'Mercury is in a strong position. So, her marriage will be celebrated in a grand manner.'

'Will she find work?'

'The planet of speech is strong and so she will get a government job. Mercury is in the seventh house. So, he will give her a position of authority.'

'How long will she live?'

'We can say seventy years. She may live longer than that as per the horoscope. Three planets are in strong positions. No planet is in a wrong position. Mars is a malevolent planet. But he is not in a position to do harm in this horoscope.'

'Is there any blemish in the horoscope?'

He picked up the paper where he had done his calculations and looked at it. 'There is no blemish. If you don't believe me, if you have something troubling your mind, go to Thirunallaru Sani Bhagavan temple, take a dip in the holy pond, and perform an archanai to the god. No harm will happen.' Saying this, he picked up the horoscope notebook and handed it to her and bid her goodbye.

The astrologer's words, that there was nothing wrong in the horoscope, no blemish at all, and that Revathi wouldn't get married for three years, gave great comfort to Amaravathi's mind, and filled her with optimism. She returned home with the peace of mind brought about by the belief that everything would become alright. Even then, she didn't rest contented with the word of the Kazhutur astrologer but spent three-four days consulting other astrologers in Arugeri, Ponneri, and Nallur. Not just that, she also consulted a parrot astrologer. All of them repeated what the Kazhutur astrologer had said.

'No fault. No malevolent planets. She will live for seventy years. Will hold a government job. If what I say doesn't happen, I will give up my profession.'

When Amaravathi asked Revathi to accompany her to Thirunallaru, Revathi asked, 'Did the astrologer say that Mercury had a malignant influence on me?' and without waiting for her answer, she went on, 'Do you know how many lakh kilometers separate Earth and Mercury? How will that planet touch me? Do I and Mercury have a fight? Why should it come and take me in its clutches?' and laughed.

'No, no, it is not Mercury. Some problem may arise because of the movement of Saturn. Let's go.'

'I am not coming anywhere.'

'...'

5

Kokila was sitting outside and drinking tea. Ganapathi was drinking tea next to her. Priyanka picked up her tea and went inside the house. Kokila said to Ravi, who was standing outside, on the street, washing his autorickshaw, 'Come and drink your tea.' 'I will drink at the shop,' he replied. His full attention was on washing his auto. Whenever he washed his auto, it would take him at least half an hour to finish his job. He liked his auto to be clean. The tape recorder fixed in his auto should play clearly. The most important of all was the horn, it should sound loud and clear. He wanted that everyone on the street should know it was Ravi's auto arriving if he just touched his horn. It was for this reason that he had fixed that horn in his auto.

'Come and drink your tea', Kokila said again. Ravi didn't pay any attention to her, concentrating fully on his job. Kokila thought, 'It is because of our quarrel yesterday that he is refusing tea now,' and got angry.

'Are you refusing tea now because we quarrelled yesterday?' she asked. He didn't reply.

'She is older than you by two years. We haven't been able to arrange a marriage for her. When a female is sitting at home you come to us and say you are in love, you are going to get married, aren't you ashamed?' she asked. Ravi didn't open his mouth. He pretended as if he was lost in washing his auto.

'You show a way for my daughter and do whatever you want. I won't stand in the way.' Kokila raised her voice. Whenever she spoke, every word would be as if she was injecting poison. Ravi's behaviour was as if it didn't matter what poison she injected, how many times she injected it, it wouldn't affect him at all.

'In Burma Nagar, in the Drivers' Quarters, there are so

many guys. How come she didn't like even one of them? Instead of eloping with one of them, she is squatting at home.' When Kokila said this, Ravi looked up immediately at her. He seemed to be very angry. 'Is that the talk of a birth mother?' he asked.

'If you and your father fixed her marriage, why would I say anything?' Kokila asked.

'Won't we do it?'

'When?'

'When the time comes.'

'The time will come for you both only after she becomes an old woman.' Kokila said this with great firmness. Ravi reacted by clenching his teeth and growling, 'Will you shut your mouth?'

'I will shut my mouth. You run after some girl in the town. All those who pass by on the street can come up our steps and tick me off. Let them insult my daughter. Do you know what that woman said to us when she came last week?'

When he realised that she was referring covertly to Amaravathi's visit and her anger, Ravi got so enraged he felt his head would explode. He ground his teeth. He gave a solid punch to his auto. 'Why do you sit here in the morning saying all this?' He glared at Kokila.

'How many years is it since your sister came of age? Find some way for her, and then drag any donkey here to live with. If you talk of love and marriage before that, I won't even see you as my own son. I will poison you to death,' Kokila shouted.

'Do that first.' Ravi said and began to wipe his auto with a wet cloth.

Ganapathi went inside the house with the tea tumblers as if what Kokila and Ravi were talking had nothing to do with him.

'Try to feed us rice that you get from the ration shop at least. You can get married later. How will you feed the girl?'

'You talk too much, that I know,' said Ravi.

When Priyanka came out ready to go to work in a textile shop, Kokila lashed out in anger, 'You go every day to work in a textile shop, don't you? How many men come there every day? You aren't smart enough to seduce one of them and elope with him?' Priyanka's eyes filled with tears. When she saw Priyanka walking away without answering her, Kokila said, 'You will have to go on like this till you die. Even after consuming the two thousand rupees that the textile shop owner gives you, no one is going to do anything for you.'

She added as if she had had a change of heart, 'You donkey, can't you go with some flowers in your hair? Not even smart enough for it. Which dog will look at you if you go like this?'

'What are you saying? Can any dog come to this home claiming that he loves my akka? If he still comes, will I let him live?' Ravi shouted.

'You won't get her married. She shouldn't marry a man herself. But you will chase after any bitch.' Kokila made a face at him.

'I will love whoever I want. But no son of a whore can love this Ravi's akka.' Ravi said as if he were boasting.

'It is your anger that will destroy you.'

'So let me be destroyed.'

'You shouldn't go near that girl's house from now on.'

'I'll see. I know everything.'

'Why I am saying this is because,' when Kokila started speaking, he snapped, 'I can't listen to your song and dance,' and whizzed off in his auto to the stand.

'If they hadn't banned the lottery, I would have celebrated my daughter's marriage by now,' said Kokila and began to find fault with the government and to curse it for banning the lottery. Her tongue was always as hot as fire when she was angry.

6

When Revathi was in college, she would never stop talking. Whatever she said, she would speak clearly and emphatically. She didn't like to whisper things. Now everything was the opposite. Upset by the way she was behaving, Arunmozhi, who had come to make her see sense, said, 'Is there any logic in what you are doing? Can you love a guy just because he is fair and handsome? Can you marry him? What you are doing is an insult to our own caste.'

'Where does caste come into it?'

'What is without caste in Tamil Nadu? What happens without it?'

Revathi didn't reply.

'One's intelligence is not only in studying well, getting marks. Have you seen your face in the mirror?'

Revathi didn't reply.

'You have got corrupted by Thamizh cinema.'

'...'

'You are dying for a chap who has nothing. And you are killing others as well.'

'You speak well,' said Revathi and tried to laugh. She found it difficult to laugh. She couldn't laugh. As if it struck her just then, she said, 'My mother is intelligent.'

'Why do you say that?'

'She has phoned and called you here, hasn't she?'

'Do you know what all you have lost now?'

'Tell me one thing, let's see.'

'No smiles. No talk. No mischief. No make-up. You are not yourself.' As Arunmozhi listed each item one by one, Revathi's face faded.

Revathi wanted to talk a lot to Arunmozhi. She wanted even more to ask her why her heart was like this and to cry on her shoulders. But she couldn't talk. Nor could she cry. She had so much in her mind that she wanted to say to Arunmozhi, so many questions to ask her. What she didn't know was how to begin, what to say, what to ask.

Amaravathi's tears, Natesan's worry, Arunmozhi's scolding and her questions, nothing saddened her. As soon as Amaravathi had told him about Ravi and Revathi, Murugan had obstinately gone off to Madras, saying, 'From now on, I won't even see her. I won't even stay in this house.' He hadn't returned home for three months. He didn't talk on the phone to Natesan or Amaravathi like he used to earlier. Even when he did, he just answered briefly the questions asked and disconnected the call. From their childhood, it was Revathi who was the obstinate one. Murugan was the type to give in and carry on in most things. But in the case of Ravi, not only did he not give in even a nano bit, he didn't ask her even once directly, 'Why did you do this?' In his anger, he didn't speak to her. He had gone without looking at her face. In these three months, he hadn't talked on the phone even once to Revathi. She would have been happy even if he had spoken angrily to her, cursed her, or even hit her. It was his behaviour that was burning her like fire. She couldn't distant herself for even a moment from the feeling of being singed. She felt the desire to request Arunmozhi to tell him to tick her off, to get angry, to come and hit her. She knew that Murugan and Arunmozhi were in love. She also knew that he would listen to Arunmozhi. Even so, Revathi didn't ask anything of Arunmozhi.

'How did you get to meet him? What did you talk to him?'

'I didn't talk anything.'

'Is that the truth?'

'I swear.'

'Then, why do you say you will only marry him? Everybody will laugh if they hear you. Will I say something to harm you?'

'No.'

'Then why don't you listen to me, understand me?'

'I want to listen to all of you, what Appa says, Amma says, Chitti says, you say.'

'Then what stops you? Tell him to get lost.'

'Can't.'

'Why?'

'Don't know.'

'Do you know who you are? Do you know your status?'

'Mmm.'

'If our friends come to know that he drives an auto, what will they say? Do you still love him even though you know his status?'

'Mmm.'

'How?'

'I like him.'

'Why?'

'Don't know.'

'What wonder of the world did you see in him?'

'Nothing at all.'

'You are an idiot,' Arunmozhi said and sat for a while as if she didn't like talking to Revathi. She picked up a book lying nearby and turned a few pages. Suddenly, as if in anger, she asked, 'What are you doing? Do you know its consequences?'

'I do think about it.'

'Then?'

'Nothing you all say stays in my mind. Only what he said.'

Arunmozhi looked at Revathi strangely. Then, she said in a tough voice, 'It is because of your obstinacy that you are going to suffer, and make others suffer. This is the truth.'

'Do you think so?' Revathi asked in a sober voice. To look at her then, it seemed as if she would burst into tears any moment. The life that had animated her eyes five-six months earlier had died. There was no brightness in her face. No glow in her cheeks. It looked like the face of one who had just finished crying. Her normal style of talking, smiling, everything had gone. Her talk and her eyes were full of secrecy. Even the way she sat, it seemed she was carrying a huge burden. It was difficult to see her so. At the same time, Arunmozhi felt sorry that Revathi was refusing to listen to her.

'What you are doing is not only about you. Many such guys follow girls all the time. Does it mean that we should marry all of them?' Arunmozhi asked angrily. Without bothering about her anger, Revathi said calmly, "As soon as I saw you, like an infant getting lost in a huge festival crowd, I lost my heart," he said that, didn't he? That is why.'

This made Arunmozhi even angrier.

'Chee. Shut your mouth. Those are only words,' she said in a rage.

Revathi didn't get angry. She didn't get irritated. She said as if she had memorised it, 'Even Appa, Amma, Anna, Arunmozhi, Revathi are only words.'

'Then what is Ravi?' Revathi didn't expect this question from Arunmozhi. So, she didn't open her mouth.

'You are obsessed.'

'You speak like a teacher,' Revathi said but Arunmozhi got up as if she hadn't heard it. Revathi didn't ask her to sit. Didn't ask her to stay. This made Arunmozhi very angry. She looked at Revathi with dislike. The way Revathi was sitting was like an orphan child begging for alms. Her eyes looked like those of a doll. She had lost considerable weight. Even the clothes she was wearing looked as if they were draped on her for the sake of appearance. When she looked at her, Arunmozhi's anger came down slightly. She went near Revathi. Holding her right hand, Arunmozhi spoke as if these were her last words on the subject, 'There will be someone for you in this world. Honestly, it is not him.'

Revathi did not say anything. She felt like sharing her plans with Arunmozhi: 'After marriage, I will take him to Madras. I will join some company for work. I will get a good salary. We won't have any major issues. I will buy him a car and ask him to drive it.' But then she thought whether she, who simply gave her advice like Appa, Amma, and Chitti, would understand. She was surprised how all of them said the same thing: 'Leave him.'

'Do you remember Akila who always said "OK fine", "OK fine" for everything, the girl who lived in the next room to us, the one who was dark, short, and flabby, the Salem girl? She said no to a boy working in an IT firm and managed to get a guy who works in the RTO, do you know?'

'Is that so? I don't have any contact with her now.'

When Arunmozhi replied, 'Oh, you have a very big contact now,' her face fell completely.

As if these were now her final words, Arunmozhi said, 'I have talked to you for an entire night and a day. I tried talking to you even now. It doesn't seem as if you are going to correct your ways. I am going back to my city. If you marry him, I won't attend the marriage.'

'I am going, leaving,' Arunmozhi said this but she didn't even move out of the room. As if she knew that Arunmozhi wouldn't leave, Revathi didn't try to dissuade her. She didn't even plead with her. She sat as usual without moving. When Arunmozhi said as if she had suddenly remembered it, 'That doctor fellow who followed you around in college. You should have chosen him. Better option.' Revathi replied in an even voice, 'Didn't feel like it.'

'This guy is the best option of all in this world, isn't he?' Arunmozhi asked and glared at her. Arunmozhi's anger, shouting, irritation—nothing seemed to have the least effect on Revathi.

7

'Don't spoil my mood, Amma.'

'A murderer, I agree. But she is your sibling.'

'I have experienced all the shame because of it.'

'It must be a fault in the planets. That is why she has lost her mind. She never troubled us like this before.'

'Leave me alone for a bit, Amma. It seems as if I am getting a headache.'

'If like you, like your father, I too stand apart from all this, I am afraid that something may happen to destroy your father's honour, your honour.' Amaravathi was close to weeping when she said this.

'Let her elope, let her get lost. We'll do her funeral rites.' Murugan spoke through clenched teeth.

'We will lose our family honour.'

'It's disgusting.' Murugan smote his forehead.

'It is disgusting,' said Amaravathi with emphasis, and sat there with her head hanging, not looking at Murugan. Amaravathi had not expected at all that Murugan would be so full of anger against Revathi. He had never spoken of her with such dislike before this. Usually, people's anger would come down as they spoke about it. But it was the opposite with him now.

'Let this filth stick to you, to your daughter,' he said and turned his face away.

'What would we have done if she had been born lame?'

'That would have been alright. This is just extremely disgusting. A disgust we will continue to feel even if she dies.' When Murugan said this his face became small. He looked at Amaravathi as if she was accused of murder.

'If we have to live with honour, we should do it in front of society, print invitation cards, and conduct the damned obsequies in a wedding hall, Thambi.'

'Do whatever you want. Just leave me out of it.' Murugan said emphatically. Amaravathi thought that even in saying this he was making a big concession. She placed another demand before him.

'If we send her with no jewellery on her ears, nose, her neck or hands, it will be a loss of honour for your father and you, Thambi.'

'Do whatever nonsense you want. It has nothing to do with me. I will not come for anything.'

'She won't commit suicide. Staying on here, she is killing me.' Amaravathi broke into tears when she said this. Through her tears, she said, 'I used to tell everyone with pride that from the time I arrived in this house as a bride, I have never shed any tears. As if to remedy that, she is making me cry every day.'

'It is only because you are speaking that I have listened to this issue so far.' Even before Murugan could finish saying that, Amaravathi burst out, 'Let her go out of this house. She will be dead to me immediately. Even if she dies, I will not look at her face.' Saying that she left suddenly for the kitchen.

The way Amaravathi cried, and the way she went off to the kitchen enraged Murugan no end. He felt like going and slapping Revathi hard. He felt as if his head would explode in this anger. He got up hastily and went to the backyard where Natesan was standing and told him, 'Do whatever Amma wants. Finish off whatever cursed rites that have to be done. Then we can give her up as dead. One way or the other this wretched one must leave the house. I am leaving for Madras.' He re-entered the house. Natesan followed him inside saying, 'You came only this morning. Stay till tomorrow.'

'I have work,' he said and picking up his bag, looked towards Revathi's room. The door was shut. He felt enraged at her. Not being able to contain his fury, he went into the hall. Seeing Murugan leaving town, Amaravathi pleaded, 'Why don't you go at least in the evening?'

'I can't stay in this house for even a minute.'

'I will make coffee. At least have it before you go.'

'I have work. I am going,' Murugan said and went outside the house quickly. As if he wanted to talk to him, Natesan followed him outside.

'Stay a moment, stay a moment,' by the time Amaravathi came out saying this, she could see Murugan and Natesan at a distance. Not knowing what to do, she held on to the gate opening onto the street and began to cry. 'She has lit the pyre for every one of us,' she lamented.

The street was very hot then. A street dog began to howl.

PART TWO

1

Amaravathi's cell phone rang. Natesan, who was sitting in the chair, picked it up and checked who was calling. The name 'Revathi' was displayed. His face fell immediately. He took the phone with disgust to Amaravathi who was lying down inside and handed it to her saying, 'Your darling daughter is calling you.' Amaravathi hesitated, not knowing whether to talk or not, and looked at Natesan. 'Talk to her, talk to her,' said Natesan with bitterness and returned to his chair.

'Why is she calling at this time?' Saying this, Amaravathi took the phone to her ear and said, 'Hello.' Since she couldn't hear clearly what was being said on the other side, she once again said 'Hello.' 'Hello, who is speaking? What are you saying? When? How did it happen? About fifteen minutes back? Where is she now? GH refused admission? You are taking her to Cuddalore?' Tears began to flow down from Amaravathi's eyes when she asked these questions. The phone slipped from her hand and fell on the floor.

Natesan, who was watching a show on the television, turned towards her room and asked, 'What does your daughter say?' There was no answer. He could hear her weeping, so he got up and went in and asked, 'What happened?' Amaravathi was sitting with her face down. He asked again, 'What happened?'

'They say she has immolated herself.'

'Who?'

'Revathi.'

'What? When? Who told you? It was she who called you now?'

'It was that dog who spoke on her phone. GH refused admission, and they are now taking her to Cuddalore in an ambulance.' Amaravathi's tongue felt dry. In a moment, her body chilled. As cold as a corpse.

Natesan couldn't stand. He perspired. His mouth dried up. He stood holding on to the door. What to say? What to do? Neither of them had any idea.

'Get up. Let's go.' Natesan couldn't say even this clearly. He found it difficult even to wear his pants and shirt.

'Lock the house. Take whatever money we have. Take the ATM cards too.' Natesan's voice sounded strange.

'Get a taxi', she mumbled. She shivered as if she was sitting on a block of ice.

Natesan rang up Kumar who usually drove him around, and said, 'Kumar, HM speaking. Where are you? At home only? Okay. Then you bring your car around to our house immediately. Need to go to Cuddalore. Don't be late. Come quickly. It is urgent.' He disconnected the call. 'The car will come. Get ready,' he said to Amaravathi. How did the six years' worth of anger, hatred, bitterness that he felt for Revathi disappear in a moment? Amaravathi looked at Natesan strangely.

'What is there to get ready for? Are we going to a wedding? Bolt the back door. Lock the house. We just have to go like this.' Amaravathi replied. She opened the almirah in some agitation, took out the money and the ATM card and went out of the house. Natesan shut and locked the back door, the door to the room, the front door, the gate, and the gate outside and gave the keys to Amaravathi.

'Call Murugan.' Amaravathi said, leaning on the front gate because her legs were giving way. A street dog howled.

'Hello, Thambi... I am Appa speaking. They say Revathi has immolated herself. They are going to Cuddalore. We just got to know. It was that dog who told us. On the phone only. We are leaving. Waiting for the car. Are you coming directly to Cuddalore? Okay, come there. Arunmozhi? She need not come. Let us assess the situation and tell her accordingly. Okay. Let's talk later. The car has come.'

The car arrived. 'Get in, get in,' Natesan hurried Amaravathi. He also got in. 'To Cuddalore. Drive fast.' Natesan said agitatedly. Kumar started the car.

When the car reached the Cuddalore road, he switched on the tape recorder and played a song loudly. 'Please no songs,' Natesan requested in a dead voice.

Kumar stooped the movie song and put on some devotional song. This angered Natesan even more. 'Don't play any songs, Kumar,' he muttered.

Kumar lowered the volume and said, 'Something should keep falling on my ears, sir. It is a habit. My customers, as soon as they get in, ask me to play songs. They ask for a variety of songs—old songs, new songs, devotional songs. So, now even I want to play songs as soon as I start driving.' Natesan was in no mood to listen to his explanation. Amaravathi was sitting as if she was unconscious to the world.

'You used to listen to old songs with interest, sir,' said Kumar. Natesan wanted to ask, 'How the hell will I appreciate music in the state I am in?' But he didn't have the heart to ask even that aloud. He didn't want to have a conversation with Kumar and so he started looking outside. How did Revathi immolate herself? Would she have set fire to herself, or would Ravi have set her on fire? What would the burns be like? Slight? Or all over the body? What was the time when it happened? Where would the ambulance be now? Various questions chased each other in his mind. This was Amaravathi's state as well. Natesan's cell phone rang. He picked it up.

'Hello, is it Arunmozhi? Yes, we are on our way. No, we don't know how. Per cent meaning? I don't understand. Oh, how much the body is burnt. We don't know. We are yet to see her. If the per centage is above thirty to forty per cent, she won't survive? Did a doctor say so? I haven't talked to that dirty dog yet. Let me talk to him and tell you. Bye.'

He felt as if a fire was searing his stomach. He felt even more tense and agitated than before. He wished that Revathi shouldn't have suffered more than thirty per cent burns. He prayed to god. He looked at Amaravathi. He could see that she had been looking towards him all the time. Her face had turned pale. Her eyes were filled with tears. He wanted to tell her. 'Don't cry, don't worry, nothing will happen.' He could articulate nothing that was in his mind. With her lips trembling, she said, 'Ask that murderer how much per cent.'

'I don't have that dog's number.'

'He talked from the number saved as Revathi on my

phone.' Amaravathi gave her phone to Natesan. Natesan, who took the phone, wondered whether to call or not. 'I haven't ever talked to that scoundrel,' he remarked. As soon as she heard him say this and hesitate, Amaravathi's expression changed. Her tears stopped. She stared at him. She almost snatched the phone from him. She called up the next instant. 'Hello, I am Revathi's mother speaking. How is she? What, they refused in Cuddalore? You are going to Pondicherry JIPMER hospital? Okay, give the phone to her. What, she can't talk? What did you do to my girl? You scoundrel. Have you killed her?' The phone slipped from her hand and fell. She didn't search for the fallen phone or pick it up. She leaned her head on the front seat and sobbed. It was Natesan who picked up the fallen phone. Whatever struck him, he closed his eyes. But he couldn't sit for long with his eyes closed. He looked outside the car. He could see a girl taking firewood on her cycle.

They had said no in Virudhachalam. And if she had been refused admission in Cuddalore and they had sent her along to JIPMER Pondicherry, she must have suffered hundred per cent burns, Natesan thought. He opened his mouth to say this. He shut it the next moment. He couldn't sit still. He couldn't talk. He couldn't look outside the car either. So, he rang up Murugan, and said, 'Thambi, I am Appa speaking. They said it wasn't possible to treat her in Cuddalore. They are taking her to Pondicherry JIPMER. Yes, that lout only said. Amma only talked to him. We are on our way there. I'll let you know when we arrive there.' Saying this, he ended the call. He spoke to Kumar, 'Go fast. Go to Pondy.' He looked outside the window to change his mood. The tamarind trees on the side of the road and other plants and creepers met his eyes. Nothing could change his mood.

'What happened, sir?'

'...'

'Sir?'

'My daughter has immolated herself.' Natesan's tongue faltered. Tears flowed.

'The one who stays in Burma Nagar, North Periyar Nagar, she?

'Yes.'

'The one who drives an autorickshaw, Ravi, isn't she his wife?'

'...'

'How did it happen, sir?'

'Don't know.'

'When, sir?'

'We just heard the news. Before we rang you up.'

'He and I were classmates till the tenth. When he gets drunk he stinks up the whole street. Why on earth did you give your daughter in marriage to him?

'...'

'Will she survive, sir?'

'No idea. Go a bit faster.' Natesan sounded angry.

'I am going at hundred only, sir.' Kumar's tone had changed completely. 'Nothing will happen. Don't worry, sir.'

Natesan didn't hear anything that Kumar said. His mind was occupied with Revathi, with various questions like whether she would have reached the hospital, whether they would have admitted her, which part of the body would have caught fire, which part would have burnt to the higher degree, would the face, arms, legs, abdomen, the whole body have been burnt. His body was hot as if he had high fever. He was sweating even in the AC car.

Amaravathi didn't cry aloud. But tears were streaming down from her eyes in strands.

Natesan looked out of the car. He could see cars, buses, autorickshaws, and bikes on the road. The car had reached Cuddalore. The phone rang. He picked it up. 'Yes, Thambi. We have crossed Cuddalore. We are driving fast only. Naturally, Amma is crying. That scoundrel hasn't talked after that. Whether to file a case or not, we have to ask our girl first before we do anything. I will ask her as soon as we reach the hospital. It will take us half an hour more to arrive there. Okay. I'll call you as soon as we reach. You don't get tense. You've boarded the bus? Okay, come.' Natesan leaned back and closed his eyes.

'If she survives, let him be, sir. If she doesn't, go after him. File a case and get him thrown into jail by the scruff of his neck. That is how he will learn a lesson. File a case that he wanted dowry. The case will be strong. Say that he harassed her for jewellery, that he harassed her for money. Enough.' Natesan didn't listen to anything that Kumar said. He didn't feel like talking to him. His only thought was to see Revathi. He was concerned that nothing should happen to her.

'Your only daughter, sir?'

'Yes.'

'Pray to Tirupati sir. Pray that nothing should happen

to my daughter, and we will come together as a family and shave our heads. Good will happen.'

'Drive a little faster, Kumar.'

'We'll be there in ten minutes, sir.' Kumar offered him a bottle of water, adding, 'You are not able to speak, sir. Drink a little water.' Even after drinking half a bottle of water, the dryness in the mouth and the heat in his stomach hadn't lessened even a bit. 'Drink some water,' he offered the bottle to Amaravathi. She was leaning her head on the front seat and didn't raise it, but she gestured no with her left hand.

'Why on earth did you give your daughter in marriage to him?' Natesan couldn't answer this question asked by Kumar earlier. The very fact that Kumar knew who Revathi was seemed dishonourable to him. He felt ashamed that Kumar knew everything. He thought he had made a mistake by calling Kumar. He felt irritated that so many knew that the Revathi in Burma Nagar was his daughter. He lowered his head on the front seat in anger.

Seeing a corpse being carried on the road, Kumar said, 'A good omen sir. When you go on important work, it will end well if you see a corpse on the way.'

'Really?' Both Amaravathi and Natesan asked together. Both looked outside the car. They could see a funeral procession.

'Crossing a body is such good omen, sir.'

Kumar's words gave both of them immense relief.

'Why do they take the flowers from the garlands on the corpse and sprinkle the petals on the road? It creates so much mess on the road.'

'Everyone does so, sir.'

'Even when they are dead, people create garbage on their last journey.'

'We have reached Korimedu, sir.'

'I don't know where they are. Have to call them.'

'They must have gone to the Emergency Ward only. If we go straight there, they will tell us.'

'Do you know where it is?'

'Yes, sir.'

'Go straight there.'

The car entered the main gate of JIPMER hospital and stopped in front of Emergency. Amaravathi and Natesan got off the car.

'Go inside and ask. They will tell you. I will take the car to the parking lot and come back.' Kumar drove away in the car.

Natesan and Amaravathi ran inside the Emergency building. A large hall. Wherever you looked, it seemed like a crowd at a festival. Three doctors were sitting in a row. Six or seven nurses were standing close to them. People seemed to be going in all directions. In their haste, they didn't know whom to talk to. Natesan walked up to a nurse and asked, 'Did you admit a girl called Revathi a short while ago?'

'What case? Fire or accident?'

'Fire.'

'Go to the fifth floor,' the Nurse said.

'Call the filthy dog and ask him,' Natesan said to his wife.

Amaravathi called Ravi. 'I am Revathi's mother speaking. Where is she? We are on the ground floor of the Emergency building. Fifth floor?' She disconnected the call immediately.

'She is on the fifth floor,' she reported and began to look for the way upstairs.

They climbed the staircase to the fifth floor. A security guard prevented them from entering. Ravi, who was standing in front of the door, said, 'The girl who was admitted just now, they are her father and mother.' The guard opened the door. Amaravathi and Natesan entered the hall. Ravi too entered with them. When they entered the hall where the attendants to the patients slept at night, Amaravathi asked, 'Where is she?'

'They are bandaging her in this room,' Ravi pointed to a room next to the ICU. Amaravathi and Natesan looked at the shut door of that room. They couldn't see anything. Then, looking at Ravi, Amaravathi asked, 'What did you do to my daughter? Have you killed her, you murdering rascal?' When he didn't answer, Amravathi pulled him by the shirt in anger and asked, 'What did you do? Why did you set her on fire? You garbage-picking stray dog!'

'I didn't set her on fire.'

'If you lie, I will beat you with my slippers, you filthy dog,' Natesan pushed Ravi. In his rage, he wanted to cut him to pieces and kill him. Seeing him stand there glaring at them, Amaravathi burst out, 'You dare glare at us after setting fire to my girl,' and gave him a tight slap. Hearing the noise, the security guard and two nurses came running and yelled, 'Keep all your fights outside.' The guard tried to eject all three of them from the room. Because Amaravathi and Natesan pleaded in turn, 'I want to see my daughter', they warned them, 'You cannot raise you voice here. You cannot make a noise.' The nurses went inside their room. The guard stood next to Ravi.

When would they finish bandaging her? When would the door open? Amaravathi and Natesan stood waiting. They glared at Ravi in anger every now and then.

In a short while, the door opened. Revathi was brought out seated on a wheelchair being pushed by a nurse. Her head was shaved. She was bandaged from her feet to her throat. The moment she saw Revathi, Amaravathi cried out 'Oh my God' and wept in panic. Revathi looked at Amaravathi and Natesan. There was no sign of recognition in her eyes. She was inert like a corpse being made to sit on a wheelchair. It was only for the one or two minutes it took to push her wheelchair from the room where she was bandaged to the ICU that Amaravathi and Natesan saw her. As soon as the chair entered the ICU, they shut the door. 'They have shaved my precious girl bald', Amaravathi covered her face with her hands and began to cry. The very next instant, she fell unconscious.

A man who was standing in the hall lifted Amaravathi and made her sit. A woman sprinkled water on her face. Another woman used her own sari to wipe her face. A woman poured water into her mouth. Natesan watched everything. But who did what, what was happening, nothing registered in his brain.

Amaravathi regained consciousness. She looked at the people gathered around her. 'Where is my daughter?' she asked. She kept asking the same question again and again.

'Only the attendants must stay inside. The rest of you

have to leave. Time's up.' The security guard announced. Nobody paid any heed to his announcement. They stood waiting to see the doctor, to see the nurse. And when the security guard began to compel them to leave, saying 'Go out', they simply exchanged places, no one left the room. When the guard started yelling forcefully, only the men left one by one. 'Only those with the pass stay inside. The rest go out of the room.' The guard kept announcing. One or two women went out. The guard opened the door and announced in a stern voice to those sitting or standing on the staircase, 'The attendants can come in but you must have the pass in your hand.' Ten odd women got up and approached the door. 'Show me your pass,' he said to each one and let them in. A woman who was eating said, 'I'll come after I finish the meal.' He nodded as if he was saying yes. 'Is that all? Has anybody gone down?' The guard shut the door after asking the people waiting outside. He then saw Natesan and Amaravathi and said authoritatively, 'You both go out.' Ravi, who was standing close, said, 'You are talking to an attendant.'

'The man?' asked the guard.

'No, her.' Ravi pointed to Amaravathi.

'Does she have a pass? What is the name of the patient?'

'No, she didn't get a pass.'

'How can you be inside without a pass? They must have issued one when they admitted the patient.'

'They gave me. Not the lady.'

'Get it first. Go to the doctor's room.' The guard said with authority.

Ravi went to the doctors' room which was close to the ICU, to the north. In four or five minutes, he returned and gave an attendant card to Amaravathi. Suddenly, in a fit of rage and madness, Amaravathi screamed at Ravi, 'What did you do my girl, you scoundrel? Why did you set her on fire?' He didn't say a word in reply. He stood with his head lowered.

Natesan, in his turn, shouted angrily, 'Come out and I will beat you with my slippers.'

'Don't make noise here. Both of you go out.' The guard said to Ravi.

'I have a pass,' Ravi replied.

'Only women can stay in this hall at night. If you wish, you go sit on the staircase. Only one attendant per patient.' The guard's voice was very stern. Ravi left abruptly as if he was angry.

'Sir, you have to leave too.'

'We just arrived. We haven't seen our daughter. We haven't met a doctor yet to find out what is happening.'

'Now, you can see the patient only early in the morning at four or five o'clock. And then, they will allow only the attendant inside. And you can meet the doctor in the morning.'

'We don't know anything that's happening. We need to know about it.'

'She has been admitted. She is in the ICU. That is all there is to know. If you wish, you go buy food and water for the attendant and leave after giving it to her.' There was not a drop of pity in the guard's voice. Spotting the hand entering the shirt pocket, he said, 'Don't do anything disgusting, sir.

Even if you offer me a crore, no one but the attendant can stay here. I am telling you nicely sir. Go out. It is past eight thirty.' The guard's voice had thickened.

'I have to see the doctor. I have to speak to my daughter.'

Without answering Natesan, the guard started checking each person, 'Do you have the pass? Show it to me.' Natesan pleaded with the guard, 'Can she at least go out for five minutes?' He wanted to spend a little time with Amaravathi before she went into the hall for the night.

'Quickly. I will shut the door if you are late.'

Natesan and Amaravathi opened the door and went out.

'What to do, whom to ask, don't know anything.' Natesan's voice broke as he said this.

'He has murdered her. The scoundrel.'

'Okay, you go inside. See the doctor if possible. See the nurse. If you can see her, meet our child and ask her what to do next. I will sit here.'

'All night?'

'What else can be done? If we had had a word with her we would have known what to do next.'

'Whatever it is we will know only after we meet the doctor. So go home and come back in the morning.'

'It is past nine now. It will take two hours to go. And two hours to come back. I will just stay here.'

'The driver has to go, isn't it?'

A man sitting on the staircase volunteered without being asked, 'There is no point waiting here. Only early in the morning at five will they let the attendant inside the ICU. Even that only for five or ten minutes. That is all. Then they allow you inside only the next morning at five o'clock.'

Natesan and Amaravathi looked at the man. The guard came out of the door and announced, 'Is there any attendant here? If there is anyone here, come inside now. I am going to lock the door.' Amaravathi and Natesan looked at each other silently, not knowing what to say.

'Please come, amma,' the guard called out to her.

'You go in. I will talk to you on the phone.' Natesan said.

'Won't Murugan be arriving?'

'I will see. I will wait outside till he arrives. I will talk to you on the phone and let you know what we are doing when he comes. Should I buy you some food and water?'

'No need. Apply for medical leave. I will ask her if we should file a case.' She handed over the bag with the money. She also gave the ATM cards. What to say next? Amaravathi didn't know. Natesan didn't know either. They looked at each other emptily as if they were not conscious at all.

'Enough, come amma. It is time,' the guard said. Amaravathi went in. The guard locked the door.

Natesan stood staring at the locked door. The glass pane on the door was black.

2

Ravi, who came out of the ICU building, looked around for his mother and sister. Since he didn't know where they were, he walked out ten or fifteen feet to check for them. He took the cell phone out of his pocket, called his sister and asked,

'Where are you standing?' He added, 'I am standing in front of the ICU. Come here,' and he cut the call. Kokila and Priyanka walked towards him from the south. When he saw them, Ravi cried uncontrollably. Seeing him cry, Kokila and Priyanka began to weep. In between her tears, Kokila asked, 'What is the situation? Where is she?'

'In the ICU.'

'How is she?'

'Don't know,' tears flowed from his eyes as he replied.

'What happened?' Priyanka asked.

'Come to a side,' Ravi said that and took them to the front of the toilet block.

'What did the doctors say?'

'As soon as we admitted her, they shaved her head and bandaged her body and took her in.'

'How did it happen?' Kokila asked. Ravi cried without replying. The way he stood and the way he cried created panic in Kokila and Priyanka. 'Will Revathi survive?' They repeatedly asked him in fear. He didn't open his mouth at all.

However large a gang confronting him, however large a gathering, and even if he was in the wrong, Ravi would enter into the fight with daring. He would shout and gather people. He would make a ruckus. He would create a racket. He would swear that the fault was not his at all. He would never be afraid. He would never give way. He would immediately pounce in attack. He would never stand crying. He would never be subdued. He would snarl at anything. If such a guy was crying, Kokila and Priyanka thought that Revathi must have hundred per cent burns to a high degree. So, in turn in they asked what happened, how did it happen, and why it happened. He answered some questions and didn't answer others. Since he was agitated, he couldn't even speak properly.

'Did you listen to us then? For everything you said, "I know", "I know", and shut our mouths. Now see where you have ended up.'

'Is this any place to say all this?' Ravi glared at Kokila.

'We'll remain silent, you send us off to jail.' When Kokila said this with great firmness, Ravi lost his temper.

'Will you shut your mouth? Who asked you to come here?' He asked with irritation.

'You are the one who is at fault. You should shut your mouth.'

'You go yourself and complain to the police and hand me over. My wretched fate, I was born to you.' Ravi struck himself on his head.

'That you were born to us, look at our fate!' Having delivered this with great anger, Kokila turned her face away as is she didn't want to look at him any longer. Like Kokila, Ravi too couldn't control his anger. So, he asked Priyanka, 'Did you guys come to see me dead or kill me?' She didn't reply, just wept.

'So why are you displaying your tears now?' He asked Priyanka.

'Is she burnt badly? Will it become a problem?'

'No idea.'

'So what if you are a female? You need to be a good wife. She doesn't know anything and kills herself and all of us!' Kokila said this crying. 'Nothing will happen, don't cry Amma,' said Priyanka who then broke into tears again. She then asked Ravi, 'Will there be a case? Will the police come?' Before Ravi could reply, Kokila jumped in.

'For what your thambi has done, what do you expect—the police or a celebratory garland?'

'I'll see who dares to come to catch me,' even if he said this with bravado, his voice betrayed his fear.

'I told you then itself, did you listen to me? The girl is educated. She looks good. Her dad has a job. They have their own house. A moneyed family. She won't suit us, how much I explained! You didn't listen to anything. All that a female needs is a personable face to roam around proudly! To roam without any regard to anyone!'

'Will you be quiet for some time?' Ravi asked in anger.

'If you had married a girl from a Burma Bazaar family, would we be in this situation?'

'Will you move away instead of killing me? I am confused what to do next. And at this time, this cursed woman blabbers anything at all!' Ravi said, his heart in a turmoil. Kokila did not pay heed to what he said and continued, 'If you had gone to work in Burma Bazaar, why would trouble come to us? You were obstinate, I won't go to Madras, I won't go to Burma Bazaar. Now, where have you reached? And you haven't come here alone, you have dragged us with you. You didn't care that someone elder to you, a female at that, was waiting to get married, and gave us a song and dance. Now you are suffering this.' Kokila wiped her eyes and nose with the munthanai of her saree. She said, 'Even my daughter is fair-coloured. She is as attractive and has the body of an actress. Not a single fault in her. Even so, not even one dog came wagging his tail to marry her. Not one dog came to our door saying he was in love with her. She is almost on the shelf now. If she had been married off at the right age, she would have given birth to two or three kids by now. My daughter is hanging around with nothing at all. She didn't even know how to seduce and catch a guy. She is standing like a clod of earth,' Kokila blew her nose.

'Where have you come to weep like this? You should have some idea what is happening here. Get lost, go back home.' Ravi said.

'Can we see her?' Priyanka asked.

'Even I was chased out by them. No idea when they will let me in.'

'When can we see her?'

'I am aware of the situation, which is why I am asking you to go. Go back and contact this lawyer.' Ravi gave them the lawyer's name, his address, and the directions to his house. He gave them the lawyer's cell phone number also.

'I educated you. You didn't study and roamed the streets. I asked you to work in the textile shop. Instead, you went with your dad to sell lottery tickets. I said go to Burma Bazaar, we too will come there. You were adamant to drive an autorickshaw. And where you went to drive your auto, at the auto stand, you had a hundred quarrels a day. As if all these faults were not enough, you got hitched to this girl. I told you not to set up your own house. You didn't listen to me. I don't know what sins I have committed.' Kokila began to cry again.

'What are you blabbing? Why sing the old dirges? It isn't clear what is going to happen. If she survives, I escape. Otherwise, it is jail for me.' As he said this, Ravi was overcome by tears. Seeing him cry, Priyanka cried as well. His cell phone rang then. He picked it up and talked.

'The nurse is calling. Why is she calling at ten o'clock at night?' Ravi ran towards the ICU building agitatedly.

Stunned, not knowing what to do next, Priyanka and Kokila remained standing there. It was so dark that they could not see each other's faces. The moon wasn't bright yet. And there was no breeze at all out there.

3

Some were lying down. Some were simply sitting with their legs extended. The hall was lit by a dim night light. No one's face was clearly visible in the half-light. To sit, or to lie down, or to knock on the door to the ICU and call the nurse and ask how Revathi was? Nothing was clear. If they had arrived ten minutes earlier, when Revathi was being admitted, they could have spoken to the doctor. She could have asked Ravi. But she hadn't because she couldn't get herself to talk to the murderer. She thought she could ask the nurse. Immediately, she walked by the southern wall, past the lifts, to the door to the ICU. She hesitated for a moment unsure whether to knock on the door or not. Her hand seemed to knock on the door by itself. The nurse opened the door and asked, 'What?'

'My daughter Revathi is inside. I want to see her.'

'You can't see her now.'

'I wasn't here when she was admitted. I arrived only when she was being taken inside.'

'This is an ICU. Also, this is the Fire Ward. You can't see her whenever you want.'

'I just need to see her face once.'

'I can't let anyone in without the doctor's permission.'

'Will she survive? Is there any danger to her life?' Amaravathi's eyes filled with tears.

'Nothing will happen. Go lie down,' she said. And generally to all the women in the hall, she announced like an order, 'No one should knock on the door just like that,' and shut the door.

Amaravathi stood like an orphaned child in front of the shut door. Darkness seemed to engulf her.

Her heart prayed to Pazhani Murugan. Revathi should have suffered only mild burns. And that burn should heal within ten or fifteen days. There shouldn't be a burn even the size of a dot on her face. She shouldn't have got burnt in her chest or abdomen. She shouldn't have had any burns on her hand, not even the size of those made by spluttering mustard. We shouldn't let her stay with Ravi now. We should file a complaint in the police station and separate them.

All women in the hall, those lying down and those sitting, saw Amaravathi standing in front of the ICU door. The woman sitting next to the lift said in a sympathetic tone, 'It doesn't matter how long you stand there, they won't let you in.'

Amaravathi looked at that woman. But she didn't speak. She looked at the doctors' room that was opposite. Only about five hundred feet away. She went straight to the doctors' room; the nurse who was sitting there asked, 'What do you want?'

'To see the doctor.'

'See the doctor in the morning.'

'My daughter was admitted only in the evening. I don't know how she is.'

'We'll take care of everything. You just be calm and lie down.'

'Can't I see the doctor?'

'See him in the morning. The doctor is busy inside now, he is picking out what is needed in the morning for each patient, the cloth needed for bandaging, ointment, syringes, and medicines. Can't disturb him now. Ask the doctor in the morning. He will tell you. Now go lie down.' The nurse spoke rudely. Amaravathi's eyes filled with tears. The tears brought her no concession. She stood still for two minutes. Since there was no change in the nurse's demeanour, she glanced into the inner room. She could see two doctors, and four nurses, selecting and arranging bandages, medicines, ointments, and syringes in each tray in front of them. The nurse said, 'Go lie down.' Amaravathi came out of the doctors' room.

She looked around the hall for a place to sit or lie down. There was a little space next to the western wall. She went and sat there. Malar, a woman who was sitting next to her, asked, 'What did they say, amma?'

Amaravathi remained silent.

'They don't let you in however much you plead.'

Amaravathi didn't open her mouth even now. If she knew how much per cent burns Revathi had suffered, she may have got some energy. She would have talked. The phone rang. She picked it up. 'Yes. I talked to the nurse. She wouldn't allow me inside. She refused to tell me how much per cent. This hospital is no good. Let us shift her tomorrow itself. They won't tell us what the status is. Has Murugan arrived? He'll arrive in fifteen minutes? How can I sleep? Okay, call again when Murugan arrives.' She disconnected the phone.

The noise of an ambulance arriving could be heard. It could be heard clearly because it was night. She looked at the eastern part of the room. Like things thrown haphazardly into a box, women were strewn around, lying down, sitting, their legs extended. It looked like a hallucinatory world. She wondered what would happen to Revathi. She felt like crying. She leaned her head against the wall and wept.

'They will call early in the morning at four or five,' the woman sitting next to her, Malar, said. Amaravathi asked, 'At four o'clock?'

'They start calling each one of us by turn at four.'

'How do you know?'

'It is three days now. I am here only.'

'Why?'

'My daughter has got burnt in a fire.'

'Will she survive?'

'It is more than eighty per cent. So, they say she won't survive.'

'The one burnt is your daughter?'

'Mmm.'

Amaravathi couldn't ask any more questions. Revathi's shaven head came to her mind. She felt like burning Ravi to ashes. Should hand him over to the police. Should file cases against him to prevent him from coming out. In her rage, she muttered curses against Ravi. Then she abused his mother and father. She then directed her fury on his caste and community. However much she abused them all, her anger did not abate even a bit.

Will Revathi survive? Will she be like she was? Will her face be alright and not ugly/repulsive? Will her face, arms, and legs be so terribly burnt that she would be confined to the house? Will people find her repulsive looking? Will she look so bad that people would avoid her? Will her burns be light? One doesn't know anything. If she could have known the per centage of her burns the fever in her mind may have come down a bit.

'Will you lie down?' She didn't reply to Malar's question.

'How did it happen?' Amaravathi didn't answer this either.

'No girl should suffer what my daughter did,' Malar said.

'What happened to your daughter?' Amaravathi asked.

'No idea.'

'You don't know?'

'That day I was herding goats in the forest. At noon, some guy came running and said this had happened. I ran directly here from the forest. By the time I reached, they had locked her in. Wouldn't let me see. They allowed me to see her only the next day early in the morning. She was lying like a piece of brinjal cooked in a stew. I lifted her to a sitting position and cleaned her. She was a bit conscious and spoke to me. When I went in yesterday, the clarity of the day before was gone. 'Do you know me? Do you know who I am?' I asked her. She said something, but it was incoherent. Her sight had gone bad, her speech had gone bad. Who knows what it will be like tomorrow morning, perhaps she will be gone?' Malar stopped talking. She blew her nose on her saree.

Revathi should not have been burnt eighty per cent. Her speech shouldn't go. Her eyesight shouldn't go. Amaravathi's heart desired that Revathi should have only some ordinary burns. She prayed to her favourite god, Pazhani Murugan, that her desire should be fulfilled. The phone rang then. She believed that if a bell rang when you were praying for something your work will get done. She picked up the phone and spoke, 'Yes, has Thambi arrived? You are leaving? Okay. Why do we need to ask her, file a case. I will feel at peace only if that scoundrel goes to jail. Why should she live with him after this? Let her stay at home with us. It is not as if she would live like a queen if she went back with him. She will live a life where it is a daily struggle to feed themselves. We didn't think that he would go this bad. We just let him be. We can't do that any longer. Even if we hit him only once it should be a fatal hit. He didn't tie a thaali around my girl's neck, it was a snake that he tied. Where in the world do you have policemen who are not amenable to bribes? Go talk to them.' She ended the call.

She felt thirsty. 'Do you have water?' She asked. Malar gave her a bottle of water and asked, 'How are you thirsty even in this cold?' Amaravathi drank the water silently.

Amaravathi's phone rang. She picked it up and talked, 'What, Thambi? How can I think of food in this state?' She cut the call. Immediately, she was filled with anger against Ravi. She thought of how all he had hit Revathi, kicked her, tortured her. As she thought of each instance her heart felt heavier. She wanted to send him to jail immediately. She could hear Malar sob. She wanted to say, 'Don't cry amma.' But she didn't. Malar spoke on her own.

'How do we account for human beings? Even cattle and goats live together. A man and a woman cannot stay together.'

Three cellphones rang all at once. The security guard came out of the doctors' room and said, 'Are you guys going to talk all night? How many times do you have to be told you cannot speak on your mobile phones here?' He returned to the doctors' room. All talk ceased only for a minute. Then like water dripping from a sieve, words began to flow again.

'From one market to another I would sell a kid and give her the money. How many kids I must have sold! When each kid was born, I would not let it fall on the floor and take it in my arms. Each one fell into my arms and grew up in my lap. From the time they were born to the time they were sold each one would run around in my shadow. They would roam around with me. The little donkeys, the kids, would never be separated from me, not even for a moment. Just the short while when we would lie down. They would lie around in the shed. At other times, even if we chased them out they wouldn't go anywhere. If they went to graze, wherever they were, I just had to make the sound "drrouw" and they would come running. They recognised my voice. I would pluck each leaf, each plant, and feed them. I would pluck karuvakkai and stuff it into their mouths. It is kids that I brought up like that which I sold. When the guy who paid me the money would change the rope and drag it away the kid would resist and run back to me. Would the guy who paid money keep quiet? He would kick them time and again in front of me. Even then they would try to run towards me dragging at the rope. They would keep bleating at me. I would be counting the money then to see if I had been paid right. Checking if any note was torn.' Malar wept a little loudly. Hearing the sound, the women in the hall who weren't asleep turned and looked at her.

Malar continued speaking through her tears, 'I felt no pity when each of the kids ran towards me pulling at the rope held by the guy who had paid money for them, when they looked at me and pleaded like cows. Every kid that I sold went away crying to me. Each one went getting kicks from the buyer. How could their lament spare me? That is the sin that has burnt my daughter.' She cleaned her mucus flowing from her nose with her saree. She wiped her eyes.

'It was only goats, let it go amma.' It didn't seem that Amaravathi's words fell on Malar's ears. As if carrying on the story from where one lets off, she carried on her talk from where she had stopped.

'They showed me money, showed me money, and snatched away every kid from me. And I kept selling them thinking the goat would foal one more kid.'

Amaravathi was astonished that instead of weeping for

her daughter who was lying burnt in a fire, Malar was weeping for the kids she had sold.

She looked at the weeping Malar. At least Malar knew what her daughter's state was, she didn't even know that. She checked her cellphone to see how much time was left. It was two o'clock. How would two more hours pass? She felt that unlike other days, the night was never-ending.

'Did you file a case against your son-in-law?'

'I am female. He is a man. On top of it, he is Maniyar caste. He also has money. Will the police listen to him or to me? The world belongs to the one with money, doesn't it? Should I cry that my daughter is going to die? Or should I file a case and roam here and there for the police?'

'But can you leave a murderer alone for that?'

'If I file a case, I will have to look at his face, isn't it?'

'What was their fight about?'

'Do a man and a woman need a reason to fight? Isn't a stone in the rice enough to cut her down?'

They could hear an ambulance come and stop. Amaravathi's heartbeat became faster every time she heard the sound of an ambulance arriving or leaving. What had happened to someone, her mind agonised. She had seen ambulances on the road so many times before this. She had heard their sound. Her heartbeat didn't quicken then. Her body didn't turn cold. Her stomach did not feel as if a stove was burning in it.'

Amaravathi asked Malar, 'Is there a restroom here?'

'I'll show you,' said Malar and got up and walking carefully not to step on anyone went to the room next to the one where Revathi had been bandaged. The toilet was to the right.

Malar and Amaravathi returned to the place where they had been sitting earlier and sat down.

'They will only call at four?'

'Mmm.'

'What will they ask us to do?'

'They will ask us to lift them and make them sit. Will tell us to make them wash their mouths. The nurses will remove the cloth bandages around the body with great speed. They will give us cotton. We have to clean the entire body. We have to hold them up. Immediately, the nurses will apply the medicines. They will bandage them again and make them lie down. As soon as that is done, they will chase us out saying "Get out".'

'Won't the nurses clean them?'

'Even a mother can't bear to look at the burnt body. Can't bear to touch. What will a nurse do? I have cleaned her for two days with my eyes closed.' Amaravathi was surprised by Malar's words. Shouldn't the nurses clean the patients, she thought.

'How many children?'

'The one who is lying there burnt, she is the only one.'

'Where is your husband?'

'It is thirty years since the earth claimed him.'

4

'You look as if you belong to a well-off family. Why did your daughter do this?' When Malar asked, Amaravathi was overcome with tears.

'Is she an educated girl?'

'Yes, she is educated, she is. She studied a brainless course!'

'Did she elope and get married?'

'After she completed her studies, during the month she was at home, she would go to the temple. It is in that month that all this trouble, this nonsense, happened. God knows where he saw her, he started following her day and night, and tattooed her name all over his body. I will die without you he said to her and slashed his arms and legs with a blade and changed her mind. As soon as I heard, I fought with her. My son, everyone, spoke to her. She didn't listen. If I marry, I will only marry him. Otherwise, I won't marry at all, she said. She received her appointment order. We told her not to join work, fearing that she would run away. When we said let us find a groom and set the date, she poured kerosene on herself. We said alright and stopped that marriage. After three months, we fixed another groom, and she went to hang herself. Then we found a doctor and fixed the match with him. She opened the gas and was about to set herself on fire with a matchstick. It was after that that we said let her at least remain alive and fixed the marriage with that scoundrel of a lout.'

'What does the boy do?'

'He drives an auto.'

'Oh okay.'

'My saar said you are saying that you don't need your appa, amma, anna, relatives, and caste. From now, you shouldn't come here. You shouldn't meet us again. It was saying this that he conducted the wedding.'

'What did your girl say in reply to that?'

'She said okay.'

'If she had slept over it, her madness would have disappeared.'

'She did all this thinking she could go to work once married, that they could leave town.'

'Was she highly educated?'

'She had studied Engineering.'

'Why didn't she follow the good path she had then?'

'The very next day after the marriage, he told her she couldn't go out. That she couldn't talk to her neighbours. That she couldn't step out onto the street.'

'Does he have any property or money?'

'Only one autorickshaw. That too bought on mortgage.'

'Oh okay.'

'We didn't have any contact with her for the first six-seven months after marriage. As soon as she conceived, he beat her up asking who was going to pay the medical bills. Hearing the news, it was I who went and admitted her to hospital. She came to our house with her child. Our saar didn't talk to her. I sent her back after ten days. He chased her out when she was about to have her second child. I again took her to hospital. She came and stayed with us for ten days again.'

'Even then your family didn't talk to her?'

'No.'

'Oh, okay.'

'After that, she would come home sometimes. When she came, she wouldn't enter the house immediately. She would wait outside checking if her father was there, whether her brother was there. I would ask why are you standing outside. It was then that she would enter the house. Even then she would keep standing saying, "I have to go. I have to go." He wouldn't even let her sit and eat. If she went missing for fifteen minutes, he would immediately take his auto and come stand outside the house.' Amaravathi sighed.

'If she stood outside, she was gone. If she stood in the street, gone. If she went to a shop, gone. He would beat her up badly. He was suspicious twenty-four hours a day, that scoundrel.'

'You daughter caught someone like that?' Malar asked in some doubt.

'My daughter would never answer back. Wouldn't fight. Wouldn't say a bad word. She wouldn't tell us even about being beaten and kicked. "Be good. Don't smoke, don't drink," she would tell him. The beating and the kicks were for that. I don't know how she withstood that beating, all those kicks. From the time she was born, neither I nor our saar had ever hit her. We had never seen her in tears. We never saw her face fall because she lacked something. Our saar loved his daughter. He wouldn't let her do anything around the house. He wouldn't let her go near the stove or even wash the dishes. She hadn't even washed her own clothes. That street lout settled the accounts for all that. She would read a lot of story books. She would read English books. The only money she spent on herself was to buy books. He would beat her up asking, "Did you come to run a family, or to read books?"'

'Even the females are not blameless. They can be short-tempered bitches.'

'My daughter isn't like that. Be it in our street, or in our community, no one said a bad thing about her. From a young age, no one ever said that they saw her here or saw her there. No one said she didn't study well. Of what use, all that? Her fate was written badly,' Amaravathi said and blew her nose.

'Be it at home or be it outside, she wouldn't talk disrespectfully to anyone, wouldn't behave badly. She earned a reputation for being really a good person. She lost everything the day she saw that scoundrel. None of us thought she would do a thing like this. Heartless. She was so obstinate. "I won't elope with him. I will only go with him if you agree to and conduct our marriage. I won't marry anyone but him," she held fast to this like a monkey. How much I had to hear from our saar and our son because of her. I gave her twenty sovereigns gold jewellery. He didn't make a living with any of it. I gave each child one sovereign gold chain each. He ate up even that. Other than the thaali around her neck he sold and ate everything, that scrounger.'

The door to the ICU opened. A nurse emerged and went into the doctors' room. In a little while five nurses and two doctors went into the ICU. Seeing that, the women who were lying down or sitting stood up. A few went to the toilet and returned. Malar stood up. Immediately, Amaravathi stood up and kept looking at the door to the ICU. All the women in that room looked excited and agitated. A nurse came out and said, 'Kasturi's attendant, please come.' One of the women who was standing went into the ICU in great haste.

Every ten minutes or eight minutes, the nurse called out to each female attendant. Every woman who entered came out crying, with their eyes full of tears. Not one of them spoke of what they did inside, how they did it. All that talk that had filled the room before four o'clock had disappeared now. Looking at the faces of the women who emerged from the ICU, Amaravathi was filled with an unknown fear and dread. As the nurse called each person, Amaravathi was filled with anxiety for when they would call her, when she would be able to see Revathi. Her body was trembling as if she were waiting to jump into the abyss from a mountain top.

5

'Who is Revathi's attendant?'

'I am here, amma.'

'Come in.'

As soon as Amaravathi entered the ICU the nurse handed her a green-coloured gown. She gave her a mask to wear over her nose. She also gave her gloves to wear. She took each of them in her hands and asked, 'What are these for?' The nurse only said, 'Wear the gown.' Amaravathi felt alarmed when she saw the objects in her hands. She wondered why she needed all of them for meeting a patient. 'Do I have to wear this?' She asked.

'Certainly. Otherwise, there may be infection. Quick,' the nurse hurried her. The nurse was wearing gloves. She was also wearing a mask covering her nose and mouth.

Amaravathi wore her gown backwards. The nurse spotted it and said, 'You are wearing it the other way round. Take it off and wear it correctly.' She wore the gown the way the nurse instructed.

'Wear the mask.'

Amaravathi faltered. The nurse helped her wear the mask. Amaravathi wore the gloves herself. The nurse saw that her hands were shaking in fear and asked, 'If you are so afraid, how will you clean the patient?' Amaravathi looked at the nurse and at the room. It was as dimly lit as the hall. The ICU was in the North-South alignment. They had left a little space in the middle and divided the room into two with a glass partition. The beds of the patients were in the western side. On the eastern side was the room where they cleaned and bandaged the patients and next to it was the doctors' room and next to that was the room for the nurses on duty. The last room had medical supplies. The nurse walked to the west following the path between two glass partitions and Amaravathi followed her. Reaching the other side of the hall, opening a door to the west, the nurse said, 'Eighteenth bed, go lift and make her sit. I'll come.' She went off to the medical supplies room.

There were nine big beds each on either side of the room. On each bed women had been placed like white cloth bundles. When you saw them they didn't look like women but like white ghosts. When she was struggling to spot bed number eighteen, a doctor and two nurses came and stood near Revathi's bed, thus enabling Amaravathi to realise that it was the one.

'Lift her and make her sit,' the nurse said.

She went near the bed. Only Revathi's face was visible. The rest of her was covered in bandages. She only saw her face. 'Oh God,' Amaravathi turned her face away.

'You can't shout here,' the nurse admonished her. Again, when Amaravathi looked at Revathi's face, the very instant that she saw her, she cried out, 'Oh God.'

'If you are easily frightened, why do you come as attendants?' the nurse asked. In her agitation, fear, trembling, to not cry at the grotesqueness/horror of Revathi's face, Amaravathi covered her mouth tightly with both her hands.

'Lift her and make her sit.'

'Take her to the dressing room.' As it didn't look as if Amaravathi had heard her, the nurse took her there. The others followed. It was only ten or twenty feet distant. The nurse removed the bandages. With skin having peeled off the whole body, Revathi looked like a plucked chicken. There wasn't a single thread of cloth on her body.

'Is this my daughter?'

'Isn't your daughter Revathi?'

'Mmm.'

'Amma.' It seemed to come from far away. That voice was the only proof that the body standing there was Revathi.

'My girl,' Amaravathi covered her face.

'What are you doing, amma? You shouldn't cry here. It will have an impact on other patients.' The doctor said softly.

'This is not my daughter.' Amaravathi cried.

'If you are so frightened, why did you come as her attendant?' The nurse spoke harshly. Seeing Revathi's bare body look slimy like a snake which had sloughed off its skin, Amaravathi slumped to the floor like a leaf fluttering down from a tree.

'Send her out. If there is someone else call her,' the doctor said angrily.

Escorting Amaravathi to the nurses' room and seating her there, a nurse opened the ICU door and called out to the guard. When he came in answer, she said, 'Is there anyone else who has come with a patient called Revathi? Find out.' She shut the door immediately.

Opening the door to the hall, the guard asked those sitting on the stairs, 'Is there someone with a patient called Revathi?' 'I am here,' said Ravi and stood up.

'Come inside.'

Ravi came to stand in front of the ICU with the guard. The guard knocked on the door. After two or three minutes, the nurse who opened the door, asked, 'Is there someone with her?'

'This is the man.' The security guard pointed to Ravi.

'What are you to the patient?'

'Her husband.'

'We can't let a man in. Please stay, I will go and ask the doctor.' The nurse shut the door. After asking the doctor she came and opened the door and said, 'Come inside.' When

Ravi entered the ICU, she shut the door and handed him one by one a gown, mask, gloves, and socks. When he had worn them, she took him to the dressing room and asked him to clean Revathi.

Amaravthi came back to consciousness slowly. She looked around at the nurses' room where she was seated. From where she was sitting, only ten feet away to the west was Revathi's bed. The door was shut. She could hear a patient crying loudly when someone was cleaning the patient and applying ointment and other medicines and tying the bandages. She could hear a nurse saying, 'Stay still, stay still.' She wondered whether she should take off her mask, what to do about her gown, about her gloves. She looked strange to herself in the gloves, mask, and gown. Everything looked strange—that place, glass doors, glass partitions, the low noise, soft murmurs, patients lying like white ghosts, and the dim light. She hadn't spoken a word to Revathi. She hadn't asked her how she was. She hadn't asked her anything, who set her on fire, how did it happen, what case to file, nothing. She lowered her face to the table. Will she survive?

The nurse who entered the room asked with solicitude, 'Are you alright now?' Amaravathi lifted her face and looked at her.

'You should leave now.'

'My girl?'

'We called Revathi's husband to clean her and she has been bandaged again and made to lie in her bed. Please take off everything and go out.'

'Will my girl survive, amma?'

'Please go out. It is time.' The nurse said and left the room. Amaravathi could see a woman attendant go out from the room where they did the bandaging. In a few seconds, she could see another woman attendant go inside. When she saw the doctor coming out of the room, she got up and went to him and said, 'I want to see my girl.' The doctor asked, 'What are you to the patient?'

'Mother.'

'Malathi,' the doctor called out. A nurse came.

'Please allow her for just a minute.'

'She fainted, sir.'

'Now she is bandaged, isn't she? Allow her in for just a minute.'

'Yes sir.'

The doctor left.

'Come, amma.' Malathi called. Amaravathi followed her. Malathi opened the door and let her in and said, 'You can't speak loudly. Don't talk all kinds of stuff to the patient.'

Amaravathi nodded her head seemingly in assent. Malathi left. Amaravathi approached Revathi's bed and stood there. Her eyes were shut as if she had no more cares left in the world. Apart from her face, no part of her body was visible. The whole body was covered in bandages. Her face was swollen. The head looked black as if covered with a charred cloth. As she noticed each thing, Amaravathi felt as if she was standing on water. She tried to call, 'Revathi.' Her mouth refused to open. Her lips refused to move. 'Why did he do this? What is happening to your body? Is it burning? Paining? What happened? What was the quarrel that grew big enough for him to set fire to you? What were you doing when he poured oil on you and set you on fire? Couldn't you have run out on to the street?' A hundred, a thousand questions rose in her mind. But not one question came out of her mouth in words. Like worms in the earth, the questions remained in her mind. She got a hold on herself and called out softly.

'Revathi…'

Revathi's eyes opened.

'Revathi…'

'Don't cry, Amma. I won't die.'

'Oh God.'

'Will my face become like before, Amma?'

'There is nothing the matter with you.'

'Don't cry, Amma.'

'I am not crying.'

'I can see you crying. Do I look so horrible? I feel like seeing my face in a mirror, Amma.'

'Nothing is the matter with you. Be quiet.'

'Why did you run away frightened earlier?'

'…'

Amaravathi struggled not knowing what to say. She couldn't bear to continue seeing Revathi's face. She felt that her heart would explode. She just wanted to run away from that place.

She tried to touch Revathi. Her hands dropped. She tried to see Revathi. Tears curtained her eyes.

'Amma,' Revathi called. She wanted to talk. But Amaravathi was unable to speak. Her mouth refused to open. She couldn't ask even one of the questions she had thought of the previous night.

'Amma, where is Appa?'

'He is outside.'

'Has Anna come?'

'He is also outside only.'

'Arunmozhi?'

'She came at night itself.'

'Did Appa cry, Amma?'

'He has been crying since the day you said you wanted that auto guy.'

'Leave that alone, Amma.'

'Should we go to a different hospital?'

'No need, Amma.'

'Your father has been going around with ten lakh rupees since yesterday.'

Malathi came back. She gestured, 'Enough, please come out,' as if even speaking a little loudly would lead to great danger.

'Please go out.'

'Muruga of the Pazhani hill, are you alive? You have done this to my daughter.' Amaravathi cried.

'Please go out. There are so many patients here. Seeing you weep, they will also cry. That is why we don't allow anyone inside. Please leave.' While saying this, Malathi pulled Amaravathi's arm to send her out. 'Amma,' called Revathi then. Neither Amaravathi nor Malathi heard her voice.

6

Revathi wanted to talk to Amaravathi. But she couldn't open her mouth or move it. Apart from her eyes, nose, and mouth, they had bandaged her everywhere. And they had put a mask on her nose. At dawn, they had applied a bucketful of ointment on her body and bandaged her. The bandage was two inches thick. Even after so much ointment, her body burnt as if she were lying in a fire pit. There wasn't even a small spot in her body where she didn't feel this burning. They put the medicines for the wounds and for sleeping in the glucose drip itself. She felt all the time as if she was sleepy, that she should keep sleeping. When the effects of the medicines receded, she couldn't stand the burning even for five or ten minutes. She would feel as is she were dying. 'It's burning, sister.' As soon as she cried out, the ward sister would come and add the sleeping medicine to the glucose. Within a minute or two she would feel as if she were flying in the sky, or buried in the ground, or drowning in water. Even that would be only for a few minutes. After that there would be no movement, no consciousness. Opening the eyes, moving the body were impossible tasks. When Amaravathi came, the nurse had removed the mask.

'Amma, don't leave. Stay here only. I won't die. Don't cry, Amma. Listen to me. After going with Ravi, I have never spoken the truth to you.

If they hadn't banned the lottery, Ravi would have been selling lottery tickets. He wouldn't have been driving an auto. He wouldn't have driven some passengers to the temple.

He must have seen me only for three days. I don't know how he found out my name, but on the fourth day he tattooed my name on his chest and both his arms and came to show me. Would a man tattoo on his chest and arms the name of a girl he had seen only for three or four days? Ravi did exactly that. He is a little mental Amma. And I a little cracked.

Are you listening to me, Amma?

What does he have? How many times you asked me, why do you like him? I always replied "I don't know" then. Even now I say the same thing. I don't know. Perhaps it was that he had tattooed my name on his chest and arms, or that every time he saw me he said, "I will die if you don't marry me", and cutting his arm with a blade. You won't believe it, but he would cut his arms just like that, do you know? When he tattooed my name and came and showed me my mind panicked as if I had jumped off a cliff. It was that moment that my fate was rewritten. Each and every day he would tattoo my name on a different part of his body and show me. He would show me where he had cut himself with a blade. I felt bad for him, pitied him. That was all. He wasn't a crane. He was a frog.

You have asked me so many questions about Ravi. I could never answer them. I would then think, "Chee, don't want this". As soon as you went away, I would remember the tattoos, him cutting his arms. Instantly, my heart would go and jump into the garbage. In the whole world, there is nothing as debased as shameless as the heart.

Appa said so much to me. Annan didn't even talk to me. He stood before me with a cut arm and a bottle of poison.

What could I do? I thought Appa and you would be at peace only if this issue came to an end. So, I thought that we should get married soon. You conducted the marriage as if you were getting rid of a tiresome fly. Even that was a big gesture. How humiliated you felt at the marriage, I know. On the day the marriage took place, no one was happy other than Ravi.

When I was at our home, my mind was occupied with him. The very first night in his house, I kept remembering our house. What can one say about the heart? I would fall asleep at our home whenever I laid down. I could never fall asleep in his house. There was no space in that house to sleep alone. Mosquitoes on top of it. Sleep would never come. Because I couldn't sleep, I would keep thinking of you, of Appa, of Annan. Only a kilometer separated our houses, I felt it was like an ocean.

How come Revathi is talking so much today, is that what you are thinking Amma? I have made you cry too much.

It is burning too much. I can't stand it. It's as if I am dying. Can't lie down. Better to die than stand this burning. I don't know why they keep this place dark always. I want to turn but can't move my body. Call the nurse and tell her to give me an injection to stop this burning. It is killing me.

Amma...

Don't go away. Stay with me.... You shouldn't cry listening to all I say.

Are you crying, Amma?

Whenever Appa called me he would say, "Amma, amma." In the whole world, the practice of calling a daughter a mother is there in Tamil Nadu only. How many years is it since Appa called me "Amma"? Why couldn't Appa get angry like Ravi, yell at me like him? Why couldn't he curse me? If I die, will you read Thiruvachakam, Amma?

Why don't you talk, Amma?

When I am discharged, I am going to come home with you. I am going to work. Whatever happens, okay. Tell Annan and tell him to give my application in his company itself.

When I was studying Engineering, I said I would work only in TCS. When I was selected in the campus interview, I thought my wish had come true. It was the day I received the order to join training in Noida that Ravi came to our house and cut his arms. You cried loudly. I got angry because of that. So, I tore up the order. The situation may have been different if I had gone to Noida. Why did Ravi choose that day to come to our house and cut his arms outside?

Amma... why aren't you saying anything?

Among my batchmates who joined TCS, many own flats, have cars. When you fall in love, you don't think that you will need money, a house, relatives. The very minute you get married you think you need money, house, and relatives. It is money that binds people together. And separates them.

Are you able to hear me, Amma? If you can't, come nearer, Amma.

Everything would have been different if Ravi had listened to me, allowed me to work. Your weeping would have become less. The minute I mentioned that I wanted to go to Madras, I wanted to work, he would get so angry. He thought I would leave him if I went to work. Do you know how difficult it is for a pretty woman? The difficulty she faces because she is beautiful can't be understood by others.

Are you crying listening to me? Tears cannot heal any wounds.

When Ravi would come back drunk and lie there, when he would vomit and lie there unconscious, how could I sleep? I would lie awake all night. Then I would remember how you and Appa told me not to marry Ravi, pleaded with me, cried. I would think of each incident and weep. I would feel like sharing it all with you. I couldn't say it in person. I thought I should at least put it down on paper. I would immediately get some paper and write. I wrote pages and pages. I would write till sunrise. In the morning, after he got up and left in his auto without any memory of having vomited at night and lying there senseless, I would read what I had written all night. Even I couldn't read it. Tears would flow from my eyes. I would think how much you would cry if you read it. I would tear it up immediately. So many nights, so many pages. If you people had read it, neither you nor Appa would have wanted to live. Every night I would fill the pages. With my weeping. With my tears.

It is only when they are drunk that many people remember their wives. All that drama was because of that.

Are you listening, Amma?

All that happened is an accident. Let it go. Don't blame anyone. Don't curse anyone. When I come home, I want to go to work. That is my desire now.

One should have luck to be alive. My greatest fortune was to be born to you and Appa.

Amma, you are near me, no? I thought that perhaps you had gone down. Tell the sister and stay here. No, you don't ask. They won't let you. I will tell the sister. Stay. I will call her. "Sister, sister…"'

Revathi called the sister without pause. Her voice didn't come out. Her lips didn't move.

7

As soon as she came out of the ICU, Amaravathi cried loudly, 'She is without any clothes in front of the doctor. Even I can't bear to see my own daughter. He has burnt her fully. Not even one god has punished him.' As soon as they heard Amaravathi crying, the women and men waiting outside on the staircase got up and came to the door to try and know who was crying, who had died. Murugan and Natesan were part of the crowd and, recognising Amaravathi's voice, they knocked hard on the door. The guard opened the door and asked, 'What?'

'My mother is crying. Have to see her, sir.' Murugan said in a panic.

The guard opened the door. Murugan and Natesan rushed to Amaravathi and asked her, 'What happened?' Even more so than before, Amaravathi felt like crying on seeing Murugan and Natesan. She cried but didn't tell them what had happened. She couldn't speak. Murugan and Natesan thought that Revathi had died. Her crying made them believe that.

'First, tell us what happened, Amma.'

'She is lying like a corpse Thambi, your sister.'

Murugan spotted a doctor come out of the ICU and go into a room with a board that read Duty Doctor, and went there saying, 'Come, Amma.' He asked nervously, 'Sir, how is the patient called Revathi?'

'Who are you?'

'I am the patient's elder brother, sir.' Amaravathi and Natesan entered the room then.

'Which case?' The doctor asked Malathi who was nearby.

'Revathi, sir.'

'Which bed?'

'Number eighteen, sir. The case that was admitted yesterday evening sir.' Malathi said.

'Where is the report?'

'Inside, sir.'

'Get it please.'

Malathi went out, entered the ICU and brought the report and handed it to the doctor. The doctor's face changed as soon as he began to read the report.

'The treatment is on.' The doctor said. Even that he seemed to say because he had to say something. Then, Amaravathi acted as if insane, and took off the bangles from her arms, and the chain from around her neck one by one and placed them on the doctor's table. She folded her hands and said with uncontrollable tears, 'We have a big house. We have three empty plots. We have thirty forty sovereign gold jewellery at home. I will sell everything and give you the money. Please give my daughter back alive.'

Seeing Amaravathi's actions, Natesan took out from his

handbag the bundles of notes that he had been carrying and kept them on the doctor's table. The doctor looked from Amaravathi to Natesan and said patiently, 'Pick up all this and keep it away. There is no necessity for all this here. We don't treat people for money here. There will be no shortcoming in the treatment. We don't check the status of a person before we treat her.'

'Should we shift her to a different hospital, sir?' When Murugan asked this, the doctor's face changed. It looked as if he was a slightly angry.

'Won't we give good treatment without charging money?'

'Sorry, sir.'

'Wherever you go, the treatment is the same. In these cases of fire, JIPMER is the best in this region.'

'Is there any threat to her life?'

'The admission was only last evening. Only now have we changed the first dressing. Let's see.' The doctor got up.

'What per cent sir? They say survival isn't possible over forty-fifty per cent.'

'Will one become alright as soon as one is admitted? Don't the medicines and tablets need some time to take effect?' The doctor said this and looked at the jewellery and the money on the table. Whatever struck him, he said in a tired voice, 'At this moment, none of this has any meaning. Right now, this money is worthless.' He left the room. All three, Murugan, Natesan, and Amaravathi came out of the doctor's room into the hall.

'Come, Amma. Let us go down. We can wash our face, drink tea and come back.' Murugan called Amaravathi.

'No need.'

Amaravathi couldn't stand or speak much. It seemed as if all the blood in her body had seeped away, and she was now an empty shell. She had no energy at all in her body.

'Don't you have to wash your face? Don't you have to rinse your mouth? Come let us go down and come back up.' Murugan said. With each stair accommodating two or three people, there were twenty odd people there. That itself irritated him. So, he started compelling Amaravathi. He didn't know that there was always a crowd out there. Natesan also said, 'Come, let us go down and come back.' Without any reply, Amaravathi began to go down the stairs. Murugan and Natesan followed her.

'Let me get hold of him, I will beat that bastard with my slippers.' Murugan gnashed his teeth.

They discovered the place earmarked for the attendants of the patients to have a bath. Amaravathi washed her face and rinsed her mouth.

'Come, Amma,' Murugan said, and walked ahead.

They went to the canteen which was two hundred to three hundred feet to the south of the Emergency block. As they reached there, Amaravathi immediately sat down on the cement bench in front of the canteen. Natesan also sat down. The sun was behind a big tree to the east.

'You didn't go home at all at night?'

'We went. Immediately, we showered, changed our clothes, and came back. We brought clothes for you also. You can change your clothes now, if you want to.'

'Why do I need to change my clothes now?'

'Did you see our child? What did she say? How is she?'

'There is nothing to say.'

'What are you saying?'

Amaravathi covered her face with the edge of her saree.

Murugan brought tea in two cups.

'Because he had tied a four anna thread around her neck, he set fire to her making her suffer so much pain, catch him and throw him into jail, Thambi,' she told Murugan.

'First, stop crying. Tell us how she is and what she said.' Murugan spoke angrily.

'That poor girl is looking for you both. She didn't speak another word. She didn't ask about anyone else.'

'Don't cry, Amma. Nothing will happen.' Murugan consoled his mother.

Amaravathi looked up at the fifth floor of the Emergency block. She spoke in a bitter voice.

'How my child must have screamed when she was set on fire.'

'I can't find where he is.' Murugan gnashed his teeth.

'Get up, Amma. Let us go upstairs. I want to see Revathi. I have to ask her and file a complaint against him. Let me see who survives, him or me.'

'Don't see her, Thambi.' Amaravathi seemed to order him.

'What are you saying, Amma?'

'She is completely burnt.'

'You get up. Whatever it is, I have to see her.' Murugan compelled Amaravathi to get up and walked towards the building with her.

Flies were hovering around the three cups of tea which remained untouched on the bench.

The sun was rising in the east above the tree.

8

Opening the door, the security guard asked, 'Who is Revathi's attendant?' Murugesan, Natesan, Amaravathi, all three ran up to him.

'Only one of you must come in.'

Defying him, all three ran inside. They crossed the hall quickly and halted in front of the ICU door. The guard who came along with them, knocked on the ICU door. The nurse who opened the door, asked 'What?'

'You asked me to call Revathi's attendant. Here.'

'Please buy the injection written in this prescription and bring it.' The nurse extended a sheet. Murugan took it and rushed away. Amaravathi asked the nurse who was about to shut the door, 'Is my daughter crying?'

'What is the patient's name?'

'Revathi.'

'I have just come for duty. I will check and let you know. Please wait outside.' She shut the door immediately. The next moment, the guard told Natesan, 'Sir, please wait outside.'

'Can we see the doctor?' Natesan asked.

'If needed, they themselves will call you.'

The guard opened the door and Natesan and Amaravathi went out.

Amaravathi sat down on the staircase to the sixth floor. Natesan sat down next to her. As soon as she sat down, Amaravathi rested her face on her knees. Hearing of Revathi's immolation in the fire, travelling to the hospital in a panic, not sleeping all night, seeing Revathi's burnt body, not having eaten, all of it had exhausted her.

Thangammal, who was sitting on the step below Amaravathi, asked, 'Burnt was she?'

Amaravathi lifted her face and asked, 'Are you asking me?'

'Yes, amma.'

'The case that came last evening as it was getting dark?'

'Yes.'

'I saw when she was taken off the ambulance at six last evening, there wasn't space to touch her with a finger. Every inch was burnt. I don't know how these sinful bitches find the nerve to set themselves on fire, and then they scream, "Help, help." When a mustard sputters and falls on your arm, it burns as if you are losing your life. When a woman burns like a house on fire, how much her body must suffer?'

'How was my daughter, amma? Did she scream when they lifted and brought her in?'

'How could she not scream when she was burnt so fully? Iron itself melts when you put it in fire, what is a human body? Only a guy with a beard was with her. Is that guy your son-in-law?' Thangammal asked. Amaravathi did not reply only to that question.

'I went down to have some tea and water and saw all this. They took her off the ambulance at that time.'

'Did she scream a lot?'

'How could she not? She screamed as if she was being killed.'

'Oh, God,' Amaravathi said and covered her face with her hands and sobbed.

'Sivane,' exclaimed Natesan.

'These males torture the women so much and beat them so much. It is only when their dicks rise up that they want their females. Otherwise, they don't want them. These bitches also run for that saying they don't want their fathers, don't want their mothers.'

'Which place do you come from, amma?'

'Karuveppilankurichi.'

'What have you come here for?'

'A daughter of my older brother set herself on fire because of a husband-wife quarrel. It is eight days today. It is not as if she is alive. Nor as if she is dead.'

'What did the doctor say?'

'Hasn't said yes. Hasn't said no. Whenever we asked, no one has said more than "Let's see." When we ask others, they say sixty per cent, she won't survive. It is with these hands that I raised her. It is with my own hands I am going to throw earth on her.' Thangammal said and asked. 'How much per cent for your daughter?'

'Don't know.'

'Didn't the doctor say?'

'No, amma.'

'If the doctor doesn't open his mouth, it is a gone case,' when Thangammal said this, Natesan and Amaravathi got angry immediately.

'Keep quiet for a while, amma,' when Natesan said this, Thangammal shut her mouth.

'In all these years, if even once we had called him and threatened him to behave himself my daughter would not have been burnt in this fire. The dog would also have learnt to behave. An auto driver, a drunkard, a mannerless fellow, you said all this and kept away from him. That is why he has burnt her,' when Amaravathi said this, Natesan grew furious.

'Do you know where and how we are?'

'Do you know how my heart is burning?'

'You talk as if I know nothing. I only know the humiliation I have felt for the last six years.'

'You gave her money. You gave her things. You never questioned whatever I gave or did. What is the result of all that? You didn't call that dog and threaten him. If he had been threatened, he would have learnt some fear. He would have behaved. "What to say to a street mongrel", you said. "We will lose our honour, we will lose our honour," you felt and kept away from him.'

'It is only humiliation for me till I die.' Natesan said with bitterness and hatred.

'That guy was no match for our daughter in education, accomplishment, status, or caste, he wasn't fit in any way for her. A mongrel of an auto driver. A dog begging for food. It is your daughter who said she wanted that dog.'

'Be quiet.'

'Now, no one will lose their honour. Nor their respect. Now, no one needs to throw stones on shit.' She spoke spitefully.

'Do you know what you are saying? Why do you speak of her as dead when she is still alive?' When Natesan asked this, Amaravathi kept silent for a little while. But she couldn't remain so for long.

He listened patiently to her accusations and finally spoke.

'If I asked him, ticked him off, I was afraid he would take it out on our girl, hit her, kick her. That is why I didn't talk to him or go to the police. If he faced this once, he wouldn't be afraid the next time. He would lose his fear forever. If we stayed away, he may still have some concern about us, I thought. I didn't get involved in this for that reason. For so many years because I wanted my daughter should live without further trouble, remain alive. If I said something, and he replied, it could have worsened and become so bad her meetings with you may also stop. If she didn't have the money that you gave her, her life may become more difficult. So, I kept quiet. If he and I had quarrelled, she may have reacted that he had insulted Appa, and may have had a big fight with him, and he may have beaten her up very badly, thinking so I kept away.' Natesan couldn't speak any more. His eyes were full of tears. He lowered his head.

Amaravathi looked at Natesan strangely. He had never spoken so many words to her. That itself was a big surprise to her. Whenever asked anything, he would only reply in one or two words. Even that would be, 'okay' or 'will do', or 'will see', or 'you see'. He was sitting there completely weighed down. She avoided looking at him and lowered her head to her knees and said in a bitter voice, 'It looks as if my daughter is going to the cremation ground.' When she heard that, Thangammal turned to look at Amaravathi and said, 'Don't say that with your own tongue, amma. She may survive. Pray to God. Good will happen.'

It was very humid there. There was no breeze at all. Everyone had started perspiring in the morning itself.

Murugan came back after giving the injection that the nurse had asked for and sat to the right of Amaravathi.

Amaravathi and Natesan asked in one voice, 'Did you ask the nurse for any news? What did she say?'

'I asked. "Wait outside," she said.'

'He has brought us down to sit like this, that garbage picking dog.' Murugan exclaimed.

'You went inside, what happened? What did she say? Did she ask us to file a case or not? Did she speak clearly? Did you ask whether we should take her to a private hospital?' Murugan asked.

'Don't ask anything, Thambi.' Amaravathi said, cutting short the conversation.

The guard came out then and called, 'Kavitha's attendant please come.' A woman sitting on the stairs got up hurriedly and ran inside.

'Shouldn't we file a case?' Murugan asked.

'A brother-in-law of one of the teacher's is an SI in Mangalampettai. I asked the teacher to speak to him. The SI said that he would speak in the police station and let us know. I want to act after we understand everything,' Natesan replied.

'We should make that dog sit inside the jail at least for an hour.' Murugan gnashed his teeth. His phone rang then. He answered the call.

Two women came down from the sixth floor and Murugan got up to give way to them. He sat down again as soon as they went down the steps. Natesan's cellphone rang then and he went towards the sixth floor with it.

'How is Revathi really, Amma?' Murugan asked as if speaking secrets.

'She is like a corpse, that is all.'

The guard came out then and ordered, 'All of you clear the stairs and go down. Not one of you should remain here.'

'Even the attendants?' A woman asked.

'Whoever it is, you have to go down. Come back up after an hour.'

A woman in a green dress came out of the ICU with a yellow plastic bag and dropped it in a big plastic bin kept near the corner of the staircase.

Another nurse said loudly to the guard in the hall, 'Tell me when you have made everyone go down. Not one person should remain.'

The guard started shouting, 'Go downstairs, go downstairs.' A few knew why he was saying that. A few were bewildered. 'We are sitting outside only, no?' They asked the guard. Some got up and walked as if they were going to the sixth floor. Some were confused whether they should go up or down. Amaravathi had the same confusion. The ones with passes were sure of themselves. Others weren't so sure and didn't know what to do. If they went downstairs. it wasn't easy to come back up. Only those with passes could go downstairs any time and also come back upstairs any time. Those without passes could only come up during the visiting time after five o'clock. If anyone still wanted to come up, then a pass-holder would have to go down and give them the pass. Murugan and Amaravathi got up and stood up, not knowing what to do. Natesan came down at that moment, having finished his phone call.

'Go down, go down,' the guard was forcing people one by one. The crowd lessened gradually. 'Only Brinda's attendant should stay,' the guard said. Malar and two women with her who were sitting on the stairs to the fourth floor got up and went to the guard and asked, 'Why didn't you call us to clean her early morning?'

'Come inside.'

Malar and the two women went into the hall. It wouldn't have been a minute since they went in, you could hear Malar crying loudly as if in mortal pain.

Three men came in a hurry from downstairs and knocked on the door. The guard opened the door and asked, 'What?'

'The girl who died now, Brinda, I am her husband,' one man said.

'Come inside,' said the guard and let all three go in and, glaring at the others still left there, said, 'Why are so many of you still standing here? Go downstairs. Won't you listen if I speak politely?' Since they had no choice, they began to go down one by one.

9

'Why are they chasing us away?' Amaravathi asked Thangammal.

'They will bring the dead body out. Whenever anybody dies, they won't let anyone stay here till the corpse is taken out. In the eight days I have been here, not one day has passed when I wasn't turned out. Yesterday, they turned us out twice. For eight days I have been waking up to the faces of corpses.'

When they reached the ground floor, an ambulance came from the main entrance and stopped in front of the emergency block. Immediately, security guards ordered those standing in the verandah and those loitering here and there to move to one side. All of them on the ground floor, including Amaravathi, stood to one side. A man and two women jumped down from the ambulance and ran in and went to the four doctors sitting in a row and said something. Immediately, the doctors said something to the nurses. A man in khaki-coloured clothes pushed a stretcher and walked out quickly to the ambulance. Two men dressed in white also ran out with him. They lowered the completely burnt body of a woman from the ambulance and placed it on the stretcher and pushed it to the doctors and halted there. Immediately, elbowing each other, a crowd ran towards the stretcher to have a look at the woman. Four or five guards controlled the crowd saying, 'Move away, move away. You cannot crowd here.'

When she saw the girl on the stretcher, Amaravathi

exclaimed, 'Oh Lord! She is burnt so badly.' Not only her but all the people who were standing aside in the verandah felt pity for the burnt girl lying on the stretcher. The stretcher was pushed into a nearby room. Doctors and nurses rushed inside. As soon as the stretcher was taken into the room, the crowd began to disperse. Those who were going in did so, and the ones on the way out began to leave.

'One died just now. The dead body is yet to be taken out. Another has come so that the bed won't remain empty.' Amaravathi stared at the face of Thangammal who said this.

'Come,' said Natesan and began to walk towards the canteen. The others followed him.

Murugan bought four tokens for tea. He first brought a cup of tea for Thangammal. He then got two cups of tea and handed them to Natesan and Amaravathi. Both of them kept the cups on the nearby stone bench without drinking their tea.

'Why did you keep the tea on the bench? Look at the flies hovering over it.' Murugan picked up the cup and gave it to Amaravathi and said, 'Drink, Amma.' Amaravathi took it from him and gave it to Thangammal, saying, 'Please drink this too.'

'You should have some hot water. It will give you some energy,' Thangammal said.

'With my daughter lying in such a state, how can I drink tea?' Amaravathi was overcome with tears as she said this.

Thangammal finished the tea and said, 'You have to drink. Does the stomach know this is food at a wedding or food at a wake?'

Thagammal's words felt like a slap on the cheeks to Amaravathi.

Natesan watched the people who had come to the canteen, people who were on the road, people who were standing or sitting under the tree. He looked at the flies hovering around the two undrunk cups of tea on the cement bench. Whatever thought came into his mind, he picked up the cups and went and threw them into the garbage bin.

Thangammal said, 'Come let us go to that tree. We have to sit down somewhere to pass the time.'

Natesan and Amaravathi didn't know what to reply and looked at each other. 'We can't go upstairs, can we?' Natesan asked. Amaravathi didn't say anything in reply.

'Okay, come,' he said and began to walk with Thangammal. Murugan was talking to someone on his cellphone.

They walked about three-four hundred feet to the east behind the emergency block. In the parking meant for doctors, about thirty-forty cars were standing in a row. There were rows of trees. There were crowds of people sitting under each tree. They searched for a place to sit. They went to a tree which had only two women sitting in its shade. Thangammal sat on the ground without any hesitation. Natesan and Amaravathi kept standing. Murugan came along still talking on the phone.

When Amaravathi said, 'Do anything to get her back alive, Thambi', Murugan burst out, 'What are you saying, Amma? Is money bigger for me than her, than Paapa? Am I the kind to think like that? Do you know how many people I have called and how many times from last evening till now?

Whoever you ask says, "We need to know the per centage of burns before we can say anything." They say, "JIPMER is better than other hospitals." It was when we were at the canteen that a friend's father called me. He said he would be here in quarter of an hour. We'll take him along to talk to the doctor. Then we can decide what to do. After we know this, I will go to file a case. If anything happens to her life, I won't leave that fellow alone.' Murugan ground his teeth.

'He has murdered my daughter. He has brought us to this state. What harm did we do to him?' Amaravathi, who said this with disgust, turned to Natesan, 'You said you would talk to the police, what happened?'

'That SI talked to me when we were upstairs itself. When she was taken to the GH with burns yesterday, the news was sent to the Station then itself. It is not necessary for us to file a case. The police and the magistrate will come on their own to take a statement from Revathi. A case can only be filed based on her statement. It is a government matter now, he said, there is no need for us to run around.'

'Will the police come?'

'Yes, it is a government case now.'

'When will they come?'

'That I didn't ask.'

'Ask them that first. If you don't give them money, if you don't give them a petition, how will the police come by itself? That creep may give them money and make them revise the case as if she set fire to herself.'

Amaravathi looked at Natesan with bitterness and disgust. How could he believe that the police would come on its own! She was agitated—what was he afraid of, what did he think would happen if he went to the police, that they would shoot him? She sat down next to Thangammal in her anger. Immediately she ranted at Revathi, 'You have made me sit here like this as if you wanted to drag me through everything!'

Natesan, who had finished talking on the phone, said, 'They say they have made all arrangements. The police may come at any time. The police have been informed by this hospital also. The SI said that if it was urgent, we should arrange a car and get the police here.'

'In that case you should take the car immediately and go and get them. He should go to jail before my daughter loses her life. I want to see that with my eyes,' she said. Natesan called his contact immediately.

'I've been living in terror from the day he tied a thread, the thaali, around my daughter's neck, the fear hasn't left me still. What news would come when, where would she be lying beaten up, in which house would she be hiding, afraid of being beaten up, every minute was terrifying. I was always in a panic. Whenever she called, I would pick the phone with fear. Only after she said "Nothing Amma, I called just like that" would my panicked shaking stop. He would shout like anything if she was delayed by a minute when she went shopping. He would beat her up like anything. If she ever went back late after coming to see me, he would punch her in her face saying, "Why didn't you stay on there? Why come back?" And look at him sitting out there unharmed. Not a line of worry in his face that he has taken a life', Amaravathi was wailing to herself when Natesan returned and said, 'He said he would talk in the station and let us know. He will try to send them today itself. I told him to tell them to hire a car and come. I will pay the rental. If we wish to give a petition we can give it to the policemen who come, he said. Give it to them in the hospital itself. They will arrest him there itself, he said.'

'Ask for the phone number of the policeman who is coming. Hit them with money and make them arrest him here itself. Only then will my mind cool down. He is sitting there upstairs, that filthy dog,' Amaravathi said. Natesan began to speak on the phone again.

'You are saying so much now, why didn't you have him arrested earlier?' Thangammal asked with concern.

'We got the phone call only at four pm yesterday. We had to see our girl first and came running here. They didn't allow us to see our girl at night. I saw her only early in the morning.'

Natesan couldn't get through to the number he had dialled. So, his face fell.

'I haven't yet seen my daughter. I haven't talked to her. If I talk to her, I can make a decision,' Natesan spoke as if he were explaining to himself.

Thangammal looked at Amaravathi and asked. 'You look like a well-off family. Couldn't you have thrown your money at the police and got him arrested earlier itself?'

'This is a six-seven-year story amma. Every time they fought, I would say, "Come back, come back." She too came back twice, saying goodbye to him. Both times he got drunk and stood outside our house and yelled so much. He wouldn't leave when we asked him to get lost. When we threatened to call the police, he took out a blade and cut himself in his arms and legs. He banged his head against the wall and hurt himself. He bought some poison and stood in front of us saying he was going to kill himself. He fell at my feet and cried. Afraid of being even more shamed, I sent her back each time. In all the six years, he didn't allow her to spend even a night outside his house.' Amaravathi couldn't speak any further.

'How often I have said with my very tongue that the problem would be resolved only when she died. I have told Amaravathi herself to tell her daughter to die, to kill herself. He bashed her up. She is too bashed up to even move. Every time I heard this, I would say that I will find peace only if she dies.' Natesan's eyes filled with tears as he said this.

'Keep quiet, Appa,' said Murugan.

Seeing Natesan weep, Murugan's eyes too teared up. Amaravathi couldn't believe that Natesan would speak like this in public, that he would cry in public. She spoke as if to calm him, 'For someone of your status, you came down so much, and went to her with a bowed head. She was in a fit of madness, that is why she stood on one leg saying she wanted only him.'

'If only he had not beaten my daughter, I would have given him so much money and supported him. We have a big house in the village. We have land. We have given out everything on lease. I said many times that I would change it, ask him to go and stay in the village. If he had gone there, it would still have been okay.' Natesan said this and sat down next to Amaravathi.

Amaravathi said to Murugan, 'You shouldn't let him go, Thambi. He shouldn't come out in this lifetime.'

'Stop crying, Amma. Drink this water. I will take care of everything. Let my friend's dad come. Let him find the truth and tell us. I will beat the bugger up with my slippers at this spot itself. I'll show him I too can behave like a loafer,' Murugan spoke in a frenzied rage. Amaravathi took the bottle of water he handed to her and kept it on the ground.

She didn't say this to Natesan. Nor to Murugan. She didn't even say this to Thangammal who was sitting next to her. She spoke to thin air, 'My daughter's story has come to an end.'

'Didn't your daughter find something other than fire to play with in this world?' Thangammal asked.

'Is my daughter mad? That murdering guy has set her on fire.'

'Is that so?'

'I kept my daughter close. He seduced her with some drug. Each time she got beaten up and cried, she would only say, "I won't die, Amma." Four days ago, she came saying they had to pay forty thousand rupees as dues on the autorickshaw and took it from me. Only twenty days earlier, I paid the fees for both the children. When she came four days ago, I asked her to eat but in her happiness at having got the money, she refused and left. If she had eaten that day, my mind would be calmer now. In these six years, how much have I given her a thousand-two thousand at a time without the knowledge of my saar or my son? He is a deep pit that cannot be filled with any amount.'

'Doesn't that guy have parents? You should have told them.' When Thangammal said this, Amaravathi replied with sarcasm, 'They are there alright, but worth nothing.'

Thangammal turned to Murugan and spoke with the authority of a high-ranking police officer, 'If you are willing to bring up the children, then get him jailed. Otherwise, let him be.'

'What are you saying amma? Don't make us angry.' Amaravathi glared at Thangammal.

'If the girl were alive, it would make sense to run around. Why should you run around for a corpse?'

Paying no heed to Murugan who snapped, 'Be quiet for a while,' Thangammal carried on, 'If you have him jailed, who will look after the children? And who will get the corpse released? It isn't easy to get a corpse released. The corpse will lie in the hospital for eight-ten days. Then you will say, "Even after dying she is killing us".'

'Why are you talking like this when the girl is alive?' Natesan glared at Thangammal.

'What do you mean, amma?' Amaravathi asked Thangammal.

'Even you parents will be forced to say it.' As soon as Thangammal said this, as if they were three race horses that were running at the same speed which tripped and fell at the same instant, Amaravathi, Natesan, and Murugan, all three looked at her.

'In the house opposite ours, there was a girl called Rukmani. Born in Arumbavur, she immolated herself within six months of her marriage and died. She was here in this hospital for four days before she died. At that time, there was no air-conditioned room like now. You weren't separated by curtains. People were made to lie down on the floor on banana leaves. We had to sit next to them fanning them day and night. Her parents filed the case on the very day she immolated herself. The police arrested him. When he heard she had died, he said, "The corpse belongs to me. Only I can receive the corpse." The police let him out for this on the fourth day itself. Then he seems to have said, "I need to do the eighth day ritual, I need to do other rituals for the dead." They let him out for that as well. He must have stayed in jail for ten days only. Then he was out. The case dragged on for three years. He threw money around and had the case set aside. Now he has married again.'

Was Thangammal saying the truth? Not only Amaravathi but also Natesan wasn't sure. 'It may not happen like this in every case,' Murugan said.

'The police will come. At that time, your girl should say this man set me on fire.'

'Definitely, she will say so.' All three said at the same time in one voice.

It looked as if Thangammal had laughed to herself.

Amaravathi asked in anger, 'Why are you laughing, amma? My girl will say so. She has suffered so much in his hands. He has troubled us so much too.'

'Only one in a hundred women dares to say the truth. Others don't say this. "We had no fights at all. My clothes caught fire." This is what they say. Even my brother's daughter said this only, the lying bitch. Because of this, we couldn't task that bastard with anything at all.'

'Our daughter won't say that. She has suffered so much at his hands for six years.'

'We think something. The dying girls think something else. We are about to die, why should we cause more trouble to our parents before we die, is what they think. That is why they say to the police, "It happened by itself. When I was cooking the sari caught fire." Should we trouble our people to death even after we die is what they think and say this.' Thangammal's eyes teared up as she said this.

'Did your niece say that it happened by itself?' Amaravathi asked doubtfully.

'She gave the testimony by her own mouth. So, the police said that our complaint was worthless.'

'Didn't you try throwing money at them?'

'Why should we spend money on a dead girl? In any case, don't we need to have money first?'

Amaravathi didn't open her mouth. Murugan also remained silent. To break the silence, Thangammal said, 'Drink at least one cup of tea, amma.'

'I can't drink even ordinary water,' Amaravathi declared.

'In the beginning, when I came here first, I stayed for two without even rinsing my mouth, without drinking even plain water. But what to do? Even if we sleep, the stomach doesn't sleep,' Thangammal said.

'I don't know why these cursed crows are cawing all the time. They keep flying around this building only,' Amaravthi complained.

Natesan glanced at the tree where the crows were sitting. A huge one. There were twenty or thirty trees like that in a row. Crows were sitting on every tree. He wondered how old the trees were.

Then, they heard one of the five women sitting under a neem tree twenty or thirty feet away suddenly crying aloud, 'She has thrown burning coals on my heart.' Everyone looked at the woman weeping aloud.

At that time, spotting Ravi coming towards the canteen, Murugan said, 'I'm coming, stay here,' and began to run towards him.

'What did you do to my sister?' Murugan yelled and pushed Ravi. Confused by this sudden attach, Ravi didn't know what to do. Murugan didn't care to listen to whatever Ravi was saying, so intent he was on hitting him. Flustered at seeing Murugan assaulting Ravi, Amaravathi and Natesan ran to him shouting, 'Don't throw stones at shit.'

10

Four security guards stood at the entrance to the emergency block. They asked each one trying to enter, 'Show your pass.' They only allowed in the ones with passes, the others were chased away. They didn't listen to the abject pleas made by people. The only reply that they gave the ones without passes was, 'Come at five in the evening. Don't stand in the way.'

The guards stopped Murugan who tried to enter with Amaravathi. The 'please, please' of Murugan's English didn't win them over. Natesan also pleaded. 'If you have a pass, you can go in. Otherwise, go out.' The guards were firm.

'Let me go up. You go see what happened to the policemen, and what happened to the doctor,' Amaravathi told them and went in.

Natesan and Murugan, angered by the guards, walked briskly a short distance away from the entrance. Neither knew what to do or where to go. They couldn't look at each other either. They couldn't even talk to each other. So, they watched the people walking on the paths or sitting under the trees or on the grass. It was quite hot. They didn't know where to stand. Because he didn't know what else to do, Murugan called Amaravathi, 'Are you upstairs, Amma? What news? Did they call you? Nothing? You are just sitting there? Okay. Bye, I'll call again.'

As soon as he disconnected saying this, the phone rang. 'Yes sir. I am standing outside only. I am standing a short distance to the south from the entrance to the emergency block. Identification? I am wearing black jeans and yellow T-shirt. I'll wait here. Come. Please,' he said on the phone. Then, turning to Natesan, he said, 'I told you my friend's father was a doctor here, isn't it? He is coming now.' That a doctor was coming gave him great courage. He thought that they could save Revathi now. He tried to spot Dhanikachalam among the people on the road. Scooters, bikes, and cars were travelling on the road without a break. It was astounding to see so many cars inside a hospital.

Doctor Dhanikachalam arrived.

'Vanakkam sir,' Murugan said.

'Vanakkam sir,' Natesan greeted him.

'The boy is ringing me without a pause,' Dhanikachalam said smiling.

'This is my father, sir,' Murugan introduced Natesan to the doctor.

'How did it happen?'

'Don't know,' Murugan and Natesan replied in one voice.

'I went to the ward to see her.'

'Have you seen her, sir?' Natesan asked eagerly.

'Will she survive?' Natesan asked.

'She is burnt fully.'

'Can we take her out, sir?'

'No, no. In this state, she cannot be taken out of the ICU even for an hour.'

'Won't she survive, sir?' Murugan's voice broke as he asked.

'I've told the doctor on duty and the nurses. They will take care. There will be no problems.'

'How much per cent, sir?' Natesan asked.

'It is a bit high.'

'It doesn't matter how much it costs, sir. Whichever hospital you tell us, we will take her there. I want my girl.' Natesan's eyes filled with tears. He folded his hands before Dhanikachalam.

'After a point, money has no meaning.'

'Does it mean that my daughter won't survive, sir?' Natesan could not control his tears.

'Drugs and medicines work only up to a point.'

'I have more than ten lakh rupees in hand, sir. Just tell us where to take her to make her survive. That is enough for us.'

'Don't give the patient hell trying to take her here or there. Just leave her alone. That is what is good for the patient. And good for you.'

'Sir!' Natesan and Murugan exclaimed in one voice. Both of them had tears in their eyes.

'There is just one way.'

'Tell us, sir. Whatever it is, however expensive it is, it is okay. We just want her alive. It doesn't matter if she looks ugly or disgusting, we will keep her home.' Murugan said, trying hard to control his tears.

'You will think that now. It is not possible in reality though.'

'What is the way, then?' Murugan asked, crying.

'We can keep her on the ventilator. We can keep her alive as long we keep her on the ventilator.'

'Is it that bad, sir?' Natesan was in a state. He felt as if his heart would stop beating.

'The blood vessels have got damaged. They have been burnt.'

'How much per cent, sir?'

'Eighty-nine.'

'Won't survive at eighty-nine, sir?'

'Very little chance.'

'Muruga,' Natesan called out and covered his face and wept. Murugan also cried aloud.

'I want to see my daughter, sir. Please help.' Natesan folded his hands to the doctor.

'They won't allow people to meet fire victims too often. I will talk to the doctor on duty. You call me.'

'Please help us in some way, sir.'

'If it were thirty or forty per cent, I could give you some hope. We can try something. This is eighty-nine per cent. It is only a matter of days. I shouldn't say this. But I am telling you because I don't want you to go here and there in false hope.' Having said this, Dhanikachalam began to walk toward the building containing the pediatric ward.

'Did you hear what the doctor said before he left?' Natesan asked and began to weep. Murugan looked away and cried.

'Will Revathi go leaving us, Muruga?' Natesan didn't have the strength to ask this.

Murugan's cellphone rang. It was Amaravathi who was calling. He wondered whether to pick up the call of not. What should he tell her if she asked what Dhanikachalam had told them? Could he repeat the doctor's words? He didn't know how to manage the situation and didn't answer the call. Since the phone kept ringing, he had no choice but to answer. 'Yes, Amma. The doctor came just now. He said he saw Revathi. He said they would take care. He didn't say what per cent. He has told the doctor on duty and the nurses that she is family. He said there will be no problems. If there is nothing to do, come down. You want to remain upstairs? Okay. Bye. If there is anything, call again.' Murugan disconnected the call.

An ambulance which came from the main entrance of JIPMER stopped in front of the emergency block. Immediately, four or five guards blew their whistles and made the people standing here and there, and those walking to and fro, move to a side. They made sure that a crowd didn't gather around the ambulance. However, a crowd still gathered to see the patient being taken from the ambulance. Not wanting to stand in this crowd, moving away from it, Natesan and Murugan began to walk towards the cancer ward. Even though they were walking silently, their minds were perturbed thinking what would happen to Revathi.

Murugan's cell phone rang. He picked it up and talked. 'We are standing to the south of the emergency block on the way to the cancer ward. Where are you? Should I send the driver? No need? If you come straight from the main gate, you will reach the emergency block. Should I come? You will come by yourself?' Putting the phone away, Murugan said to Natesan without being asked, 'Arunmozhi is coming.'

Natesan was looking at the sky without any expression, not hearing a word of what Murugan was saying.

Even though Natesan and Murugan were standing together they didn't look at each other. They looked in different directions. They didn't notice the people on the road, or the scooters, or the bikes. It was hot. But that didn't bother them. There were people wherever one looked. They didn't notice them either. They stood there unaware of their surroundings. They weren't even aware why they were standing there.

Arunmozhi arrived. She asked with urgency, 'What happened?'

'Don't know clearly,' Murugan said without any further explanation. He felt like sharing with her what Dhanikachalam had said, but he didn't.

'Did you see her, Uncle?' She asked Natesan.

'They aren't allowing us to see her. They permitted only the attendant at dawn. That too only for ten minutes. Your Aunty only saw her.' Natesan spoke lifelessly.

'Did Aunty talk to her? What did Revathi say? Did he set her on fire?'

'As soon as she saw Revathi, your Aunty seems to have fainted.' Natesan couldn't speak any further. His eyes filled with tears. He turned his face away.

'Why are you standing outside?'

'You can go in only if you have a pass. Even if you go in, you can't see her. They don't allow anyone into the ICU.'

'When can we see her then?'

'Tomorrow morning.'

'What are you saying?' She was astonished.

'If we could see her, why would we stand outside?' Murugan asked with anger.

'Did your friend's father come? Did he see her? What did he say?'

'He said it was eighty-nine per cent.'

'Eighty-nine?' Arunmozhi asked in shock. She kept silent. Her eyes teared up. She asked angrily, 'Where is he?'

'No idea.'

'Didn't you ask him why did you do such a thing?'

Because there was no life left in Natesan or Murugan after hearing what Dhanikachalam had to say about Revathi, they couldn't reply to Arunmozhi.

Arunmozhi was enraged. She gritted her teeth. 'What is the meaning of not asking him anything? He has set her on fire, burnt her. Shouldn't you have beaten him with your slippers? See if she survives. Otherwise, hand him over to the police. Cuddalore is close by. Go there directly and write a complaint to the SP that he demanded money, jewellery, and tortured her. How long should we be quiet because he is a lowlife, a criminal, a mad man?' She exploded agitatedly.

'The police have been spoken to. They say it is a government case already. They will come by themselves.' Natesan said.

'Will she survive or not?'

'We don't know.'

'Oh God!' She covered her mouth with both her hands.

'Can't we see her now?'

'They don't allow anyone in.'

'Should I try talking to them?'

'They won't allow you. Keep quiet for a while, I am already so irritated by all this.'

'Where have they kept her?'

'Fifth floor.'

'Okay. I'll come.' Saying this, Arunmozhi began to walk fast towards the emergency block.

Even when she was ten feet away from the entrance to the emergency block, a guard intercepted her and asked, 'Do you have a pass?' Arunmozhi asked, 'Pass for what?'

The guard said in a stern voice, 'You can't go inside if you don't have a pass. Go away. Don't stand in the way.'

'It is very urgent, sir. I have come from Madras. I didn't know I need a pass. Please allow me, please. My friend has immolated herself.' She pleaded in tears.

'Come at five o'clock. Now stand at a distance.' The guard did not make any concession.

'Please allow me in, Anna,' she asked making him her sibling.

'If people come like this hundred to the hour, how can we allow them in? Please go away.'

Arunmozhi returned in frustration. She asked in great anger, 'Why do they act like this?'

'Didn't I tell you they won't let you inside?'

'How does one go in then?'

'We can call Amma and take her pass and you can go up with it. But there is nothing to be gained by it. There is a huge hall in front of the ICU. But they keep the hall locked. You can only sit on the steps of the staircase in front of the hall. Amma is sitting there only. It will be very crowded there.'

'Is it true that she won't survive?' Arunmozhi asked. Murugan did not reply. He kicked the ground two or three times in anger. He swung his arms into the breeze.

Arunmozhi spotted Ravi searching for somebody in front of the emergency block. 'I'll just come,' she said and walked straight towards Ravi.

'Why did you set her on fire? You showed your true colours, you lowlife.'

Ravi didn't contradict her, nor did he move away. He kept standing without raising his bowed head. He looked as if he was high on ganja. He stank of brandy as well.

'Have you been drinking?' She asked, enraged.

Ravi didn't open his mouth.

'Chee, when your wife is about to die, all you can do is

get drunk and come stand here at the hospital! Are you a man? The girl for whom you tattooed yourself and wandered all over the place, that is the very girl you have burnt now. Don't stand in front of me. Go away. I will not rest till I hand you over to the police. Bloody.' She screamed at him.

Ravi's cellphone rang. He picked it up and talked.

'I am downstairs, sir. I am talking to them only. I will bring them along.'

Arunmozhi asked through her clenched teeth, 'Which goon is calling at this time?'

'The police has come. They are calling.'

'Whom?'

'Revathi's father, and brother.'

'Where are the police?'

'Near the ICU, on the fifth floor.'

'You go. I will bring them. I won't stop till I get you arrested by the police. You are fit for jail.' Saying so, Arunmozhi moved to where Murugan was standing and said, 'The police have arrived. They are calling.' Immediately, Murugan and Natesan ran towards the emergency block.

When the security guards blocked them, 'Fire case, sir. The police have arrived. They are waiting on the fifth floor,' Arunmozhi explained.

'Are they recording the testimony?'

'Yes.'

'How are you related to the patient?'

'He is the father, he the elder brother. I am his wife. It is urgent sir. Please allow us inside.'

'Do you have a pass?'

'The pass-holder is upstairs. They are calling for the patient's father and brother. If you want, you check with them,' Arunmozhi said agitatedly. In her nervousness, she slurred her words. It seemed as if she felt that if they met the police every problem would be resolved. Murugan and Natesan too believed this.

'Okay, go in.'

All three, Murugan, Natesan, and Arunmozhi, went up to the fifth floor. As soon as they reached, Murugan knocked on the door. The guard opened the door and asked, 'What?'

'The police have called us. We need to go in.'

'What's the patient's name?'

'Revathi.'

'Wait a minute,' said the guard and shut the door. He opened the door in a few moments and said, 'Come in.'

Natesan, Murugan, Arunmozhi, and Amaravathi entered the hall in a rush. Ravi entered last. Murugan then snarled at him, 'If anything happens to Revathi, it is your corpse that will go out first.'

11

Head Constable Ganesan and Constable Anandha Kumar were standing in front of the ICU door. Natesan and Murugan said vanakkam to them. 'We have come from Virudhachalam police station. We need to take the testimony from the immolated girl. The magistrate is inside taking her testimony. We can take her testimony only after he finishes.' Head Constable Ganesan explained.

'Did SI Kannan speak to you, sir?' Natesan asked.

'Yes, he did.'

'We haven't filed a complaint at the station yet, sir?'

'It is not necessary for you to file a complaint. We got a call from GH. Now, we have received information from JIPMER as well. Now, it has become a government case.'

'Do we also have to give our testimony to the magistrate, sir?'

'The magistrate will ask only the concerned woman. It is us police who will take the statements of the girl's father and mother.'

'We have our doubts, sir,' Murugan sputtered.

'Include that in your statement. It is the girl's testimony that is important. The testimony given to the magistrate and that taken by the police have to be similar. If they are similar, the court will order the arrest of the concerned party.'

'Arrest him, sir,' Amaravathi and Arunmozhi spoke in one voice.

'Is our statement important, or the girl's statement?' Murugan asked.

'Your testimony will have currency only if the girl is unconscious. If the concerned girl gives her testimony, then your statement has no power. "So and so poured oil on me and set me on fire," should be said to the magistrate rather than the police. It is the testimony recorded by the magistrate that has legitimacy, the statement taken by the police doesn't have much power. They will accuse us of having taken money and changing the testimony. The girl who has suffered the burns has to simply tell the magistrate that he set me on fire, and the magistrate will order the arrest of the party as soon as she comes out of the ICU.'

'She will take his name sir. He should suffer what she has suffered. Look at him, standing hale and hearty. When she was on fire, why couldn't she grab hold of him? He is standing there without even a tiny wound, or sore, or even a bit of pain!' Amaravathi said this and wept softly. Arunmozhi, who was standing next to her, also teared up.

'How did it happen?' Head Constable Ganesan asked.

'No idea, sir.'

The Head Constable then asked, 'Which one is the guy?'

'The one standing in that corner, that is the one sir.' Arunmozhi pointed to Ravi. Ganesan called out immediately, 'Hey, come here.' When Ravi came and stood close to them, Ganesan smiled slightly and sarcastically and asked, 'You?'

Ravi's face changed.

'Scram. I will talk to you later,' the Head Constable said.

Ravi returned to the spot he had been standing in the western corner of the room.

The Head Constable said in an angry tone, 'This guy is a loafer. He can't sleep if he doesn't come to the station at least once a month and stand there with folded hands. How did you give your daughter to him?'

'It was destiny, sir,' Amaravathi said firmly.

'He is a sewage drain.'

To Natesan and Murugan, the words of the Head Constable stung like being hit with slippers. They stood with bowed heads in their humiliation.

The Head Constable asked Natesan, 'What do you do?'

'I am the HM of the Mangalampetta Higher Secondary School.'

'He should be thrown inside the jail, sir,' Arunmozhi said. The Head Constable asked her, 'And what do you do?'

'I am a Team Leader in INFOSYS in Madras.'

'And what does he do?' The Head Constable asked about Murugan. Murugan did not reply. It was Arunmozhi who replied for him.

'He is also in TCS. He is also a Team Leader.'

'All of you are educated. All of you are doing well. Even then, you didn't care about the girl.'

'He should be caught and jailed somehow, sir.' Arunmozhi was emphatic.

'It is only with the testimony of the girl that we can do anything,' the Head Constable said and continued with a sarcastic smile, 'He is the kind who should be inside.'

'Our daughter will give a strong testimony, sir. So much torture she has experienced.' Amaravathi said.

'Right. Please stand away from us. If the magistrate sees us standing close to each other when he comes out, he will take it wrongly. On top of it, that loafer of a dog will give a petition saying you people gave us money to change the testimony. And two goons will come to stand witness for him. And four lawyers will come to give him company. Four autorickshaw driving dogs will block the streets in sympathy,' the head constable spoke with irritation. The four people moved away at once and stood staring at the ICU door. Each one started praying to their favourite gods that Revathi should give her testimony correctly to the magistrate. All four prayed that Ravi should be incarcerated for at least ten years.

'Can she forget what she suffered for six years? He has spoken to me even words that should never fall on our ears. How badly he has spoken about her father and her brother. Will she forget all that? "It is because of me that Appa and Anna have to face filth in their lives, they have felt humiliated." How many times she has said this to me. Will she forget even that? How many times he locked her in the house and went out! How many times has she been lying on the street badly beaten up by him, how many times has she run to hide in the neighbouring house, how many times has she gone and sat in the temple her heart broken, how many times has she wandered the streets to kill time not knowing where to go, and then come home. Can she forget all that?' As if is she was reciting something she had memorised, a weeping Amaravathi listed the complaints one by one.

All that Amaravathi said was new information. All that Natesan and Murugan knew was that he would come home drunk and beat her, that they would fight every day. Even that they knew because of Amaravathi. Only now they realised that she hadn't told them even ten per cent of what had taken place. Each fact, every bit of news enraged Natesan and Murugan.

'Is it so? She didn't tell me anything,' Arunmozhi said, and she felt like slapping Ravi in the face at once. 'Beggar, bloody beggar,' she cursed.

Murugan's phone rang. He answered it. The guard moved to him quickly and said authoritatively, 'You cannot speak on the phone here.' 'Okay sir,' said Murugan and cut the call immediately.

'With her body burnt fully, that she had to stand without even a thread on her in front of the doctor, can she forget that?' When Amaravathi was saying this, the door to the ICU opened and the magistrate came out. Without even glancing at the police personnel, he went directly to the lift and stood there. The policemen followed him and stood at attention a little apart from him. The lift arrived at their floor. The magistrate entered it. The Head Constable and Constable Anandha Kumar entered after him and the door closed.

It was like watching a movie. Having seen all this, Arunmozhi and Murugan looked at each other. Amaravathi and Natesan did the same. However, no one spoke even a word. Natesan looked at Ravi. He screwed up his face as if he was seeing a piece of shit. 'Swine', he said.

Arunmozhi walked towards the door to the ICU. The guard followed her and said forcefully, 'You can't stand here. Come away. Go out.'

Arunmozhi thought of what she could tell him and said, 'They still haven't taken our statements.' She spoke as if Revathi would become alright if she just continued standing there.

'Then, stand to a side.'

Arunmozhi returned silently and stood next to Amaravathi as before.

'So many times, I have thought of punishing him. I kept quiet because Revathi was living with him. She shouldn't stay with him any longer. I won't leave him if she loses her life.' Murugan spoke threateningly.

'Why should we send her with him now? We will get a lawyer to issue a notice for divorce. She should not spend even a minute with him.' Arunmozhi spoke even more emphatically than Murugan.

'Now everything is in her hands. Only her statement would have legal sanctity say the police,' Natesan said.

'She won't let him go free. Can she forget the slaps and punches and the kicks? That he hawked and spat at her face, that he asked if her father and brother could do fuck all, will she forget all that? Staggering home after drinking, how many times has he asked her to feed him herself and spat out at her face the food she gave him. Will she forget that our townsfolk told her that she had been trapped by a lowlife? Can she ever forget that after a severe beating, not knowing where to go, she went and cried in the temple? When she got beaten and kicked ten days ago, she went twice to the bus stand and returned not having a place to go to—will she forget that?' As she narrated these incidents, Natesan and Murugan became more and more enraged as if a fire was spreading across their bodies—anger like fire spread through the bodies of Natesan and Murugan. All that Amaravathi said was new to them. If they had known all this earlier, they could have had him arrested by the police. Could have got her a divorce. 'Just a fight. Just words. He beat her.' This is what Amaravathi had told them so far. Murugan asked angrily, 'What are you saying, Amma?'

'There are a thousand things like this, Thambi. All of it is in this heart!' She beat her chest to show.

'Let one more hour go by. I will see to him.' Murugan clenched his teeth.

The Head Constable Ganesan and Constable Anandha Kumar came out of the lift. Natesan and Murugan went to them immediately. 'Wait for a while,' the policemen said and knocked on the door of the ICU. The nurse who opened the door asked 'What?', and they replied 'Need to take a statement,' and she allowed the two of them in, and shut the door.

'Justice will listen,' Amaravathi said.

'Drink some water,' Arunmozhi offered the bottle to Amaravathi, who pushed it away with her left hand. She sat down as soon as Arunmozhi said, 'Sit on the floor.' Arunmozhi sat down as well. 'Don't worry. She will give the correct statement. His story will end today.' Arunmozhi said confidently.

'Will she forget that our relatives asked "Is this the only guy you could get?", or that her classmates ridiculed her for the match? Will she forget that our neighbours and our townsfolks asked her, "You married *this* loafer?" All the tears I shed for six years are going to get an answer only today.'

12

'How could you booze at this time?' Siva Kumar asked him. Ravi stood silently without replying to Siva Kumar, gazing at the Orthopaedics building. His behaviour and mood had changed completely since the police and the magistrate had arrived to take testimonies. He couldn't stand in one place.

He couldn't speak four words coherently. He perspired continuously. Now and then, his body trembled. He smoked one cigarette after another. He drank one bottle of water after another. Without even considering that he had come to offer him help, he spoke rudely to Siva Kumar.

'It is because of your anger and short-temper that we have such complications. What should not happen, happens.' Siva Kumar said. Ravi didn't hear him at all, so intently was he looking at the ICU building to see if the police were out searching for him. Then as if speaking to himself, he said, 'Within a month of our marriage, that bitch said that one day or another she would send me to jail. She must have carried out her threat today.'

'Move to a side and smoke your cigarette. Someone will yell at you here.' What Siva Kumar said didn't seem to fall on Ravi's ears.

'Wonder what she is telling the police, that stinking slut,' said Ravi and ground his teeth. Then, he said filled with rage, 'The day I saw her was the beginning of my bad time.'

'You were the one who chased her. The one who said I will give up my life. Didn't you tattoo your entire body and roam around like a mental case?' Ravi lost his temper when Siva Kumar asked him this. 'Shut your fucking mouth,' he said and glared at him. Then he looked at the ICU building again. He watched the people walking to and fro. 'Ask the lawyer when he is coming. I don't know what statement that daughter of beggars has given. Those dogs will give in writing that I set her on fire. As soon as they get their statements, the police will search for me to arrest me. Only if the lawyer comes before that can we decide what to do.' Ravi said this and asked Siva Kumar, 'Should I stay here to be caught by the police or should I run away and hide?'

'Don't be stupid and run away. The case against you will become stronger. If you go into hiding, they will take it as proof that you did it.' When Siva Kumar said this, Ravi replied, 'The lawyer said the same thing on the phone.'

'Having got that girl, you could have really risen in life, become a big guy. Instead, you get caught in problems and involve us as well.'

'Don't you know when to say what?' Ravi glared at Siva Kumar and said with urgency, 'Ring up the lawyer and ask him when he is coming.' Siva Kumar called the lawyer and spoke to him, 'Sir, where are you now? You've reached Gorimedu? Can you speed up sir? The police have come as also the magistrate.' He reported the conversation to Ravi.

'They have reached Gorimedu bus stand. They are about to come in. Should I go and bring them here?'

'Don't go. If they see you, the police will look for me.' Ravi said this and went to a nearby tree and stood behind it. Siva Kumar went and stood next to the tree.

'The way you stand, talk, behave, all testify that you are a criminal. Don't open your mouth to the police. If you do, you will go to jail. You won't get bail easily in a burning case. Don't think that this is like your fights in the auto stand. Don't open your mouth even if the police beat you.' Siva Kumar spoke as if he was teaching a lesson to Ravi. Ravi did not respond. All his attention was on whether the police were searching for him. He leaned against the neem tree to lessen his trembling.

'Don't lean against the tree, there are many ants there.' Siva Kumar's warning went unheeded.

Siva Kumar looked at Ravi. Ravi looked like a mad man. As soon as Revathi had set herself on fire, taking her in the auto and rushing her to the hospital, then in ambulance from there to Cuddalore and then Pondicherry, and keeping awake the whole night, not eating anything at all, drinking more and more brandy as its effects wore off, not having washed, not having changed his clothes, smoking incessantly, the worry that he could get arrested any minute, all that had come together to turn him really insane. Feeling pity at his appearance and the way he was standing, Siva Kumar said, 'Somehow, I don't think that girl will get you caught.' Siva Kumar's statement gave some hope to Ravi. 'Will that be true?' he asked eagerly.

'I feel that somehow.'

'It's okay that the police came. Why did the magistrate come? That is what makes me doubtful. Will they have given money and made out a big case against me?'

'Even I don't understand why the magistrate came.'

'The biggest mistake I made in my life was marrying that girl.' Ravi cried as he said it.

'Chee, shut your mouth. Just like today, you looked like a mad man then also, running after that girl. You tortured everyone saying that you would kill yourself if you didn't get that girl.' When Siva Kumar said this, Ravi felt intense anger. 'Will you stop giving me tension?' He asked and glared at his friend.

'She is an educated girl, a well-off girl. We kept telling

you no, she is not for you. But did you listen?' Having said this, Siva Kumar wanted to offer some sympathy to Ravi and said, 'I don't think those people have filed a case against you. If they had, why would they speak to you?' As soon as Siva Kumar said this, Ravi's temper burst forth. 'You don't know fuck all. Just shut up. If they hadn't filed a case, how would the police be here? Why would the magistrate be here?' He asked in turn.

'Why are you getting angry with me? Am I the one who set her on fire? You make every bloody mistake in your anger, your intoxication.' Siva Kumar glared at him in anger. Ravi kept quiet for a short while and then said, 'Find out where my appa and amma are. Tell them that the police haven't arrested me yet. Tell them that you will let them know if I am arrested. Tell them to pawn my akka's chain and bring the money. Tell them that no one should call my number.' He spoke in a rush. Siva Kumar heard everything and remained quiet.

'If I hadn't met her, I would have married an auto driver's daughter and lived peacefully.' Ravi said this and began to cry.

'You only did every bloody mistake.'

'I feel I am going mad and on top of that you keep giving me tension.' Ravi kicked the ground.

'Couldn't you get a different lawyer? You have called this guy.'

'This lawyer doesn't argue well in the court. He won't create scenes in the police station. He isn't very brainy. But he figures out what the judge wants, what the police want, and he will do it secretly. Among the lawyers in our town, he is the one who manages matters without going to court all that much. Even if he grabs a lot of money, he gets the job done. He is the original thief.'

'The lawyer is coming. Our Auto Union chief, Anbu, is also coming with him.' When Siva Kumar said this, Ravi glanced quickly at the ICU building. He could see the lawyer and Anbu coming. 'I will go behind the building. Bring the lawyer along without anybody knowing.' Ravi said this and began to walk hurriedly towards the back of the building.

PART THREE

1

Ganesan and Anandha Kumar came out of the ICU. Murugan and Natesan hurried to meet them. Amaravathi and Arunmozhi got up in some disarray and went to them. All four asked in one voice at the same time, 'What happened?'

Ganesan said as if he were spitting on all their faces, all four of them, 'What kind of daughter have you given birth to?'

That one question turned their hearts to ashes. Their pulse quietened down completely.

'Come downstairs. I need to take your statements.' In his anger, Ganesan kept pressing the lift button. The lift arrived. The door opened. Ganesan got in first, Anandha Kumar entered after him. Murugan and others got in after that. The lift began to go down. Murugan said, 'Sir.'

Ganesan didn't look at Murugan.

'Sir!' Arunmozhi called. Ganesan didn't open his mouth. It was clear that he was very angry.

'What was her testimony like?' Neither Ganesan nor Anandha Kumar replied to Natesan's question. It was Ganesan who exited the lift first. The others followed him. Without speaking a word, Ganesan went out of the emergency block and went and stood under the neem tree which was on the way to the Neurology department. He snatched the testimony from the hands of Anandha Kumar and, as if throwing it at their faces, thrust it at them. It was Murugan who took and read it.

'I was cooking at 3 pm. Kuzhambu was simmering on the stove. I was stirring the kuzhambu. When I turned to pick up the bottle of salt, the kerosene can that was on the counter toppled and the kerosene fell into the kuzhambu and on the stove and the fire engulfed me. Hearing my screams, my husband who was watching TV came running and poured water on me and put out the fire. He covered me with a sack and rushed me to the hospital in his auto. I was given first aid at Virudhachalam Government Hospital. He brought me from there in an ambulance to Cuddalore Government Hospital. They said they could do nothing for me there and sent us to JIPMER Hospital. My husband and I had had no quarrel on the day of the fire accident. We hadn't even spoken harshly to each other. Neither did I set myself on fire, nor did my husband set me on fire. The fire was accidental and unexpected. Nobody is responsible for this. This testimony has been read back to me. It is entirely correct; the testimony is as per my conscience. No one has forced me to give this statement.' Revathi's fingerprints were below this statement. Revathi W/O Ravi was written within brackets. The time and place were also recorded.

Murugan didn't speak a word. He just sat down on the ground. He felt as if his head would burst. He kept punching hard at the ground like a mad man. Arunmozhi took the paper from his hand and read it. After she finished reading it, she simply said, 'Chee.' Her face expressed disgust. Natesan read it next. 'This is what we deserve for giving birth to this girl,' he said. He gave the paper deliberately to Amaravathi in his bitterness. She read the testimony and said, 'She has killed us.' She curled up on the ground as if she had fainted and began to cry.

What would happen with the testimony that Revathi had given? How Murugan and Natesan would bully and torture her citing the words that Revathi had used in her statement! What would Arunmozhi think? What would their relatives, neighbours, and people known to them say now? The whole town laughed at them when Revathi married Ravi. Now they would laugh because of Revathi's testimony. Amaravathi cried.

Murugan and Natesan had stopped talking to Revathi from the time she had said adamantly that she would only marry Ravi. When they found another match for her, she poured kerosene all over her body and threatened to immolate herself. From that time on, Murugan and Natesan not only did not talk to her, but they also avoided even looking at her. They stopped looking for another groom. Fearing that if they allowed her to go out to work she would elope with Ravi, they kept her at home. Amaravathi threatened that if she married Ravi, they wouldn't attend the wedding, that they would no longer talk to her and that they would cut off all relations with her. The only answer Revathi gave was, 'That's okay.' Amaravathi kept her in sight for twenty-four hours a day since the time she threatened to immolate herself. Not for a second did she ever feel free of the fear that Revathi could hang herself, take sleeping tablets, immolate herself, or run away from home. She would get up at night and go check on Revathi. Only after she saw her lying down would she be able to feel at peace, breathe regularly. If she heard any sound at night, the sound of a door opening, her heart would come to a standstill. Revathi knew that Amaravathi checked on her many times every night, but she wouldn't utter a word. She would lie down silently.

Afraid that Revathi would kill herself, Amaravathi came to a decision and told Murugan and Natesan, 'Let us get her married off just for namesake in some mandapam. We don't need to do any of the other rituals like going to the groom's house or visiting the girl's house or engagement. Just the marriage. After that it doesn't matter to us if she dies, and she need not bother if we die.' She argued with them for three months. They had no rituals at all, not visiting the home, nor engagement, nor writing the marriage agreement, nothing at all. They took the girl to the mandapam the night before the wedding. The marriage was held the next day. Only Arunmozhi accompanied Revathi to Ravi's house.

The eighth month after marriage, he beat her up brutally. Hearing that she was lying unconscious on the road, Amaravathi went. She took the unconscious Revathi to hospital. An intoxicated Ravi came and fought with her, 'Who are you to admit my wife in the hospital?' It was only that day that she realised that he could speak such profanities, that he could speak so vulgarly even in front of people. Only after Amaravathi had admitted her to hospital and had her treated and she was sent home, Revathi began to talk to

Amaravathi on the phone. She began to visit Amaravathi at home, choosing times when Natesan wouldn't be there. It was only then that Amaravathi began to give her money and things. Natesan knew only half of what Amaravathi gave, he didn't know about the rest. It was then that Amaravathi began to lie to Natesan.

Whenever she asked for money to give Revathi, Natesan and Murugan would throw money down and yell, 'For whatever crap it is, take it.' Knowing that she couldn't protest, Amaravathi would pick up the money from the floor.

Natesan would yell at her every time she reported that Ravi had beaten Revathi, kicked her, had started a fight in the auto stand, that the police had taken him away. Murugan would shout even louder. So, she would tell them only one per cent of the things that happened. Even for that the house would be in turmoil for a week. But Amaravathi wouldn't tell any of this to Revathi. Whatever she gave, she gave saying, 'Appa gave this, your anna gave this.' Even when she gifted her new clothes for Deepavali or Pongal, she would say such lies. Natesan and Murugan knew that Revathi asked for money, that she asked for things. 'Whatever inauspicious thing it is, you take care of it. You do it. Don't come to me.' The two of them would say similarly. They kept aloof from Revathi's affairs, but they never stopped any of this. They would never talk to her if they saw her outside, nor would they say anything if she came home. Only Revathi would come home, not Ravi. Not once had Revathi brought her children along. Natesan and Murugan were keen to avoid this happening and would warn Amaravathi, 'She was born in this family, that woman can visit our house. No other low born dog should step inside.' Amaravathi hadn't breathed a word of this to Revathi.

From the time the phone call came, 'She has immolated herself,' Natesan has been going around with more than ten lakh rupees in his bag. Murugan has been going here and there saying it doesn't matter if it costs a crore to save Revathi. They had forgotten all that had happened and only wanted her to survive, and she had given such a statement! What would Natesan and Murugan think? How could she meet their faces now? This was what made Amaravathi cry in a public place. This was what made her curl up on the ground. This was the moment that made her hate Revathi for the first time. The moment that she wished that Revathi would die.

'She has shamed me even in this situation. Let her die. It is better that she dies quickly. How could she make me, her birth mother, tremble in fear for six-seven years? There is no one like me in this world, giving birth to such a girl! Even now, she hasn't lost her desire for her man. She has shown so much loyalty to a road-side loafer.'

Natesan took the paper from Anandha Kumar and read it once again. Tears blurred the words on the page. He looked again and again at the fingerprints. He then returned the paper to Anandha Kumar. 'This is enough reason to die,' he said simply.

'If she had said even one word, I would have arrested him by now. And the SI keeps calling and asking, "What happened? What happened?" She saved him. It is not wrong to save someone. But she has saved a criminal. Alright, it is getting late. You give us your statement. We have to leave.' Ganesan said with some irritation. He turned to Anandha Kumar and said, 'We need to take a statement from that asshole as well. Finish fast, we have to go. Phone him and call him here.' Anandha Kumar took out a folded white sheet from his diary immediately and handed it to Natesan.

Natesan took the paper and asked Amaravathi, 'What should I write?' Amaravathi sat up immediately and burst forth angrily, 'She has thrown dirt on us, that prostitute, that slut. Show we suffer such indignity even further? Just write that you don't know her. Why should you suffer more humiliation because of her? You don't need to say that she is your daughter any longer. You don't need to go to court and the police station saying, "I am the father of that shameless whore," and lower your head having lost your name and honour. Let her die quickly. That is what I pray for now. She should die. Turn into ashes. Become part of the soil. What work she has done! As far as we are concerned, it is six years since she died. What are we going to gain by filing a case on behalf of a corpse?'

Natesan had never heard Amaravathi speak so passionately, so arrogantly before.

'What should I write pa?' Natesan asked Murugan.

'Whatever you wish.' Murugan turned his face away immediately. He punched the ground in anger. His body was burning in the fire of his anger.

'Will it work if our statement is different from hers?' Arunmozhi asked pathetically.

'It will have no power.'

'What then is the way, sir?' Arunmozhi asked in tears.

'Give a different statement. We can keep him inside only till the Magistrate's copy of the testimony comes to the court and the station. This will be so because your girl would have given a similar statement to the Magistrate as she gave to us.'

'He should be inside at least for one day, sir.' Arunmozhi pleaded.

'You look like educated people. Well-off as well. Why did you go and fall on this shit?'

Natesan stood looking down, feeling humiliated like a criminal. Since no one spoke, Anandha Kumar told Natesan, 'Please write, it is getting late.'

Natesan took the paper and sat on the ground and began to write, but he could only write 'Natesan'. He couldn't write any more. His hand trembled and he couldn't hold the pen steadily. His eyes filled with tears. Seeing him sit there unable to write in his disturbed state, Ganesan spoke to Murugan, 'You take the paper and write.' Murugan took the paper from Natesan and asked, 'How do I write, sir?'

'Write as if it is your father writing.'

'Cuddalore District, Virudhachalam Town, 414 Kurinji Street' was all that Murugan could write. He couldn't write beyond that. His hands trembled. They couldn't form letters which became just scratches on paper. Seeing this, Arunmozhi took the paper from Murugan, saying, 'Give it to me. I will write.'

'There is a different handwriting on the top of the page, we can't have a different handwriting below. It won't work. Tear that paper up. Write on this sheet.' Saying this, Anandha

Kumar gave her a new sheet of paper. As soon as Arunmozhi took the paper, Natesan intervened, 'Give it to me, I will write it myself. I am the one who fathered her. Don't I have to do her funeral rites?' Natesan took the paper with irritation and began to write fast.

'I, Natesan, resident of Cuddalore District, Virudhachalam Town, Periyar Nagar South, 414 Kurinji Street, give this statement. My daughter Revathi, resident of Cuddalore District, Virudhachalam Town, Periyar Nagar North, Burma Nagar, Rojappoo Street, was cooking on 24.06.16 when she suffered severe burns in a fire that occurred accidentally and is under treatment in JIPMER hospital, Pondicherry. No one is responsible for this unexpected fire. I state that this was an accident.' He wrote and signed the statement and gave the paper to the policemen.

'Please get your wife's signature as well,' Anandha Kumar said.

Amaravathi drew a line as her signature. The very next instant she beat her face as if her life was going and cried loudly.

'You two please sign as witnesses.'

Murugan and Arunmozhi signed as witnesses. Only Arunmozhi hesitated. Reading Natesan's statement, she said, 'We could have made him sit in jail at least for a day. That rabid dog can come out on bail after that. Are we going to let him go scot free?' Her voice broke.

Natesan said decisively, 'Give them the paper.'

Head Constable Ganesan who received the paper said, 'It is because educated people, decent people, move aside that the loafers proclaim themselves kings.'

'She shamed me for six years. And now as well. What kind of a girl did I give birth to? And I thought her to be the Mahalakshmi of the house!' Amaravathi beat her face again and again.

'I am the kind of person who wants to avoid police stations entirely, never wanted to be a policeman!' Natesan said this and shook with tears.

'She has slit our throats, that monster,' Amaravathi hawked and spat enraged.

'In a way, the decision you took is right amma.'

'We don't want to be alive, sir. Whatever we deserved for having given birth to her, we have already suffered it.'

'Your girl has given you release in a way. No need to spend your time at the station, in the lawyer's house, in courts, no need to spend so much money and suffer so much tension. Your daughter has saved you all that.'

'All these years I wanted her to live. Especially after she married that good for nothing loafer, I would pray every day for her life. But now all I want is that she should die quickly and her corpse taken to the cremation ground. That is my heartfelt desire.' Tears streamed down from Amaravathi's eyes.

Ganesan spotted Ravi coming towards the emergency block along with three young men. 'Look at him coming there. Call him and take his written statement. Let's go. It is getting late.' Anandha Kumar went immediately and brought Ravi. His three companions greeted the Head Constable. 'Give a written statement,' Head Constable Ganesan said to Ravi.

'Why are you asking me to write, sir? Take whatever the girl's family is saying in writing.' Ravi said softly.

'What are you speaking? You haven't come to your senses even now. You have snuffed out a life and you don't even have the brains to plead, save me please.'

'I know that you are speaking to me having taken money from them sir,' Ravi hadn't even finished saying this when Ganesan gave him a tight slap.

'You son of a whore, who do you think you are talking to? The magistrate who came, did he also come to take money? You street dog! Do you look like a man who has lost his wife? You are stinking of alcohol, no one can bear to stand next to you. I'll drag you to the station right now, rascal!'

As soon as Ganesan stopped, Anandha Kumar began to yell at Ravi.

'You are the fucker who took her to the General Hospital yesterday when she was burnt in the fire. Don't you know there would be a case filed if you go to GH? It is our job to get your statement now. If the Head Constable wishes he could drag you in chains right now to the station. We have come with handcuffs. Write your statement or we'll throw you into jail.' Anandha Kumar extended the paper to him. It was Siva Kumar who was standing next to him who received it.

'Don't mistake him, sir,' Siva Kumar said with humility and asked, 'What should we write sir?'

'Did that girl immolate herself? Or did someone else set her on fire? Who was at home when the event took place? Write everything in complete detail.' Anandha Kumar said harshly.

'Okay,' said Siva Kumar and took Ravi to the shade of another neem tree at ten feet's distance and sat down. In a minute or two the lawyer who was standing at a distance came and joined them. He was the one who took the paper and began to write. In ten minutes, Siva Kumar brought the paper and gave it to Anandha Kumar.

'Give it to sir,' Anandha Kumar said.

Siva Kumar handed the paper to the Head Constable. Ganesan took the paper and began to read it.

'I, Ravi, resident of Cuddalore District, Virudhachalam Town, Periyar Nagar North, Burma Nagar, 11 Rojappoo Street, am giving this true statement as per my conscience. On 24.06.16 afternoon my wife Mrs. Revathi was cooking at home. At that time the kerosene can toppled and caught fire. Hearing my wife scream, I rushed to the kitchen. The fire had engulfed her body. I immediately poured water over her and put off the fire. The fire had caused slight burns to my wife. I took her in my auto to Virudhachalam Government Hospital. There she received first aid. They instructed us to take her to Cuddalore for further treatment. Accordingly, I took her in 108 Ambulance to Cuddalore Hospital. There they refused her admission and asked me to take her to JIPMER Hospital. Accordingly, I brought my wife to Pondicherry and admitted her to JIPMER Hospital at around 6.40 pm. On the day of the fire, there had been no fight between my wife and me. No fisticuffs or arguments took place that day. The fire was accidental. Nobody planned it. My wife did not do it deliberately, nor were I or any of my relatives involved in this. Yours truly,' it said and was unsigned.

'Why haven't you signed it?' Ganesan asked.

'I'll get it, sir. I gave the paper just to check if it was alright, sir.' Siva Kumar said and took the paper politely and went to Ravi to get his signature and returned it to Ganesan.

'Why, wont that asshole give it to me?' Ganesan took the paper and flung it away. Siva Kumar picked up the paper from the ground with some trepidation and said, 'He didn't come to you because of fear, sir.' He went and gave the paper to Ravi. Ravi walked up to the Head Constable and offered the paper. He didn't take the paper but shouted instead, 'Do you think this is something ordinary? A magistrate visiting, two policemen coming here, do you think this is for nothing? Do you think the law, the police, the court, are like driving an auto?'

'Sir, don't repeat again and again that I am an auto driver.' Ravi had just finished saying this when Ganesan turned on him like an enraged animal and kicked him from where he was standing.

'Please stop, sir. Please stop, sir.' Siva Kumar and Anbu fell at Ganesan's feet and pleaded. Even so, Ganesan stopped kicking Ravi only when his anger had abated.

'Filthy dog. Do you know who you are talking to? You arrogant buggers will immolate yourselves and die. And we have to suffer for it in the sun? We should have given you the run around, never allowed to see us, made to wait for two or three days. If we had done that, you would have brought money, organised a car, been in attendance, ready to suck any dick, and waited outside the station. I didn't do that. So, you think you can talk. As if you are driving a ship rather than an auto. How did that girl marry you knowing you are filthy dog, a lowlife!' Ganesan hawked and spat at Ravi's face.

All that had happened—the kicks, the slap, and the abuse in front of Murugan and Natesan—kindled Ravi's anger. 'You are speaking whatever you want, sir,' he said. The Head Constable immediately punched his face hard. The way Ravi stood, spoke, and acted as if he had no fear, all of it seemed as if he was acting to someone's instructions. It enraged Ganesan even more. Siva Kumar and Anbu pleaded, 'He is a bit cracked sir. Don't take it wrong. Forgive him sir.'

'Who are you? I think I have seen you somewhere.'

'From Virudhachalam only, sir.'

'You are the bee that burrows into shit. That is why you are standing like this. You don't know what a terrible fate you have escaped from. From now, if you pray to any god, fold your hands and pray to that girl. She is the one who has let you go free.' Ganesan said to Ravi.

Ravi walked away without saying anything. The others said vanakkam to Ganesan and left. Anandha Kumar kept Ravi's statement safely.

'He thought that you had given us money and brought us here. If he had been born to a good whore, he is the one who should have given us money, brownnosed us, fallen at our feet, prayed and pleaded to us to see that the case disappears. He doesn't even know that. Knowing that you would call the police, he has come with a lawyer, did you notice?' Ganesan asked Natesan.

'Really? I don't know who that was.'

'The one who came last and talked to us. That is the one.

They must have taken pre-emptive bail as well. That is why so much arrogance.'

'We are the fools, sir.' Natesan said pathetically.

'Your girl took the right decision. It is good if she dies early. Why should she live with this piece of excrement?' Ganesan hawked and spat again.

Natesan didn't open his mouth. His face was shrunk. He felt like dying.

'Okay, it is getting late. We will leave now.' Ganesan said.

Natesan folded his hands. Murugan did as well. Amaravathi and Arunmozhi stood up and folded their hands.

'Settle things and come along. I will go before you.' Ganesan instructed Anandha Kumar and began to walk briskly towards the main gate.

2

'We asked the magistrate to come by bus. He said he would come only by an AC car. The car rent was a thousand five hundred, make it a round four thousand including the Head Constable and me. Normally, he should give. That is how it is in a fire accident case. But he is a loafer, so I have to ask you.'

Amaravathi said with bitterness filling her heart, 'The auto driver has all the luck.'

'Your daughter is saying this so firmly. What can we do when it has been recorded on tape?'

'She is a murderer. What else can she do but kill us?'

'Even now, give me a different statement. We can throw him in for two or three days. He can come out on bail after that.'

'Can we change the statement now?' Arunmozhi asked eagerly.

'Yes, you can. We will have to ask the Head Constable though.'

'Should we change it, mama?' Arunmozhi asked Natesan longingly.

'It doesn't matter if it costs money. Change the statement. She has written her testimony against us. We don't need to think of her as ours any longer. Let us also give a statement against hers.' Amaravathi poured out all her resentment and anger.

'It is not correct for me to say this as a policeman. I will say this, nevertheless. The decision you have taken now is right. It is also wrong in a way. Now all that you have to do is write that you suspect him. "Our daughter wasn't in her senses when she gave her statement. He only burnt our daughter. He used to torture her for dowry." If you do that, we will arrest him right away and take him off. We will produce him in court and have him sent to jail. It will be some botheration for us, but that's all. If we arrest him, he was jumping around now, tomorrow he will fall at our feet and offer us money. The girl will die today or tomorrow. As soon as he hears of her death, he will file for bail within two days of going inside saying, just to make trouble, that he will only cremate his wife. What does the magistrate know? He will give him bail. Because you had him arrested, he will not allow you to come near your daughter's body. You will insist. This will lead to verbal and physical fighting and become a police matter. A case will be filed. We will arrest both parties. He is capable of anything. He has no sense of honour, no sense of shame. The body will remain in the hospital because of your fight. If the body is released even so, he will file a petition that the body has to be buried, that the milk ritual has to be done, that the eighth day ceremony has to be performed, and all the rituals be observed. The court will admit it. The court needs only a case number. Even if we fight the case, he will be inside only for ten odd days. He will obtain bail. Then he will fight the case. He will drag it out for two or three years. Even though they may know that he burnt his wife, four lawyers will turn up to argue that it is false. Things will go on like this for two-three years before a judgement is delivered. During that time, you will die running from the lawyer's house to the police to the station to the court.... We didn't let him go today because of what you wrote and felt. We did so because we wanted your girl's body to be released to go to the cremation ground. The Head Constable hit him for that only. If we thought your daughter could survive for ten more days, his story would have been different. We would have handcuffed and taken him. We would have said we never met you people.'

Anandha Kumar must have been only twenty-five years old. He spoke every word with deliberation, slowly, as if he was repeating something he had memorised.

'Do they have children?'

'There are two.' Arunmozhi replied to Anandha Kumar.

'How old are they?'

'Four, five.'

'Where will they stay now?'

'Let them stay anywhere, let them die anywhere.' Amaravathi replied with a heart full of rage.

Anandha Kumar looked intently at Amaravathi. Then, 'Don't speak like that, please. A child can be without a father, can even live without knowing who the father is. But the child shouldn't be without a mother. From now, those children will yearn for every meal till their death and die crying. How will they sleep at night now? Whom will they lie down next to? Your daughter will die today or tomorrow. But what about those children, what will be their state? They say the biggest thing in the world is the ocean. That's wrong. Amma is the biggest in the world.' Anandha Kumar's eyes filled with tears. To hide his tears, he looked up at the sky. He wiped his eyes with his handkerchief. Even then, the tears didn't stop flowing. He snuffled. He looked everywhere but at the people in front of him. He took Arunmozhi's bottle of water and drank some.

'It is very wrong to ask you for money after seeing that girl. The Head Constable paid the money for the car the magistrate used. When he asks me to collect the money, I can't refuse. In the police, you have to obey your superior officer. That's it. You can't question the order, you can't speak against it. I have just joined service. If you can't pay fully, give a thousand rupees less. I will say you paid the entire sum.'

Amaravathi got up and approached Anandha Kumar.

She looked at him keenly. She held his hands and said with clenched teeth, 'You are a stranger. She didn't have your heart, your sympathy, the monster. She saved him and made us live in shame and humiliation forever.'

'Please don't abuse that girl. In the condition that she is, she doesn't deserve to be cursed.' Anandha Kumar's eyes teared up again. He looked away again. He gazed at a distant tree. He looked at the people walking the street in the heat. He kept quiet for a short while.

'It is getting late. If you can, please give the money. If you can't, it is alright. I will give from my pocket.'

'I am willing to give you any amount for your good nature, Thambi.' Amaravathi said.

'Even now we can go and tell him that they have filed a case against you. If you want to escape arrest, give us some money, he will give us five thousand, ten thousand happily. Such things do happen in the police force. There are instances of taking money from both parties. But Head Constable is a good sort. On top of it, the Mangalampettai SI is calling us time and again. That is why we didn't extend our hand to him. And then, I have seen him at the station for two years. He talks big. The station knows that. If he gets angry, he may not even have the body released. He will do anything once he is drunk. You are the parents of the girl. Can you stand her corpse stinking to high heaven?'

'Why couldn't you have been born to us?' Natesan held his hands and teared up.

Murugan gave the money.

'If anything happens, they will call the police station first.

The police has to be here before they can take the next step. If you need any help, call me.' Anandha Kumar gave them his cellphone number.

'Will she die, sir?' Arunmozhi asked. Anandha Kumar did not reply.

Natesan folded his hands in salutation to Anandha Kumar. Amaravathi also folded her hands to him.

'Sir, a moment,' Arunmozhi gave ten thousand rupees from her shoulder bag.

'Why?' Anandha Kumar asked in surprise.

'We have the money. But we couldn't abuse him. We couldn't give him a beating. You could abuse him, beat him, in a public place, in the middle of the road. You could hawk and spit on his face. This is for that.'

'Oh, that?' Anandha Kumar laughed softly.

'We didn't hit him or abuse him. It is this uniform that did all that. Only the uniform has that authority. When we saw the girl, the Head Constable sir and I became very angry. We wanted to break his arms and legs. He could have chased her away saying, "I don't like you, I don't want you." Instead, he set her on fire. He must have been drunk when he did it. Or the girl could have done it herself trying to frighten him. In any case, he is responsible for what happened. So, we beat him.'

Not just Natesan and Amaravathi, even Murugan and Arunmozhi looked at Anandha Kumar strangely. His talk had taken away all their anger, made them emotionless.

'This money cannot save the girl. If it could, I would have given ten thousand myself. She is not even thirty, fully burnt. She didn't even think of her children. How hurt her heart must have felt, in how much pain her heart would have been, for her to forget her own children? You all think that the girl has made a mistake. She has done the right thing. She hasn't given him freedom, she had dealt out a punishment to him, till death. From now on, he will die every moment. Even if had been arrested and jailed, he would not have been punished like this. Your daughter is a good girl, sir. She has saved even a murderer. Only the good will have the heart for this. He has killed a life. He has orphaned two lives. She has saved even such a man. No woman will die leaving her little children behind. If she still chose to die, how wounded, how charred her heart must be. I know. I have suffered this. My mother also died like this.' Anandha Kumar cried, which made Natesan and Amaravathi cry as well.

'Because of the mistakes the parents make, children become beggars, thieves, and prostitutes. From now who will worry that the children haven't eaten? Who will ask them to sleep at the right time?' Anandha Kumar began to walk away. Natesan and Amravathi folded their hands to him as they would to a god.

3

Amaravathi's sister, Latchumi, and her husband, Sivapatham, arrived. They asked immediately, 'How is she? Hope there is no threat to her life?' Not only Murugan and Natesan, even

Amaravathi didn't say anything in reply. Amaravathi leaned on Latchumi's shoulder and sobbed.

'Can't we take her to a private facility? Is a government hospital good enough?' Sivapatham asked.

'We must see.' Natesan replied. His voice showed no emotion at all.

'What do the doctors say?'

'They say they will see.'

'If something happens to the girl's life, we shouldn't leave him alone. We should finish his story.' Sivapatham said in a raised voice.

'We should have got her a divorce earlier itself. It was wrong not to act.' Latchumi spoke harshly. 'What has she done!' She added and clenched her teeth.

'We should have had him arrested earlier. Because we let him be, he has now burnt our daughter alive.' Sivapatham said with some regret.

Latchumi and Sivapatham asked question after question for about ten-twenty minutes. At least Murugan tried to answer them for some time. Arunmozhi stood as if her mouth had been sealed shut. Unable to answer their questions with any coherence, Natesan said to Murugan, 'Thambi, take them for some coffee.' Even though Latchumi and Sivapatham said no to the coffee, Murugan compelled them to go along with him to the canteen.

'You should also go and drink something.' Amaravathi said to Natesan. He didn't say anything in reply but looked at a neem tree in the distance. The leaves of the tree were fluttering in the breeze. The tree seemed to be shrouded in the heat.

'At least you go and drink something.' Amaravathi said to Arunmozhi.

'I don't want,' Arunmozhi replied and looked at the people walking on the road.

Arunmozhi's father Sundaram and mother Kamalam arrived. Amaravathi felt like crying when she saw them.

'How is she?' Sundaram asked.

'We can say nothing. From what the police say, it is difficult for her to survive.' Natesan replied.

'Haven't you seen her?'

'No.'

'Why not?'

'They didn't allow us in.'

'How did the police come? Have you filed a case?' Sundaram asked with concern.

'There is no need to file a petition now. The police came and took our statements.'

'How did the police come by themselves?'

'They said because it was a fire accident it became a police case automatically.'

'Is that so?'

'Yes. The police came. The magistrate came too. They took statements and left.'

'Who gave the statements?'

'Revathi gave and so did we.'

'What did you say?'

'That it had happened by itself.'

Sundaram was surprised. 'What? Why did you do like this?' Kamalam asked. Latchumi and Sivapatham returned from the canteen just then. Sundaram told them about the statement. Both of them asked again and again, 'Is it true? Is it true?' Natesan didn't open his mouth to say anything. He wanted to run away somewhere. He wanted to be by himself. His face showed no sign of life. Latchumi asked Amaravathi with some vehemence, 'Why did you give such a statement?' Amaravathi replied with deliberation, 'Because our brains are addled.'

'Why did you give a statement that it happened by itself?' Latchumi asked again.

'He is such a saint. He has done so many good deeds. That's why, because of that only, he is standing there whole and hearty without even a pinhead of a sore on his body. She had done evil deeds, no? That is why she is lying there fully burnt, all her flesh cooked, dying a terrible death.' Amaravathi's voice did not shake. Her lips did not tremble. Only tears flowed down from her eyes.

Natesan became angry because Sivapatham and Sundaram kept saying, 'You have made a mistake, a mistake.'

'If we filed a case, I would have to go to the police station, lawyer's house, court, each one of them. At each place I would have to admit this is the guy who married my daughter. All of them would ask why the hell did your daughter marry such a lowlife and hawk and spit on my face.' Natesan snapped and turned his face away. He gazed at the tall building to the west. The sun was setting behind the building. There wasn't a single cloud in the sky. Even in the evening it was very hot.

'Aren't we there for you? Wouldn't we have taken care

of the case?' Sivapatham and Sundaram asked. Natesan did not reply.

'If you give birth to a good girl, you can go and tell four people. How can those who have given birth to a bad daughter speak to anyone?' Amaravathi questioned them. Sundaram was about to say something when Natesan preempted him with, 'Please don't trouble me. As it is, I am standing here with no life in my body.' He turned his face away again.

'Why don't we discharge her from here and have her treated elsewhere?' Latchumi asked Amaravathi.

'The doctor should agree, isn't it? If we ask they say no. Her per centage of burns is very high they say.' Amaravathi spoke reluctantly.

Murugan's phone rang then. He picked it up and spoke to the caller. 'Is that so?' He asked and cut the call in anger.

'Who was it?'

'That rascal.'

'What did he want?' Arunmozhi asked disinterestedly.

'She is saying that she wants to meet me.' When he said this Murugan's face showed his utter disgust.

'Please go and see and her.'

'I am not going,' Murugan said in great anger.

'What are you saying?' Arunmozhi asked in surprise.

'How can I even see her face after her testimony? She is shaming us even in such circumstances. Do I need to go and see such a woman?'

If she had been in front of him, he would have himself set her on fire, his heart was so filled with rage at her perfidy in giving her testimony in favour of Ravi. The rest were also filled with the same rage. Murugan had expressed it aloud, the others hadn't.

'Should I go and meet her?' Natesan and Murugan glared at Arunmozhi in anger when she asked this. Amaravathi glared at her too, pouring out all the rage in her heart, 'No one needs to go. Let her go for her funeral without anyone seeing her.'

Arunmozhi remained quiet for a little while and then asked, 'Shouldn't we ask her why she gave such a testimony?' Neither Murugan nor anyone else answered her.

Arunmozhi said to Amaravathi, 'Give me the pass, please. Let me go at least to abuse her,' and forcibly took the pass from her and began to walk away. Murugan intercepted her and asked with uncontrollable rage, 'What are you doing? Isn't the shame she has heaped on us so far enough?'

'Shouldn't we ask why did you give such a testimony and humiliate us?' Arunmozhi asked.

'It is my bloody fate. She does all the wrong things and I suffer the humiliation.' Murugan turned his face away in extreme bitterness. Arunmozhi said to placate him, 'You shouldn't go, I will.' Murugan burst out, 'How much more should I be shamed? Only what females think, do, is right, isn't it?'

After keeping silent for a little while, he said, 'Give it, let me go die,' and snatched the pass from Arunmozhi's hand and began to walk briskly towards the emergency building. Arunmozhi walked along with him.

The guards allowed only Murugan inside. They wouldn't

allow Arunmozhi however much she pleaded. 'Only one hour is left in the time for visitors. Please stand away. Come back after an hour,' they told her with finality. Murugan then told her, 'You wait outside. I will go up and see her and come back.' He went in and stood near the lift. The lift was on the seventh floor. Instead of waiting for it, he took the stairs.

Ravi was standing in front of the door on the fifth floor. As soon as he reached him, Murugan asked with distaste, 'What?' Ravi looked down and said, 'The guard said that Revathi wanted to meet you.' Murugan knocked on the door immediately. The guard opened the door and asked, 'What?' Before Murugan could reply, Ravi said, 'You asked me to call Revathi's anna. This is him.'

'Come in.'

The guard allowed only Murugan inside, shutting the door on the face of Ravi who also tried to enter along with Murugan. Murugan entered and stood in front of the door to the ICU. The guard followed him and knocked on the door. The nurse opened the door and asked, 'What?'

'This is the patient Revathi's anna.'

'Come in.' The door was shut as soon as Murugan entered the ICU.

The nurse handed him a gown, mask, and gloves one by one. He wore each one following her instructions.

'You shouldn't speak. Just look at her and come back.' The nurse seemed to be laying down a martial law. Murugan nodded his head to say okay.

The nurse walked in front; Murugan followed her. She opened the door to the room where the patients were and said, 'Go in. Hers is the last bed, number eighteen. Don't take too much time.' She let him go in and shut the door.

Where was Revathi? Where was bed number eighteen? Murugan looked around confused. It was only after a few moments that he began to understand the layout of the room. All the beds were occupied. You could see only the faces of the patients. Their bodies were covered in bandages. The light was very dim, and the AC was very high. He searched for bed number eighteen.

'Anna.' The voice seemed faint as if she was calling from a distance. He looked for where the voice had come from.

'Anna.'

He approached Revathi's bed. When he saw her face, he couldn't control himself, covered his eyes, and exclaimed in horror, 'Oh God!' Flesh that had charred in the fire, he could not see that face again. He should run away without looking at her face again. He began to tremble as if he had been abandoned in the middle of an ocean. He felt his head was spinning. He was afraid to open his eyes.

'Anna.'

'…'

'Anna.'

Murugan did not remove his hands from his face. His arms and legs trembled uncontrollably. His mouth became dry. His head was spinning, his eyes dimmed. Tears streamed down his face. He should escape from that place and run away. That is the only thought he had.

'Anna.'

Murugan hit his own face. 'Oh, God!' Hearing the noise,

the nurse entered and looked at him as if asking what had happened. Then she raised a finger to her lips to say quiet and gestured to him to keep peace. Murugan covered his mouth with both his hands but he couldn't control his tears or the trembling of his body.

'Anna.'

'…'

'You can speak,' said the nurse.

He couldn't ask any of the one, two, ten, hundred, thousand questions he had prepared to ask Revathi. All the questions had turned to ashes the moment he saw her. He couldn't even ask her why she had given such a testimony. He couldn't even be angry now. He tried to speak. His lips wouldn't move, his mouth wouldn't open, he could only cry.

'Anna.'

'Aiyo, God!'

'Please forgive me, Anna.'

Murugan couldn't even mouth, 'Don't say that.'

'Call me by name, say Revathi, Anna.'

'Aiyo, amma.' He cried.

'Please sir. Quiet.' The nurse said strictly.

'Take my name, Anna.'

Murugan couldn't speak. His lips were stuck together. He tried to open them but couldn't. He couldn't stand firmly on his feet. It seemed as if he was standing on a block of ice. He was trembling even more than before. He couldn't bear to see Revathi's face. He closed his eyes.

'Are you angry with me, Anna?'

'No, no. I swear.'

'Stay with me, Anna.'

'I will stay, I will stay. I won't go anywhere. I've talked to the doctor. However many crores it costs us, I won't go home without you.'

'Don't spend your money, Anna.'

'…'

'Don't cry, Anna.'

'I am not crying.'

'Call me Revathi, Anna.'

'Aiyo amma.' Hearing Murugan cry, the nurse who was standing by the next bed said, 'Go out, please. Time's up. There is a risk of infection.' She glared at Murugan.

'Sister,' Revathi called.

'Enough, Revathi. You shouldn't speak too much. We can talk once you are better. Stay quiet now.'

'Please, sister!' Revathi pleaded.

'I will save you even if I have to give my life.'

'Please forgive me, Anna.'

'Don't say that. I will lose my life.' He bit his fingers but still couldn't control his crying.

'Say my name, Anna.'

'What are you asking, what are you asking?' Murugan asked repeatedly.

'Anna….'

'Aiyo.'

'Sir, go out. We have to attend to other patients too.' The nurse held Murugan's hands, tried to pull him away.

'Forgive me, Anna. Stay here, Anna.'

Murugan couldn't hear Revathi's words. The cold breeze of the AC had swallowed her voice.

Murugan tried to take off his gown, mask, and gloves to return them, but he couldn't do anything. The nurse helped to take them off, did it all herself. As if her remembered suddenly, he pleaded, 'My thangachi asked me to call her by her name—Revathi. I forgot to do that. Can I please go and call her Revathi and come back?'

'No, sir. If they hear you speak loudly, the other patients will start crying.'

Murugan took out a thousand rupee note from his pant pocket and offered it to the nurse. The nurse's face changed. She said disdainfully, 'This is shameful, sir. Go out, sir. It is only because Revathi was crying from the morning to see you that I allowed you inside.'

'Please, madam.'

'Get out, sir.'

Showing no pity, the nurse went quickly to the door and opened it. Having no other choice, Murugan moved out. The ICU door shut behind him immediately.

As he came out of the ICU and walked across the hall, the guard stood ready with the next door open. When he came out, he could see Ravi standing there. 'You bastard! You set her on fire and have the guts to stand here in front of me! You bloody loafer. Don't stand in front of me. If you do, I will murder you. My thangachi is lying there like charred wood. Get lost or I will beat you up with my slippers.' Murugan pushed hard at Ravi. All those standing and sitting on the stairs were dumbstruck. They just stared at Murugan. Everyone thought that a girl related to Murugan had died. An impatient woman asked, 'Is everything over?' Murugan looked at her. Her form didn't register in his eyes.

He began to walk down the stairs one by one. Ravi was coming down three-four steps behind him.

When they reached the ground floor, Ravi caught up with him and said, 'She will survive somehow.' He was crying.

'How dare you speak to me after setting her on fire? Get lost. Don't stand in front of me, don't force me to become a murderer. If you stand here, you will get a beating with my slippers. You are no better than a stray dog.' Saying this, Murugan pushed Ravi with all his strength.

Without waiting to hear what Ravi, who had fallen down, was getting up to say, Murugan left the emergency block.

As if she was waiting for him to come out, Arunmozhi ran towards him in some panic. She asked rapidly, 'What happened? What did she say? Did you ask her why she gave that testimony?'

Murugan did not answer any question of Arunmozhi's. She kept asking him questions. As if in answer to all the questions, as his final words, Murugan said, 'She should not survive.'

Murugan wept loudly. He didn't care for the road, the people, the crowds. All his anger at Revathi for falling in love with Ravi, her obstinacy to marry him, her unexpected testimony, had disappeared the moment he saw her. Now he had no anger, no regrets at her behaviour. He only felt pity for her. He wanted her to survive.

'Come,' said Arunmozhi and took him to the north of the emergency block, the way to the Paediatrics department. Natesan and others were sitting under a large neem tree.

Sivapatham, Sundaram, Latchumi, and Kamalam asked in one voice, 'What happened?'

'I think every spot in her body is burnt fully. I couldn't even make out where her eyes are, her nose or her mouth. The face is puffed up like a poori. She is unable to speak. It is difficult to hear what she is saying. It seems like she is speaking from a great distance. The only thing she said was, "Forgive me, Anna." She kept saying that only. There is a cut wound on her shaven head. He must have pushed her down in the fight. She kept asking, "Call my name, Anna".' Murugan spoke to Arunmozhi and kicked hard at the ground.

'Should we leave him alone even now?' Sundaram asked with uncontrollable anger.

'What else did she say?' Latchumi asked.

'She will live, such a golden heart she has. She will survive. Please don't cry like a small child.' Kamalam said.

'Sit down, appa.' Sivapatham said.

'Some filthy dog roaming the streets somewhere entered our family and destroyed us. He is a pucca rowdy. He and his bloody face.' Latchumi shouted.

'Please sit down.' Arunmozhi told him.

Murugan couldn't stand, so he sat down. The others sat around him. Murugan lay down on the ground. He hit the ground, punched it, and cried. Seeing him crying, Natesan suddenly told Sundaram, 'You should leave now for home.'

'We came just now. We will leave in some time. What is the rush?' When Sundaram said this, Natesan turned to Sivapatham, 'At least you should leave now.'

'What is the rush now? How can we come all the way and leave without seeing the girl?' Sivapatham said a bit incensed.

'At least in the other wards, they would allow people

in now and then. In this ward, they don't allow anyone in, anyone.' Amaravathi said.

'It is good that they don't allow anyone in. No one who sees the people lying there can remain alive.' Murugan said.

'Buy them some tea, coffee. Take them with you.' Natesan said to Arunmozhi.

'We don't want anything.' Sundaram said.

'I'll also accompany you. Come.' Natesan stood up and thus forced the others to get up. Natesan's talk and actions seemed new and puzzling. It seemed astonishing that he was so adamant in what he wanted.

When they were in front of the emergency block, an ambulance arrived from the main gate. Six-seven guards surrounded the ambulance. A guard shouted again and again into the mike he was carrying, 'Please stand aside. Nobody should stand in the way. No one should enter the area that we have roped off. Please go away, no crowds allowed here.' People who were coming in from the main entrance, people going out, people on their way to different medical facilities, people sitting and talking to each other under trees here and there, all began to congregate around the ambulance. In a few moments, a large crowd had gathered.

They brought out six people from the ambulance. Two men, four women, and a child. All of them were fully burnt. They brought them out with urgency, placed them on stretchers, and immediately took them inside. This was done very fast. It was done smoothly without a single misstep or confusion. The ambulance left. The surrounding crowd gave way by itself without being asked to do so by anyone. Arunmozhi was surprised. As soon as the ambulance left, the guard began to shout into his mike, 'Please disperse. You have created a traffic jam. Cars, bikes, drive slowly. All of you disperse.' Hundreds of people began walking in obedience to the voice on the mike.

In a few moments, in some manner the crowd knew what had happened. Some people had fallen into the fire because of the push and pull of the crowd at a temple festival near Senchi where devotees were performing the fire walking ritual. Two women had died on the spot. Those who had been burnt slightly had been admitted to Vizhupuram Hospital. Only those who suffered severe burns had been brought to JIPMER.

It seemed unbelievable that they would have to announce in a mike to disperse crowds at a hospital. Within five to ten minutes, a furlong-long line of cars and vehicles had backed up outside the main gate. Not able to believe her eyes, Arunmozhi said to Murugan, 'Everything is so surprising.'

'I have been seeing from last night. An ambulance arrives every ten minutes. It doesn't matter if it is day or night. It is like a big company.' Amaravathi said.

'You should go,' Natesan said to Sundaram.

'Yes.' Sundaram replied.

'Okay, come. I will accompany you to the bus stop and see you off.' Natesan began to walk towards the main gate leading the way. Even though they wondered why Natesan was acting like this, why he was adamant that they should go back immediately, the others had no option but to follow him.

'Even though we came such a long way, we couldn't meet Revathi.' Kamalam expressed her regret.

'Do you have money for your expenditure?' Sundaram asked.

'There is no role for money here.' Murugan replied.

'Are you coming? Are you going to stay here?' Sivapatham asked Latchumi.

'I am not coming. You go by yourself.' Latchumi replied.

'Will you have anything to eat?' Natesan asked.

'No,' said Sundaram, and added, 'It was a big mistake to let that street dog go free. If there is a way, have him arrested and thrown inside. I know a lawyer; he will take care of the case.'

'If something happens to Revathi's life, I will myself hit that filthy dog with my slippers.' Sivapatham said in anger.

'It was our fault to give our girl to a loafer.' Kamalam said.

'As If there was no other man in the world, she caught hold of an auto driver!' Latchumi's words burnt Natesan, Amaravathi, and Murugan like fire.

After reaching the main gate and till they boarded the bus, Sundaram, Sivapatham, and Kamalam said various things, asked many questions, but Natesan did not open his mouth. He remained quiet. Murugan didn't speak either.

4

When they were walking back, Natesan stopped suddenly and said, 'You people go. I will join you.' Everyone looked at him to find out what the matter was. He wondered why they were all looking funnily at him. He said again, 'Go on, I will join you.'

'Okay, join us quickly,' Amaravathi said and continued walking. Murugan, Arunmozhi, and Latchumi began to walk with her.

As if he had some important work, Natesan began to walk towards Gorimedu bus stand. He looked at both sides of the road leading to the emergency block. People were walking in and out of the gate. It was crowded like a temple chariot pulling event. For a while, he stood in the shade of the banyan tree near the main entrance. He watched the people waiting for the bus. He looked at his watch as if he had some important work. He wondered what he needed to look at the time for. What was the reason that Revathi fell in love with Ravi, for her being so adamant in her decision to marry him, and for suffering beatings every day from him after marriage, and then for her self-immolation?

From the time he remembered he hadn't touched meat, eggs, or fish. He had always had vegetarian food. He had never tried black magic or sorcery of any kind, never even thought of doing any harm to anybody. He had never given money on interest to his fellow teachers. He examined his conscience to see if, from the time he joined service to the time he became Headmaster, he had ever done anything harmful, behaved badly with any students, especially girl students. He wondered if he had failed any student without any reason. He didn't think he had done any harm to anyone so far.

He wondered if he had ever behaved badly with his

family. When his father died, his mother died, he had taken the entire responsibility for the expenditure. He hadn't taken a single paisa from his thambi. How could people divide and share the expenditure for their parent's death? He had refused to take money saying this was crass. When they divided the property, he had given his thambi not just the land, house, orchard, enclosures that he asked for, he gave his thambi an additional three acres of land because he was unemployed. When his thambi died from cancer, Natesan paid for everything.

He had never taken a loan from anyone. Hence, he had never cheated on a loan. He hadn't gone late to school even one day. He hadn't ever missed teaching even a period in all his years of service. He was a believer in God from his childhood. He had great devotion to Vallalar. He would go walking to Vadalur every Thai Poosam. He had been feeding at least a hundred people every Thai Poosam since he got his job. He had never missed the annual Muttrothal at the Chidambaram Natarajar temple. He had never sent away empty-handed those who came home saying that they were going to Tirupati and asking for some money as offering. He had never said he had no money to those who had come asking for money for the marriage thaali. He would always take a hundred rupees in coins when he visited any temple. He had never returned without giving some money to every mendicant who asked for alms there. His mother Parvathambal had told him often that he should never say no to those who asked for alms, 'It is a great sin to do so. God will never grant you a good release.' Whenever he gave alms, whenever he offered food, he would remember his mother. He had never done any harm to anyone. How was it then that his daughter was undergoing such torture? Would one's ancestors have done some awful sin? Perhaps someone had tied a worker and beaten him up for missing a day's work. They may have sold milk diluted with water. They may have sent away empty-handed holy mendicants. They may have borne false witness. What would they have done?

'Even the food I offered at Thai Poosam hasn't saved us.' Natesan murmured to himself and then wondered if had done any wrong in his previous birth. A man bumped into him then and walked past. Only then did he seem to come back to his senses, and he looked at the road and began to walk back to the emergency block.

'She has caused her own death,' when he said this to himself, tears began to flow from his eyes. He said finally, 'This too is fate. Everything is fate.'

5

A good crowd had collected in front of the emergency block. Murugan and Arunmozhi walked towards the crowd. Arunmozhi asked a woman, 'Why is there such a crowd?'

'To go inside, why else?'

'What time does the Visitors' Hours begin?'

'At five.'

'Is it already five?' Arunmozhi looked at her watch in

surprise. She then looked at the crowd. She looked at the seven-storied emergency block. The building was west facing. It was in front of the main gate. The road from the main gate to the emergency block had been divided into two by flowering plants in a raised bed that they had constructed. One side of the road was for coming in, the other for going out. On both, you had a broad pavement for people to walk on. Neither pavement was unused even for a moment. Wherever you looked, you saw buildings. Wherever you looked, you saw people. Wherever you looked, you saw trees. The hospital looked as if twenty-thirty thousand people on an average visited it every day. There were no signs to indicate that it was a government hospital, a free hospital. It looked like a private corporate hospital. They had marked off with ropes enough space for ambulances to come and stand in front of the emergency block and to leave with ease. Not just that space, the entire block was under the constant surveillance of security guards.

A large crowd had gathered in front of the emergency block, outside the area reserved for ambulances. There was no movement in the crowd, no fighting for space. No one was crying, shouting, or lamenting loudly. Unlike other times, not one person pleaded with the guards to be allowed inside. No one quarrelled. The crowd was peaceful as if people believed that once it struck five o'clock, all their work would be done. It was then that they could see an ambulance coming from the main gate. Without anyone saying anything, the crowd split into two to give way. Without slowing down, without any obstacles, the ambulance sped to the entrance of the emergency block and came to a halt. They took out three bodies disfigured in a car accident. They were placed on stretchers and the hospital staff ran inside with them. The whole crowd was moved by the appearance of the three injured people. People exclaimed, 'Poor things!' The ambulance started back. Without any instructions, without any announcement, the crowd parted to give way to the ambulance.

'It is so surprising.'

'What is?' Murugan asked.

'The way people gave way to the ambulance. I haven't seen people so peaceful even in temples.'

'I can't believe it. Are these people citizens of our country?'

The guard announced on the mike, 'Visitors can go in now.'

The crowd began to enter the emergency block. But there was no pushing or pulling. No one ran in frantically. They all entered slowly. They gave way to each other, kept their distance from each other.

Arunmozhi and Murugan were the first to reach the fifth floor. Natesan and Latchumi joined them. The door to the hall was shut. About thirty-forty people were standing next to the door and on the staircase. There was no space even to stand on the staircase. A man who lost his patience knocked on the door. The security guard opened the door after a little while. The one who knocked on the door and two others approached the guard. The guard asked dismissively, 'What?'

'I have to go in.' The man who knocked on the door said.

'Did the doctor or nurse call you inside?'

'No.'

'Then why did you knock on the door?'

'A girl of ours is inside, have to see her.'

'We will call you if you are needed.'

'I have come from Tindivanam. Our relative is inside, I need to see her. Please, let me inside.' A woman in a creamish-sampangi-flower-coloured saree pleaded.

'I have come from Chidambaram and have been squatting here since the morning. They told me I could see her in the evening at five. Please open the door.' An older woman was in tears as she asked.

'I am coming from Kallakurichi. I have been sitting here for two days. Haven't been able to see our girl. I need to go back home. Please let me in.'

Arunmozhi joined her voice to that of the men and women pleading with the guard, 'Anna, please let us in for a short time, anna.'

'This is not like other wards. Only serious cases are admitted here. There is no visiting time for this ward. If people from outside go in, there is risk of infection. Even if I allow you in here, they won't allow you into the ICU. You will have to stand in the verandah. No one can go further. I can allow you in only if nurses or doctors call you.' The guard explained clearly.

'At least allow us to stand in the verandah.' A woman asked.

'Please listen to me, amma. No one can see the patients in the condition they are in.'

'Let us stand in the verandah just like that.' Two women pleaded.

As if his heart had melted, the guard stood aside without saying anything. First, two women went inside. Then, in the next few moments thirty-forty people had entered the hall. The guard hit himself on his forehead in exasperation. Arunmozhi went in along with the crowd. Murugan, Latchumi, Natesan, and Amaravathi followed her in one by one.

All the thirty-forty people standing in the hall were looking only at the ICU door. There was no sign of the ICU door opening. Even though they had entered the hall after winning the tussle with the guard, all their faces were listless. A few tried to look in through the ICU door. A few went directly to the doctor and asked about the status of their patients. All the relatives that had come to see the patients stood in the hall. The woman from Tindivanam dared to go and knock on the ICU door. Only after she knocked two or three times did the door open. The nurse who opened the door asked, 'What?'

'I am coming from Tindivanam. My mama's daughter immolated herself four days ago. She is inside. I need to see her. I have stayed put here since the morning.'

'Is that so?' The nurse asked politely.

'Yes, amma.' The Tindivanam woman said. Based on the nurse's politeness she thought that the nurse would allow her in.

'Security,' the nurse called.

The guard came and asked 'Yes, amma?'

'Why do you allow anyone and everyone to knock on the

door? You should stand next to the door, understand?' She banged the door shut. The Tindivanam woman's face fell.

'All of you stand away. Nobody should stand next to the door. No one should knock on the door. Only those who have to meet the doctor can go inside. The rest of you, leave.' The guard said with authority.

The nurse opened the door and said, 'Guard, please send Mangai's attendant if they are here.' Thangammal who was standing in the crowd ran immediately to the door.

'Are you Mangai's attendant?'

'Yes, amma.'

'Come inside please.'

The ICU door was shut as soon as Thangammal entered. Thangammal returned almost as soon as she went in. Immediately, her granddaughter and two men asked her, 'What happened?'

'They want us to buy three bottles of perfume.'

'Did you see her?'

'They have drawn curtains around her bed. They told me strictly not to go near her.' Thangammal couldn't finish what she was saying and burst into tears.

'That is why I said I will go inside.' Thangammal's granddaughter Kala scolded her.

'It is not as if I refused to see her.' Thangammal replied and then told the man standing next to her, 'Why are you standing like a wooden block? Go quickly and buy some bottles of scent.' He ran out immediately.

The nurse who came out of the ICU asked, 'Who is Pazhaniamma's attendant?' Three-four people ran towards the nurse.

She gave a chit and said, 'Buy the injection written on this.' The man who took the chit asked eagerly, 'How is she, amma?'

'She is alright. First get the injection.' She said rudely and shut the door. All the nurses were like each other in the way they shut the door.

'The doctor is calling Latha's attendant.' The guard announced. Four-five people ran into the doctor's room.

'Why are they asking them to buy perfume instead of medicines or tablets or injections?' Amaravathi asked.

'She has started stinking, I think.' Thangammal wept and Kala cried with her.

Amaravathi was shaken to the core. Her arms and legs began to tremble uncontrollably. She turned to Murugan and asked, 'Shouldn't we meet the doctor?'

'It is so crowded there.' Even though Murugan said this, Arunmozhi, Natesan and he went to the doctor's room. But the doctor got up and left the room and entered the ICU.

The nurse who opened the ICU door said, 'Guard, clear the room. That's all for today.' And she entered the ICU again.

Amaravathi asked Murugan who returned from the doctor's room, 'What happened, appa?'

Murugan replied in a lifeless voice, 'There was a complication with a case inside. He went to the ICU urgently.'

'When will he come out?'

'I don't know.' Murugan replied in a weak voice.

'It is five forty-five now. All of you go out.' The guard announced. Not one person moved.

'However much you stand, it can be only for ten more minutes.' The guard said sarcastically.

'Couldn't meet the doctor,' Arunmozhi said dejectedly.

'It is time. All of you go out.' The guard announced. This time he spoke harshly. In a short while, he began to try to clear the room one by one.

'I want to meet the doctor.' One man said.

'What were you doing till now?'

'I have to ask if we can discharge her from here and take her to another hospital.'

'Whatever you want to ask, ask tomorrow morning. Now, go.'

'Is this a private hospital? You are quoting so many rules and regulations!'

The guard got angry. 'Whatever it is, come back in the morning. Don't argue law with me.' He took him by his arm and dragged him outside.

Pazhaniammal's attendant who came out of the ICU began to wail loudly. The people in the hall surrounded her immediately. 'What's the matter?' Some asked. She kept crying and said nothing in reply.

'Did you listen to me? This is why we ask you to go out. You don't know about this ward. Please go out.' The guard said. Not one person in the crowd thought of going out. The doctor came out of the ICU.

'Why is there such a crowd here? Clear the place.' As soon as the doctor said this, the guard began to move them out one by one. Murugan and Arunmozhi attempted to go to the doctor's room.

'Time's up. Leave the room. You can't see the doctor now.' The guard stopped them and tried to send them out of the hall. They moved hesitantly to where Amaravathi was standing.

The guard approached Ravi who was standing in a corner. 'Does one have to speak to you separately? Go out.'

'I want to meet the doctor. You haven't allowed me to meet anyone after admission. Haven't even met the doctor so far.'

'See him in the morning.'

'Are you the big doctor?'

'What are you talking? Go out.' The guard grabbed Ravi's hand and pulled. Ravi shook him off and went quickly to the doctor's room and said, 'Sir, my wife is struggling between life and death. I haven't seen her since yesterday. Haven't talked to her. I don't know what is happening.'

Ravi's tone enraged the doctor. The nurse standing behind the doctor gestured with her finger to her lips as if to indicate, 'Don't speak loudly.' He didn't pay any heed. He moved quickly to the door and called out authoritatively to Arunmozhi, 'Please come here.' Arunmozhi hurried into the doctor's room. The doctor looked strangely at Ravi.

'What do you want?' The doctor asked in irritation.

'I haven't heard anything about my wife, sir.'

'What do you want to know?'

'I haven't seen her since yesterday, sir.'

'It is not good to see a patient in the ICU time and again.'

'Speak in English, akka.' Ravi said to Arunmozhi.

Controlling herself, Arunmozhi said to the doctor, 'I am

Arunmozhi. Team Leader, TCS at Chennai', and she went on to ask about Revathi's condition, whether she would survive, how much per cent burns she had, whether she could be taken to a private hospital, which was the best hospital for the treatment of burns in Tamil Nadu, which part of Revathi's body was burnt most severely, could surgery help in her case, all in English. The doctor listened to all questions patiently without making a face and replied, 'The treatment is going alright. There is no better hospital for burns than JIPMER in this area. It is not good for the patient to shift her out in the state she is in.' Ravi didn't speak a word once Arunmozhi started speaking. He stood looking down with his arms folded.

'How is she compared to yesterday? Is there any progress?'

'It is only one day since she has been admitted, isn't it?'

Suddenly, Arunmozhi felt like crying. She said, weeping, 'She is my friend, sir. Both of us studied Engineering together. She was better at it than I was. She scored ninety-eight per cent and I ninety-three in Engineering. I am married to her anna. There was a small mistake in her marriage. So, she didn't go out to work. If she had, she would have been in a better position than me by this time. I get a salary of seventy thousand. If she had gone to work, she would have earned more than me. I studied hard because of her. But her life was spoilt. If there is any possibility, please tell us. Money is no concern. We want her alive, sir.' She spoke through her tears.

The doctor spoke to the nurse standing nearby, 'Please bring me Revathi's report.' The nurse went briskly to the

ICU and returned with the report. When he read the report, the doctor's face fell. He gave the report back to the nurse and said calmly, 'It is not good to shift the patient in her condition. We will tell you ourselves if it is good for her to be shifted from here. Let two-three days go by. We will see her progress and then decide. We cannot rush.' The doctor got up and began to walk towards the ICU.

Arunmozhi and Ravi came to the hall. There was no one there. The two of them then went out of the hall. Like an obedient schoolboy, Ravi went and sat on the staircase to the fourth floor. Arunmozhi went and joined Murugan, Natesan, and Amaravathi on the staircase to the sixth floor.

'What does the doctor say?' Natesan asked.

'He said the treatment is going on. Let us wait two-three days. Then we'll see.'

'How did the guard allow you inside?'

'He fought with him.'

'He fought with him even here? Nothing matters to this loafer!' Amaravathi said.

'Nowadays, only a KD, loafer, rowdy like him can win. We keep sitting in the pride that we are educated, isn't it?' When Arunmozhi said this, Murugan scolded her, 'Be quiet.'

The new guard who came out opening the door said, 'It is eight o'clock now. The attendants should come in.' Many women among those sitting there got up and went in one by one.

'Who is going to stay?' Murugan asked.

'I can stay.' Latchumi said.

'I can stay.' Arunmozhi said.

'You stay with Amma, Chitti. Let Arunmozhi stay here.' Murugan decided.

'I want to see her, Thambi.'

'You stay here tomorrow, Chitti.' Murugan said and speaking to Arunmozhi said, 'You go in.'

Arunmozhi got up and went to the door. 'Where is your pass?' The guard asked. 'One minute,' said Arunmozhi and returned to take the pass from Amaravathi. She said to Murugan, 'Please give me your phone. There is no charge in mine.'

Murugan gave his phone to her and took hers.

'Whatever happens, call us.' Murugan said.

Arunmozhi nodded her head and went into the hall.

'Is there any other attendant left outside? Has anyone gone to eat? I am about to shut the door.' The guard announced.

As if he shouldn't break the law, he shut the door immediately.

'Come, let us go.' Murugan said.

Amaravathi began to go down the stairs. The others followed her. While still on the stairs, Murugan called the driver Kumar and said, 'Please come to the entrance.'

The car arrived just as they were exiting the Emergency Block. They got in one by one.

When the car crossed the main gate of JIPMER, Amaravathi asked Murugan, 'Would Revathi have slept by now, Thambi?'

'She must have slept, Amma.'

'Let my girl forget the word and sleep.' Amaravathi began to cry.

'Let it go, Akka.' Latchumi said.

'How many times I must have told her, "If he hits or abuses you, go straight to the women's police station." She would say "Yes, Amma, yes Amma," to everything but did nothing.'

'Lie down and rest quietly, Akka.' Latchumi said.

'Now there is no North or South for my daughter, no East or West, no day or night.'

'Amma, will you keep quiet? Why are you torturing everyone?' Murugan asked and glared at her.

'She didn't listen even to me.' Natesan said and wept.

The car was going fast towards Virudhachalam in the dark.

6

Early morning five o'clock. The cellphone rang. Natesan picked up the phone. It was Arunmozhi who had called.

'What's the matter, amma? Are you scared? Should we come immediately? Tell me the truth. Did you go in? Did you talk to her? What did she say? We will leave in five minutes. Wait, Murugan wants to talk to you.' He gave the phone to Murugan.

'Hello, what happened? Why are you crying? Give the phone to her. What, she can't talk? Nothing else, right? We will leave immediately. If anything happens, call us immediately. Okay, bye.' Murugan placed the phone down.

'What happened, Muruga? Did she go in?' Amaravathi asked in a panic.

'She cleaned Revathi and came out just now. She called up to tell us that only. It seems Ravathi asked where we were. She asked us to come early. Let us get ready quickly, Amma.' Murugan rushed to bathe saying this.

'Please call the driver and ask him to come immediately.' Amaravathi said to Natesan. Natesan called Kumar. Kumar didn't answer the phone. Latchumi asked, 'Should I make tea?'

'No need. You also get ready to go immediately. There is no time.'

'Have at least a sip of tea.'

'No.'

She then asked Murugan who had had his bath and was dressing up in his trousers and shirt, 'Shall I make you tea, Thambi?'

'I don't want anything. There is no time. You get ready, Chitti. Has the driver come?'

'I called him, he didn't answer.' Natesan replied.

'Why are you standing around without going for your bath?' Murugan asked.

'I forgot.'

'You forgot?' Murugan looked at his father strangely. Natesan didn't say anything and went for his bath. Murugan, combing his hair, went out to look for the car. It hadn't arrived. He got angry as if it was the car's non-arrival that was an obstacle to solving all the problems. 'These drivers are all the same. Only those boys who are useless for any work in the world will become drivers. How many times I told the idiot come at five am, come at five am. And has he come? Stupid bugger.' He entered the house again enraged.

'Aren't you ready yet, Amma?'

'I thought I had already had my bath and changed my saree. It is okay, I will come like this, Thambi.'

'The driver hasn't come yet. You go for a bath.'

'I don't know how I am forgetting so many things.' Amaravathi said and went to have her bath.

After her bath, Amaravathi said, 'We shouldn't keep any jewellery or money at home. Take the ATM cards as well.'

'I kept them ready last night itself. Who knows when they will give up. We may need money then immediately to take her to a private hospital, so I have told two teachers as well. That money will also come today itself. I've kept everything in this bag. Take it.' Natesan handed over a bag to Amaravathi.

'Can't see the driver guy even now.' Murugan went briskly to see if the car had come outside. It hadn't. He entered the house again and said, 'Call the driver.'

Natesan called the driver Kumar. He didn't answer.

'What happened?'

'He didn't pick up.'

'Car drivers, auto drivers, they are the same. Loafers. If they agree, they should come. Otherwise, they should refuse.' Murugan shouted. They could see a car come and stop outside then. Natesan went out to check and called to people inside, 'The car has come. Come out.' Then he asked, 'Why didn't you pick up the phone, Kumar?'

'I was having my bath sir.'

'Alright. Start the car.' Natesan got into the car. After Latchumi, Amaravathi, and Murugan had got in too, the car started.

Not just the four passengers, even driver Kumar did not open his mouth. Even motormouth Latchumi didn't speak a word.

They could have forced a divorce. They could have complained to the police. They had done nothing. Natesan thought he had done wrong by keeping away saying, 'Name, honour, vulgar.' Everything seemed like a dream to him. Was it right to have given in statement that the incident had happened by itself? How low he had to fall because he wanted Revathi to live. What was it that stopped him from acting even in the most dire of circumstances?

It was when they were crossing the Cuddalore bridge that the phone rang. It was Arunmozhi. Murugan who picked up the phone said, 'Tell me, what's happened? We have just crossed Cuddalore. Don't get tense. We will be there in twenty minutes.'

Keeping the phone down, Murugan said by himself, 'It was Arunmozhi.'

No one asked, 'What did she speak? What did she say? How is Revathi? Did she talk to Revathi?' Murugan looked out of the car. An ambulance overtook the car at speed. Murugan murmured, 'Someone is dying every moment.'

The car reached Gorimedu, entered the main gate of JIPMER and stopped in front of the emergency block. 'Get down here, sir.' Kumar said.

All of them got out of the car.

'Here, there is two thousand rupees in this. Keep it. Use it to fill petrol. Have some tea, coffee. Don't expect me to look after you. Stay in the car. If we need, I'll call you. Don't go anywhere.' Natesan gave the money to Kumar and, turning to Murugan, said, 'Find out if Arunmozhi is downstairs or upstairs.'

'She is upstairs.'

'Come, let us go.' Natesan went into the emergency block briskly. The others followed him. Since it was early morning, the guards did not stop them.

Arunmozhi was sitting in the corner of the staircase that led to the sixth floor. When she saw Murugan and others she burst into tears. Seeing her weeping, all four of them thought that Revathi's health had deteriorated and asked in panic, 'What happened? What happened?' Arunmozhi continued to cry and didn't speak a word. Spotting Ravi sitting on the staircase to the fourth floor, Murugan called out to him loudly, 'Hey you, come here.' Ravi got up and came but stood three steps below them.

'What happened at night?' Murugan asked.

'Akka only went inside. From the time she came out, she has been crying. She hasn't spoken a word since then.'

'Where were you in the night?'

'Here only.'

'Did the doctor or nurse call?'

'No.'

'Have you been drinking?'

'...'

'You have boozed even in this situation! Who the hell opens his shop for you at six-seven o'clock in the morning?'

'...'

'Won't you ever change?'

'...'

'Having lit the fire that burnt her, now look at you fucker acting so innocent! Just wait, I will hand you over to the police.'

'...'

'Even then, I let you be because of her. Now too, I am letting you be because of her. Otherwise, I would have beaten you like a stray dog and killed you. Get lost. Don't stand in front of me. Don't stand here and turn me into a murderer.'

Ravi didn't move. He stood with his arms crossed and head lowered.

'What now?' Murugan asked angrily.

'I want to take her to a private hospital for treatment.' When Ravi said this, Murugan's anger could not be controlled. Forgetting that there were people sitting on the staircase, that this was a hospital, he began to shout in anger.

'You are the guy who didn't know how to live with her. Now you want to help her live? If you ask her to come alive after having killed her, how can she? I would have caught and shoved you into jail yesterday itself. I didn't do that because she said no. Get lost. Don't stand in front of me. Aren't you scared for your life, you filthy dog?'

Ravi cried but didn't leave. He didn't raise his head either. He didn't move his arms crossed across his heart. An enraged Murugan asked him, 'Is this how she was when we gave her to you, you shit-eating bastard?'

Ravi didn't speak.

'Don't stand in front of me. I don't know what I will say. Get lost, you loafer!' Murugan pushed him hard.

Ravi walked down step by step and went and sat down where he had been sitting earlier.

'I feel contented only now, Thambi. You made that dirty dog stand there and asked him hard-hitting questions, that's enough for me.' Latchumi said.

'What is the point of asking questions when everything is over?' Amaravathi asked with a grimace.

'You should have beaten him with slippers much before all this.' Latchumi said.

Murugan did not pay attention to whatever Amaravathi and Latchumi were saying and turned to Arunmozhi and asked, 'What did happen inside?'

'I went in. I cleaned her. That's all. It was tough to see her.' Arunmozhi said mechanically.

'How did the fire happen? Did that dirty dog set her on fire?'

'I asked her. She didn't answer me on only that.'

'Okay, wait. Let me go and check if we can see the doctor.' Murugan said and walked to the door. Natesan went along with him. When she saw them pleading with the guard to allow them in, Amaravathi burst forth in anger.

'Whenever she tried to talk to you, you avoided her as if she was a ghost. You always walked on the streets you knew she wouldn't frequent. "We won't talk a word to her," you said from the time she declared, "I will marry only him!" Now look at where you are! It is your anger that has burnt her. Today, you are going here and there with your money, how is this going to matter? She doesn't need any of this now she said and has gone and died.' When Amaravathi said this, Latchumi got angry with her. 'What are you saying, Akka? Why do you speak like this when she is still alive? Keep quiet for some time. Don't speak whatever comes into your mouth.' Amaravathi wasn't bothered by Latchumi glaring at her.

'He is parked there like black granite. He goes on public roads. He comes back on public roads. In this country so many people are hit by cars and die. Couldn't that have happened to him? Is he such a good man?'

'Akka, please keep quiet for a while.'

'His heart wasn't moved. His body wasn't shaken. Not a teardrop in his eyes. He is acting as if he is a good man, crossing his arms and looking down, that thieving rascal!'

'Will you please keep quiet? You haven't eaten. Haven't had tea or coffee. You are unable to swallow. Where do you get the energy to talk and cry?' Latchumi glared at Amaravathi.

Since the guard hadn't allowed them in, Murugan and Natesan returned with fallen faces. Unable to decide whether to sit or stand, they kept standing.

'I am not able to hold my daughter, to lift her and make her sit. I haven't been able to give her any medicine at all. I can't ask her what is happening. She is lying there senseless. Is she a moringa tree? That you can break it off today and it will revive tomorrow. Her whole body is burnt, full of sores. Even if she has some disability, it would be good if she could live.'

Natesan sat next to Amaravathi on the staircase. Murugan went to Arunmozhi and stood watching the men and women sitting on the staircase. All of them were talking, about the women who had immolated themselves, about the ones who had died, about the ones who were about to die.

Natesan said something but it didn't fall on Amaravathi's ears who carried on talking what she wished.

'She never once said what was in her mind when she came home. She was an obstinate bitch. Her whole lineage is like that. It was I who would talk, I who would ask. For everything all that she had to say was, "Let it be, Amma," and not another word beyond that. When I asked her what about going to work, she said, "I can die for that." What burnt her was her thought, "I have committed a mistake." How many people return the very first month after marriage saying they don't like their husband! How many return with two or three children saying "I won't live with him any longer." Couldn't she have come back like that? Everyday some woman complains in the Women's Police Station and take off their thaali. Couldn't she have come back like them?'

'What are you saying? Don't you realise where you are sitting?' Natesan said softly.

'Say that again, make her understand.' Latchumi said. It didn't seem that anyone's words were falling on Amaravathi's ears.

'If a goat goes to the butcher, how will he not slit its throat? He just did his job.'

'Amma.'

'Each person echoes the other and says, "Cannot survive,

cannot survive". I've been listening to this for three days. Couldn't the per centage of burn have been twenty per cent? When you say ninety per cent, they immediately say it is a matter of days. Everyone says that in her condition, the sooner she dies, the better for her.' Amaravathi cried silently.

'Get up. Let us go down.' Murugan said to Amaravathi and lifted her by her hand. 'You also get up, Chitti.' He said to Latchumi. He supported Amaravathi and took her down step by step. The others followed.

Arriving at the canteen, Murugan bought five tokens for coffee. First, he picked up two coffees and went and gave them to Natesan and Latchumi. The next two he gave to Arunmozhi and Amaravathi. He then went to get his coffee, finally.

Amaravathi and Arunmozhi placed their coffee on the cement bench. Flies started hovering around the coffee. Latchumi saw this and tried to force Amaravathi to have a sip, 'Take a sip, Akka. Let some hot liquid go to your stomach.' Amaravathi refused to drink. When Murugan and Natesan insisted, she took a sip. She vomited the very next moment. Latchumi made Amaravathi rinse her mouth and have some cold water.

'Is this the only hospital in the world? Why can't we take her to another hospital?' Latchumi asked.

'Come, let us go where we were sitting yesterday.' Murugan said.

Amaravathi hadn't even taken two steps to the east when Malar appeared in front of her.

'What happened amma?' Amaravathi asked.

'My daughter died yesterday itself. We got into a fight with that guy's family. Because of that, we couldn't go call the police. They went only late in the afternoon. It became dark by the time they reached there. The police said that the hospital wouldn't release a body in the night, that we can do it the next day. The corpse will be released only if the police are here. When will the police come, when can we take the corpse and light the pyre, who knows?'

'Where are you going now?'

'I have been sitting since yesterday morning in front of the place where they store the corpses. This is not a place to live, it is a place where people die.' She went on her way to the mortuary, crying.

They walked to the place behind the emergency block where there was a row of trees. There were seven or eight women sitting there. A few were eating. Latchumi headed for the neem tree that was about seven stretched feet away from the women. There was a cement bench under the tree. Latchumi and Amaravathi sat on the bench. Natesan sat on a block of stone nearby. Arunmozhi and Murugan didn't know what to do. They looked at the cars parked in a row a little distance to the east. There were many big trees next to the car park and many crows on the trees.

Two women who came from the direction of the canteen searched for a place to sit down. They sat down close to the bench on which Latchumi and Amaravathi were sitting. When they opened the packets in their hands and began to eat, the woman in the purple saree asked, 'What did your man say?'

'Like every day, he asked, "Why did you come? Why did you come?"' The yellow saree woman said tiredly.

'Did you give him the idli or not?'

'I shoved two idlis into that cursed man's mouth and then only returned. I only help him rinse his mouth, brush his teeth, clean his wounds after raising him to a sitting position, change his waist cloth, I do all the shit. Even then that sinful bugger asks, "Why did you come?" It is not as if his community or family is doing anything for him.' She burst into tears as she said this.

'What happened?' Arunmozhi asked the woman in the purple saree.

'This girl's man got burnt in a fire.'

'How did that happen?' Arunmozhi asked.

'This girl's husband got drunk the night before and was tottering in the street. He seems to have pulled the hand of a woman walking by. Lifting her saree, she said, "Lick it you dog"' and lifted her saree fully and showed herself to him. There was a big fight because of that. Because this girl asked him, "Why did you behave like that?" he bashed her up, breaking her head. "He is no good at all, I am going to my father's house," she said and left with her clothes packed. "If you go, you will go as a corpse, you won't go alive," he said and poured kerosene all over her and tried to burn her. She ran out of the house. That drunk dog didn't know she wasn't there and lit the matchstick. The kerosene on the floor caught fire and burnt him. He just got cooked." The purple saree woman laughed when she told the story.

'Will he survive?' Arunmozhi asked and sat down next to her.

'Only God knows. It has been twelve days. They haven't said he won't survive; they haven't said he will. Burn injuries are said to kill a person even after a month. The sores keep growing inside.'

Arunmozhi said, 'They say if it is forty per cent the person will survive.'

'That is why it is stretching out for so many days. If it had been fifty or sixty, we would have started readying for his funeral. I believe he has been burnt close to the heart. That's why they are doubtful of his survival.'

'What will happen if it is eighty-nine per cent?' Arunmozhi asked as if she were an innocent child.

'I am saying even fifty-sixty per cent won't last, and you have reached ninety! It think one day, three days at the most.' The purple-saree woman answered and then asked Arunmozhi, 'Which is your town?'

'Virudhachalam.'

'Have you come to see a relative? Burnt in a fire?'

'Mmm.'

'How much?'

'More than eighty.'

'Oh God!' The purple-saree woman exclaimed and covered her mouth with her hand as if she had heard something astonishing.

Arunmozhi said, 'I was the attendant at night. I didn't see you?'

'I was on the fourth floor. All those with under fifty per cent are kept on the fourth floor. Those cases that cross fifty will be on the fifth floor. On the third floor you will find cases for plastic surgery, other operations, the cases that are being sent home.'

'Don't any of those on the fifth floor ever return home?' Arunmozhi asked doubtfully.

'I have been parked here for fourteen days. Only one or two cases die every week on the fourth floor. On the fifth floor, one or two die every day. The fifth floor is where life flickers out, isn't it? They say that not one in hundred cases that go there return alive. From there they go straight to the Ice Room.'

'Ice Room?'

'Where they cut and tie up corpses.'

'Do you mean the mortuary?'

'Yes.'

'Any children?'

'How can it be otherwise?' The purple-saree woman laughed. 'It is only after giving two or three children as soon as they tie the thaali that they rest, don't they? It is only after you give birth to children that they begin to beat you saying, "I don't like you, get lost." They set you on fire and burn you alive. They marry women only to have children. The women should have children. Yet their parts must be brand new! How is that possible?' Arunmozhi did not give any answer to this question.

Murugan's cellphone rang. It was Doctor Dhanikachalam. Murugan picked up the phone, 'Hello, sir. I am Murugan only speaking. I am downstairs only. You are standing near the canteen? I'll come immediately, sir. Please stay there.' Murugan got up in haste and said, 'Amma, the doctor is standing near the canteen. I'll meet him and come back.' Saying this, he began to run towards the canteen. Arunmozhi, Latchumi, Amaravathi, and Natesan, all of them began to walk to the canteen, following him.

7

'I've talked to the doctor. Come, let us go meet him.' Dhanikachalam walked ahead, the others followed him.

When they entered the emergency block, the guards allowed only Dhanikachalam inside and stopped the rest of them.

'It's okay. Let them come in.' Dhanikachalam said.

'All of them, sir?'

'Yes.'

The guards didn't say another word. Dhanikachalam walked ahead and the rest followed him. Dhanikachalam got into the lift.

'It's okay, come in.' He asked all of them to get into the lift with him.

When they entered the hall on the fifth floor, Dhanikachalam told them, 'Wait for a while,' and went into the doctor's room. He came out only after ten minutes. He gestured to them to wait and knocked on the ICU door. The door opened only after the third knock.

'One minute,' he said and entered the ICU.

Natesan, Amaravathi, and Latchumi were standing

together and Murugan and Arunmozhi stood a little apart from them. Ravi, who had been sitting on the stairs, had come into the hall and was standing in the western corner. Murugan got enraged as soon as he saw him. He clenched his teeth. Arunmozhi looked at him with disgust as if she was seeing a mangy street dog. As if they had spotted some faeces nearby, Amaravathi, Latchumi, Natesan, none of the three looked in Ravi's direction.

Ten minutes must have passed. When Dhanikachalam came out of the ICU, worried about what he would report, Murugan and the other four went and stood around him.

'The treatment is going well. I have put in a word with the doctor and the nurses. There should be no problem.'

'Any progress, sir?' Murugan asked.

'We will see how much is possible. Call me if you need any help. Don't hesitate.'

'Thank you, sir.' Murugan said.

'Will they allow us to see her?' Latchumi asked.

'Who hasn't seen her?'

'Appa and Chitti haven't seen her, sir.'

Dhanikachalam said, 'One minute,' and went and knocked on the ICU door. 'Sir?' The nurse who opened the door asked.

'Please permit one person just for a minute.'

'Sir.' The nurse said.

Dhanikachalam turned to Murugan and said, 'One of you can go in.'

'I'll go in.' Latchumi said eagerly.

'You can be the attendant tonight, Maami. Let Maama go in now.'

Latchumi's face fell even as she agreed.

'Him,' Dhanikachalam pointed out Natesan to the nurse. 'Go in.' Natesan went into the ICU immediately.

'I'll come, then.' Dhanikachalam said and began to walk towards the lift. Murugan and Arunmozhi accompanied him. The lift arrived at their floor. When Dhanikachalam got in, Murugan and Arunmozhi got in as well. The lift began its descent.

He didn't ask why they were accompanying him, didn't speak a word when they came out of the emergency block and walked towards the Paediatrics department. When they were in front of the building housing the Paediatrics department, Dhanikachalam said, 'Keep courage.' That too seemed as if he was saying it for the sake of saying something.

'Is there any other way, sir?' Arunmozhi asked.

'If one has blocked all the ways and then come here, what can we do? What will tonics, tablets, or injections do then?'

'It doesn't matter if it costs all our money, sir,' Arunmozhi cried. Seeing her, Murugan too began to weep.

'Money can only stretch the number of days she lives. She can be kept on a ventilator. We can keep her so for a week at the most. We can keep her further of course. For that you have to be a big billionaire. But it will be of no real use. It is not the right way either. Right now, they are only giving morphine to your girl. That is only so that she doesn't feel the pain. They can't continue giving her morphine for long. That will weaken the heartbeat. Morphine is given only to lessen the patient's pain. It is an end-of-life decision. Neither morphine nor ventilation can be given forever, it is neither good nor right medically.'

'We'll bear the expense even if it is a lakh a month, sir. Please organise it, sir.' Murugan folded his hands to the doctor.

'We can give her Fentanyl. It will cost more than ten thousand rupees a month. Is is not a tablet or an injection. It is like a plaster. If it is stuck on a part of the body, it is enough to stop you feeling any pain. Through a small operation we can keep morphine in the body itself. There won't be any pain for four months. We also have Codeine that works similarly. But even that won't work well after some time. Everything should get over in peace. That is what is good for the patient. And for you.' Dhanikachalam explained with sensitivity.

Murugan's mouth dried up and his body trembled. He couldn't stand.

'Please don't get tense. It is problematic even when there is a wound in the abdomen area. If the blood vessels aren't affected, we can save the person. A lot of oil must have been poured on her. She must have burned for a long time.' Dhanikachalam held Murugan's trembling hands.

'Sir!' Arunmozhi exclaimed.

'If you need any help, call me.'

Arunmozhi cried along with Murugan.

Without speaking another word, the doctor let go of Murugan's hands and entered the building.

Murugan and Arunmozhi gazed at the path that the doctor had taken and at the Paediatrics building. Tears blurred their vision, veiling everything.

Arunmozhi looked down at the ground and spoke.

'She is dying.'

'Were we the ones to force her to decide on this guy? Did we stop her from going to work?'

'That was his biggest mistake. We could also have compromised a bit. Now look at where we are. From now, none of us can see her. We cannot speak a word to her. Even if we spend crores, we can do nothing.'

'Will you please keep quiet!' Murugan snapped in anger.

'Now, in my heart I don't want her to live. I only want her to die quickly. I can't stand to see her lying there. I have even forgotten the statement she gave.' Arunmozhi looked down to hide her tears.

'Just be quiet.' Murugan said bitterly and looked away.

Murugan's phone rang. He didn't have the energy to talk. He gave the phone to Arunmozhi. Taking it, Arunmozhi spoke, 'What happened maami? Maama has been crying since he came back from inside? How can we come in without a pass? Doctor? He didn't say anything. Come down. We will go to the same place where we were sitting earlier. Yes. Come. Cut the call now.'

'Your chitti called. She said that your appa has been crying from the time he came out of the ICU.' Arunmozhi said.

Murugan didn't say anything.

He sat down under a neem tree nearby looking like a mad man. 'Why are you sitting here? Come, let us go.' Arunmozhi called him. Murugan did not reply but cried with his head down. He then lay face down on the ground.

'I feel like dying. When I think of how she and I were

when we were young, my heart refuses to beat.' Murugan continued talking about Revathi. Arunmozhi wanted to change his mood. So, instead of letting him talk, she pulled him by his hand and said, 'Get up. Let's go.' They went to the place where they were sitting earlier at the back of the emergency block. The cement bench was unoccupied. Murugan lay down on it immediately. Arumnozhi sat on a corner of the bench. Three-four crows went to and from the dustbin about ten feet from them. Each and every tree had crows perched on them. The breeze was filled with the sound of crows. There was a flowering tree nearby. She didn't even feel like seeing what tree it was.

Arunmozhi looked towards where the purple-saree woman and the yellow-saree woman had been sitting earlier. Four other women were sitting there now.

Arunmozhi got a call. She picked up the phone and talked. 'Have both the kids gone to school? Hope there was no problem? Is the girl crying for me, "Amma, Amma"? I am coming, I will come. Get them to talk to me once they come back from school. Here? Nothing much to say. We are waiting. Okay, talk to you later.'

Looking at the crows sitting at a distance, Arunmozhi said, 'The maid amma spoke to me. The boy isn't creating any problems. The girl, I believe, is crying for us. If possible, can we take a car and go spend the night at home and come back?'

Murugan did not say anything. Nor did he look at Arunmozhi.

Natesan arrived there. Murugan and Arunmozhi got

up and stood. 'Please sit down,' Arunmozhi told Natesan. Natesan, seemingly drained of all emotions, sat down on the bench mechanically. He was looking awful. His eyes were rimmed with gunk. His nose was running. He didn't wipe his eyes. He didn't wipe his nose. He didn't wipe his sweat. Arunmozhi gave him her handkerchief. He took it and kept it next to him without saying anything. She offered him the bottle of water. He took that too and placed it next to the handkerchief. It looked as if he had aged ten-twenty years in two days itself. He looked so weak.

Amaravathi and Latchumi arrived there as well.

'Please sit down,' when Arunmozhi said this, they sat down next to Natesan. Murugan was sitting on the ground gazing into the distance. Arunmozhi asked Natesan, 'You went inside—did you see her? Did you talk to her? What did she say?'

'Her face looks like a ghost's. She says something but one can't hear it. I said I, Appa, have come, but she didn't seem to understand. She just looked at me blankly, didn't say Appa even once. I called her again and again, "amma, amma". She just glared at me. That's all.' He cried loudly. People sitting here and there turned around and looked at them, hearing the noise.

'Please be quiet. Everyone is looking.' Latchumi said. Neither Amaravathi or Murugan spoke a word. Nor did Natesan's wailing stop.

'Please lie down.' Arunmozhi said to Natesan. Amaravathi and Latchumi stood up. Natesan lay down on the bench and sobbed.

Natesan's cellphone rang. He picked up the phone and handed it to Latchumi. She handed it to Murugan. Murugan spoke on the phone, 'Hello, who is it? I am sir's son speaking. Murugan, yes. The situation is the same. Are you coming? Where are you? Do come behind the ICU building. We are here.' He then informed everybody, 'Appa's school staff were speaking. They are coming.'

Feeling worried looking at Murugan's face and demeanour, Arunmozhi said, 'Please have some tea at least.'

'Okay, come.'

Murugan got up and called Latchumi, 'You also come along, Chitti.' All three began to walk towards the canteen. Murugan asked Latchumi, 'What happened to Appa?'

'When he saw Revathi inside, they said he beat himself on the face and created a scene. It took three nurses to hold him and bring him out. The nurses scolded everyone saying that was why they allowed no one inside.'

'You saw her in the morning, how was she?' Murugan asked Arunmozhi. As if he had asked her an impossible question, Arunmozhi covered her mouth with her hands and tears streamed down her face. 'Aiyo, God, no one in the world should suffer like this.' Arunmozhi said this and covered her face.

'We can talk later. Be quiet now.' Murugan said and asked, 'Tea or coffee?'

'I don't want anything. I can't even drink water. I can't have anything for a week. Just seeing her, I felt like dying. Everything was burnt. Not a spot was left. Her whole body was slimy. I was the one who lifted and made her sit in the morning. When I removed the bandages, she looked like a peeled potato. She had egg sized boils all over her body. She was bleeding from many places. I think her flesh has started bursting. I can understand your amma fainting yesterday. No one can bear to look at her, or remain alive if they look at her. Your appa must have seen only her face. And he is crying like this. He would have died there itself if he had seen her whole body. No one in the world should have a death like hers. She shouldn't live now.' She cried from her heart. He avoided looking at her and gazed at the main road instead. All the people looked like insects.

'Why did you give such a statement? Why did you humiliate your appa and anna? Did you ask her that?' Latchumi asked.

'I did.'

'What did she say?'

'She cried. There is something troubling her mind, but she is not telling us. She gave the statement deliberately. She may have thought that she shouldn't create problems for us any longer.'

'Who lit the fire?'

'I asked her many times. She didn't open her mouth. She just said, "He is an idiot, doesn't think beforehand."'

'Why was she obstinate to marry an idiot then?'

'When I said it doesn't matter how much it costs but we are going to take you home, she cried, "Don't spend any more money. What you have done is enough." When I cried, "You didn't listen even to me," she cried too. I couldn't stand watching her cry, I wanted to die.' Arunmozhi wailed like a child who has received a beating. 'I was so sad that I didn't have a life to spare. Do you know how she and I were for four years? How many guys roamed around her? A doctor's son was mad for her. Even I told her he was okay. "Chee, don't be so vulgar," she would say, and she ended up in the clutches of a loafer and is lying there burnt alive.' Arunmozhi cried as if in great pain.

'Is her speech clear and audible?'

'Only if you bend down to her mouth. Her voice is gone, I think. Even her eyesight is getting dimmer, I think.'

'Did you ask her who should raise her children?'

'What would she think of me if I asked her that in the state she is in? I asked her what I should do for her, should I bring her children to see her and she gestured no with her hands.'

'She refused to see her children?'

'Yes.'

'What is the point in hating him now? All that we said then, did it fall on her ears? She stood so obstinate not even thinking about his caste, that turncoat girl, and went to that outcast guy and learnt how to cook meat and fish to please him, I can't take that.'

'I could stand near her only after she was bandaged. If I describe what I saw, you won't be able to bear it. One should beat him up with slippers.' She said with uncontrollable rage.

'A street side loafer has made our family stand on the streets.' Latchumi cried.

Because he couldn't think of anything to say or think of any questions, Murugan asked Arunmozhi, 'Will you drink some water?'

'I'll wash my face. I have vomited four times since the morning.'

He bought her a bottle of water. Arunmozhi washed her face. Only Latchumi drank coffee.

'Three cases died in the night itself.'

'Really?' Latchumi asked as if she couldn't believe Arunmozhi.

'They didn't call three attendants in the morning.'

'Is that so?'

'When I went in in the morning to clean her, three beds had curtains drawn around them. When I asked, they said, 'Just like that!' The people outside had their doubts when they didn't call the attendants and began to cry immediately.'

The three reached the place where Natesan and Amaravathi were sitting.

'One of you go upstairs.' Murugan said.

'Give me the pass. I'll go upstairs.' Latchumi took the pass from Arunmozhi and began to walk towards the emergency block.

Murugan and Arunmozhi sat on the floor.

'You saw her early morning, how was she?' Amaravathi asked Arunmozhi.

'She asked where you were.'

'Did you ask her, "Why did you give such a statement?"'

'I did.'

'What did she say?'

'Nothing. She just cried.'

Amaravathi didn't ask any more questions. Arunmozhi had also turned her face away as if unwilling to answer any other questions.

Murugan's phone rang. He picked it up and spoke, 'Yes, sir. I am still in the hospital. Yes, the condition is the same. Nothing can be said now. Can I talk later? Okay, bye.'

Latchumi could be seen coming at a distance. Murugan got up in a panic. Seeing him, Arunmozhi also got up. Even though she was still at a distance, Murugan couldn't restrain himself and asked loudly, 'What's the matter, Chitti?' Before Latchumi could reply the thought entered his head that Revathi had died. He felt a sharp pain in his chest as if seared by fire. His body began to tremble. His mouth dried up. Tears began to flow. Everybody grew panicky.

'They are shouting at everyone on the fifth floor, "Go down, go down." They didn't allow anyone to stand there, they sent everyone downstairs. Three people have died. They are going to bring the corpses out.' Latchumi sat down next to Amaravathi saying this. It was only after listening to what she had to say that everyone could breathe. Their panic died down.

8

Natesan's phone rang. He picked it up and spoke, 'You are standing next to the ICU building? Come to the back of the building. It will take three or four minutes. I am waiting here.' He put the phone away. He got up from the cement bench and went and stood on the tarred road leading from the canteen. A van arrived and stopped in front of him. About fifteen-twenty teachers stepped out of the van and immediately surrounded Natesan and began to ask him questions.

'How did it happen, sir?' A male teacher asked.

'Can't you treat her in a private hospital, sir?' Another teacher asked.

'He should be grabbed and shoved into jail. That is the only way he will learn a lesson.' A third teacher said.

'Have you filed a case, sir? You should book him in a dowry case, sir.' A female teacher said.

'You have a good heart, sir. Nothing bad will happen. Please don't worry.' Another female teacher said.

Natesan answered questions by a few people, to some others he nodded 'yes'. He didn't answer anything to some people, just stood there silently. Slowly he became quiet, answering no one. Some of the male teachers began to question Murugan. The female teachers surrounded Amaravathi and asked her questions.

'You don't raise the kids. Let him keep them and die. That is how filthy dogs like him will learn their lessons.' A teacher told Amaravathi.

'These guys who burn their wives alive should be made to stand in the street and shot.' Another female teacher said.

The fact that so many people had come for him was of some consolation to Natesan but on the other hand he didn't like being surrounded by people, firing questions at him. He felt irritated. Now, Natesan wanted to send all of them away somehow. So, he said, 'Muruga, take all of them and buy them some food.' Murugan also began to call each one, 'Come, sir.' Not one of them wanted to eat anything. All of them were truly disappointed and worried that they couldn't meet Revathi.

'How can we eat when the girl is like this, sir?' One of the male teachers asked.

'They don't allow anyone inside; they are very strict about it. They allow people in only during the visitors' time of five to six in the evening. But, even then, they don't allow anyone into the burn ward. If they allowed people in it would be alright, one could say stay till five o'clock. It makes no sense to wait, knowing that they won't allow you in however long you stay. Better to leave.' Natesan said firmly.

'We'll wait till five and see. We have come such a long way.' A teacher called Renganathan was adamant. Natesan was worried what they would say if they heard about the police coming and the statements given by Revathi and them. Amaravathi and Murugan had the same worry. So, Natesan was steadfast in his desire to see them leave.

'You must have tea at least.' Natesan forced them and took them off to the canteen. Murugan accompanied them and bought juice for everyone. As soon as they finished the juice, Natesan said, 'You should start now. I will keep you updated on the phone.'

All the teachers expressed their disappointment, 'Couldn't see her even though we came such a distance.'

'You should start. I will let you know if anything happens.' Murugan told them.

It was only after Natesan was extremely insistent that each teacher boarded the van. The van left and Murugan and

Natesan were able to breathe only then. Natesan returned to the cement bench and lay down. Murugan sat on the ground.

Murugan's phone rang. He picked it up. 'What? They are asking for a signature? Don't know why? Didn't you ask? What were you doing? Jerking off? Okay, disconnect the call. Let me talk to the doctor and find out.' He was disturbed and disconnected the call quickly. Immediately, he called Dhanikachalam, 'Vanakkam, sir. I am Dinesh's friend speaking. I believe they are asking for a signature on some form. Should we sign, sir? We don't know why they want the signature. Can you find out and let us know, sir? Please don't think that we are troubling you unnecessarily. Yes sir, you can call me later.'

Murugan's limbs trembled uncontrollably, and he perspired profusely. It seemed as if the ground was slipping away from under his feet. His head felt heavy, and he felt as if he was about to go mad.

'What happened? Who called you?' Arunmozhi asked.

'You go upstairs immediately. They seem to have asked for some signature. Go and find out what it is about, ask the doctors, ask the nurses, and then call me. Go now, go quickly.' Murugan hurried her in his panic.

'Please give me the pass.' Arunmozhi took the pass from Latchumi and took off at a run.

'What's the matter, Muruga?' Amaravathi asked.

'They asked for some signature,' he said baldly. As if the ground and he were bitter enemies, he kicked again and again at it.

'Did they ask for a signature?' Latchumi asked.

'Yes, Chitti.'

'Then, perhaps her life is about to come to an end.' When Latchumi said this, Murugan flared up in anger.

'Just keep your mouth shut, Chitti.' Murugan said harshly. Latchumi didn't speak another word. Her face fell.

'Who told you?' Amaravathi asked.

'That loafer only.'

'Look at our fate, still speaking to that filthy dog!' Amaravathi said.

Murugan's phone rang. He picked it up and spoke, 'Yes, sir. Is that so? Okay, sir. Thanks. I hope you don't mind my calling you so often and troubling you.' Murugan then rang up Arunmozhi. 'Have you reached upstairs? Is that filthy dog standing near you? Tell him to sign the form immediately. It is urgent, believe her breathing is being affected and they want to give her oxygen. Let me know as soon as he signs. Stay there with him.' What should he do next? He couldn't sit. He got up and walked ten feet in front and then walked back. He walked away again; he just couldn't stand still. But he couldn't walk either. There was a good breeze, sweat was pouring down his body. He couldn't even breathe regularly.

He got a call from Arunmozhi. He picked up the phone and said, 'What happened? He has signed? Okay, but you stay there. Call me immediately if anything happens. Don't talk to that filthy dog. Okay bye.'

'What happened, Thambi?' Nastesan asked pathetically.

'Nothing. They asked him to sign allowing them to administer oxygen to her. I told him to sign.'

'Nothing else is the matter?'

'Nothing else. You take rest for some time. Lie down on the bench.'

Natesan lay down on the bench like a little boy. He looked like a corpse that had been laid out.

'It is all our fault. We should have said let her be at home or we should have said let her die and left her alone. At least, she would have died without suffering so much. We would also not have lost our name and honour. At the end of it all she is dying suffering so much, with our name and honour lost. This is what really saddens me.' Murugan said.

An old man was taking out handfuls of rice from a box and placing it for crows near the dustbin at little distance from Murugan. Six-seven crows flew down and began to peck at the rice without any fear. A crow pooped on the old man's back. The old man was serving the rice to the crows without being aware of the crow poop on his back. Murugan thought he would tell the old man about the poop. But he didn't say anything and continued watching the old man giving food to the crows.

Murugan looked at his cellphone without any reason. The phone didn't ring. He looked around, he wanted to get up and go somewhere. But he didn't know where to go. He worried whether the oxygen would regularise Revathi's breathing or whether her breaths would slow down further. It was quite hot, but because of the number of trees one didn't feel the heat. However, it was quite humid and sweat poured down.

Arunmozhi came back. 'Why have you come?' Murugan asked.

'He signed and they have begun to administer oxygen. They wanted an injection to be bought and we did and gave it to them.' Arunmozhi said.

'Who bought the injection?' Amaravathi asked.

'He did.'

'Who paid for it?'

'I did.'

'That filthy dog shouldn't spend even one rupee for my daughter. Even if she dies, that sin will haunt her.' Amaravathi said through gritted teeth.

'Did you see the nurse? Did you ask her how it is going?' Latchumi asked.

'They say her body is wracked by jerks and she is screaming a lot.'

'Oh God...' Amaravathi exclaimed and began to cry.

'His amma, appa, and akka, all have come.'

'What does it matter to us which dog has come?' Amaravathi asked angrily. 'Did you talk to those dogs?'

'They didn't speak and I didn't speak either.'

'Beggar dogs!' Amaravathi hawked and spat in arrogance.

'They must have come to check whether she was dead or alive, the dogs.' Latchumi said in anger.

'A case arrived just now. I saw when they were taking the stretcher inside. My heart nearly stopped beating when I saw. The security guard said the case would die today itself. She was eight months pregnant and they had operated to take the baby out but couldn't save it. It is so crowded there and it is impossible to stand anywhere.'

'Will you eat something? You haven't eaten since yesterday.' Murugan asked.

'No. When you sit upstairs, people tell you so many stories and cry. Last night itself I heard the stories of three-four people; the stories are frightening to hear. You wonder why you are alive in this world. If we stay here for a week, I am certain to turn mad.'

9

A man and a woman came from near the emergency block. They looked like a newly married couple. They came towards the bench that Natesan was lying on and sat down a little away to the west. They began to eat the food they had brought in a wire basket. They had a newspaper in their bag. Seeing it, Arunmozhi asked, 'Can you lend me the paper for a while? I will look at it and return it.' The woman gave the paper to her silently. Arunmozhi, who began to read the paper, saw the headline that said 'MOTHER DIES BY SUICIDE AFTER POISONING HER THREE CHILDREN', showed it to Murugan immediately, 'Look at this.' Murugan made a face as soon as he saw the news, 'Wherever you see, you see only death. And all the people who are dying are women.' Arunmozhi read the news item and said, 'All three children died. The woman also died.'

'Let them go.' Murugan said angrily. Arunmozhi stopped reading the paper and folded it.

Natesan's phone rang. He picked it up and spoke, 'Is that so? Why have you come so far? Okay, come here. We are behind the emergency block.' He turned to Amaravathi, 'Our next-door neighbours spoke. They are coming.'

'Where are they?'

'They are standing in front of the emergency block.'

'One of you go upstairs. We don't know what is happening.' Murugan said. 'I'll go,' Latchumi said immediately and, taking the pass from Arunmozhi, began to walk.

'If anything is the matter, call me, Chitti. I will come up immediately.'

'Okay.'

About seven people, next-door neighbours, people from the house across the street, women who lived on their street, had come as if they were attending a marriage. Amaravathi could not control the tears that burst forth when she saw them. Each woman, by turn, held her hands and enquired about Revathi.

'Did he set her on fire?' The woman from next door asked.

'She had the education and the talent. Why should she have stayed with him? She should have taken a divorce and told that filthy dog to get lost.' The woman from across the street said.

'Fate did not will it.' Amaravathi said.

'I know him too well. Even when driving the auto on the road he would create a big show. He would honk at any woman he saw. His beard, his face ... a pucca loafer. It was a great mistake to give the girl to him in marriage.' The next-door woman said.

'We didn't know he would be this bad,' Amaravathi said for the sake of saying.

'Such a good girl, she would always talk to me wherever she saw me. Was that guy suitable for a girl of her colour, her form, and her education? It is as if you threw gold into the drain.' Another woman said.

'She is gold.' Amaravathi said.

'Have you filed a case?' Another woman asked.

'...'

'You shouldn't let him get away. You should accuse him of demanding dowry. You should involve his appa and amma as well.' One of the women said.

'Everyone should be jailed.' Amaravathi said in a lifeless voice. She couldn't look anyone in their eyes.

'When can we see her?' A woman asked.

'You can't.'

'Why not?'

'They don't let anyone inside.'

'But we have come all this way.'

'They only allow a designated attendant inside early in the morning, that too only for five or ten minutes. They don't allow anyone else in after that. We ourselves are unable to see her and are standing around outside.'

'This is so strange.' The woman from the house across the street said.

They talked to Amaravathi for more than half an hour. They expressed their concern to Natesan, Murugan, and Arunmozhi as well. They explained in detail how to file a case and who all to involve in it. They maintained that Revathi should have divorced Ravi earlier itself, and that it was a mistake not to have done so. No one had any answers for some of the questions. Since they couldn't reply, they said, 'It is getting late, you should leave.'

Natesan took them all to the canteen and bought them tea.

10

Murugan's phone rang. He picked it up and spoke, 'Yes, Chitti? The nurse is calling? Okay, I'll come immediately.' He began to run towards the emergency block. Natesan, Amaravathi, and Arunmozhi were terrified immediately that something had happened to Revathi. All three ran after Murugan, asking, 'What happened? What happened?' Murugan only said, 'I'll come, I'll come,' but said nothing more. This really terrified the other three.

'The nurse is calling. I need to go up, sir.' Murugan told the guard.

'Come at five.' The guard said.

'It is very urgent, sir. Please!' Murugan pleaded with the guard, almost falling at his feet.

'Come at five.'

Arunmozhi who had joined him by that time said, 'If they don't allow you in, call your chitti and ask her to come down with the pass.' Immediately, Murugan called Latchumi and said, 'Come down immediately.'

Murugan looked at Amaravathi and asked, 'Why did you two come here?' He couldn't bear to see them in the state they were in. They looked like beggars on the street.

'We got afraid seeing you run.' Amaravathi's body was trembling slightly. Natesan's was trembling even more. Arunmozhi, whose eyes were brimming with tears, asked, 'Did you ask why they called you?'

'No.' Murugan couldn't talk any further. He stood like a very weary old man.

Latchumi, who came down after a while, told the guard, 'The nurse called them.'

'Which floor?'

'Fifth.'

'They said it was urgent.' Latchumi added and the guard didn't ask her anything more.

'You can go.' He said to Murugan.

Taking that as blanket permission, all four entered the building. Seeing their faces, the guard did not have the heart to intercept them and send them out.

Murugan knocked on the door on the fifth floor. The guard who opened the door asked, 'What?'

'You said to call Revathi's family, so.' Latchumi said.

'Come inside,' the guard told Murugan. But everyone entered the hall along with Murugan. Murugan was about to knock on the door to the ICU at the same speed as he entered, but the guard came up quickly saying, 'Please don't knock. I will do it.' He knocked on the door and the nurse who opened asked, 'What?'

'You called for Revathi's attendant. They have come.' The guard said.

'All these people?'

'They wouldn't listen to me.'

'Who are you?' The nurse asked Murugan.

'The patient's anna.' Murugan replied.

'Isn't the husband here?'

'He is here, amma. I only didn't allow him inside. From the time I came for duty in the morning, that guy has been drinking and harassing me, "Let me go in, let me go in." That is why I called for the others.' The guard explained.

'If he creates a ruckus, complain to the police. Let them arrest him.' The nurse said. She then turned to Murugan and said, 'Please buy three bottles of scent, and also a spray.'

As soon as they heard those words from the nurse's mouth, all of them recoiled as if they had fallen into fire. They didn't even say we will get the stuff. None of them had the energy to say even that. It seemed to them as if the floor was descending slowly along with them. It was Arunmozhi who asked, 'Anything else?'

'Nothing else.'

'Injection?'

'Not needed.'

'Can we stay here?'

'No need.'

The nurse shut the door.

It was always difficult to get an extra word from the mouths of the nurses. As if they were trained like this as per a programme, no nurse spoke in an agitated manner. Each nurse spoke as if they had gained expertise in speaking briefly. Nurses and doctors who replaced each other as their duty hours ended, all seemed as if they had lost their speaking ability. They shouldn't let what the relatives of the patients spoke fall on their ears. They should not see with their eyes the crying relatives. They should not allow the relatives into the ICU even if the patient was dying, even the security guard were one in thought with the doctors and nurses on this. The faces of the nurses, doctors, and the guards always looked weary. They acted as if to speak agitatedly, or even to sneeze, was highly dangerous. They didn't even walk fast.

Murugan sat down as if he was feeling faint. Amaravathi held on to the wall and began to weep. Natesan covered his face and cried. They didn't talk to each other. They didn't look at each other. Latchumi cried stuffing a cloth in her mouth. Arunmozhi, whose head started spinning, sat down next to Murugan and lowered her face.

'He is sitting outside only. Should I ask him to buy this?' Arunmozhi asked Murugan.

A furious Murugan said, 'That loafer shouldn't buy anything. I'll buy it. My sister's body has begun to stink. I will buy the scent to cover it.' He slapped himself in the face.

'I'll give him the money.'

Murugan was overcome by blinding anger. 'That son of a whore shouldn't even touch my thangai's corpse. And you are going to ask him to buy the scent!' He got up and ran to the door as he finished shouting.

The guard didn't ask any of the four, Amaravathi, Latchumi, Arunmozhi, and Natesan, who were sitting in the hall and crying, to go out.

In a short while, Murugan returned with the bottles of scent. The guard took them from him and handed them over to the nurse in the ICU.

'It is just ten minutes to the visiting time. Can we stay here?' Arunmozhi asked the guard.

The guard didn't reply in words but gestured to them to stay there. Arunmozhi went to the doctor's room to check if he was there. He wasn't. She returned and sat on the floor again. Murugan sat down next to her. All four of them sat as if they were in a house of mourning.

'Why do they ask for scent bottles in a hospital?' Latchumi asked.

Not just Murugan, none of the other three opened their mouths.

Some people who had been sitting on the stairs outside came in now. Ravi and his appa, amma, akka, all came in. Amaravathi got fiercely angry when she saw them. She turned her face away and murmured, 'Beggar dogs.'

'It is so surprising that instead of asking us to buy tonics or tablets or injections they are asking us to buy scent!' Latchumi said.

'Keep quiet, Chitti.' Murugan said.

Seeing Murugan, Amaravathi, and others sitting there crying, Ravi went to the doctor's room and then stood outside the door to the ICU and asked the guard something. Then he began to walk round and round again to the doctor's room and the ICU. Irritated by this, Murugan kept muttering, 'Beggars, beggars.' He suddenly said, 'I can't stay where he is. I will go and sit outside.' He went out and sat on the staircase leading up to the sixth floor. Since the attendants and others were standing inside the hall, the staircase was deserted. In a short while, Arunmozhi came out and sat next to Murugan.

On the way to the fourth floor, on the corner adjoining the staircase, two young men were standing. One was dressed in jeans and T-shirt and the other was wearing ordinary trousers and shirt. Both had two or three chains around their necks. They were wearing amulets on their arms. They were wearing holy threads in three or four colours. There was a plastic drum for garbage in the corner on the way to the sixth floor. It was when the jeans clad youth came and spat into the drum that Arunmozhi noticed him. He spat out the sticky saliva formed by chewing pan masala and went back to talk to the other youth as before. He returned within a minute to spit again. Arunmozhi began to watch the young man. He came back to spit every one or two minutes. She pointed out the jeans clad youth to Murugan and said, 'Watch him.' In three or four minutes itself, Murugan felt intense anger. 'Pig!' He exclaimed. People who were standing around and those standing on the staircase showed their disgust by screwing up their faces when they saw the youth spitting so often. The boy didn't seem to care for their expressions. What Arunmozhi wondered about was how saliva seemed to be constantly filling his mouth as if from a spring.

'These guys should be beaten with slippers. How he spits continuously without caring that there are so many people standing here! What an accursed habit!' Murugan hit himself on his forehead.

'People like this also exist.' Arunmozhi said.

Both felt like giving him a tight slap. Whenever someone died in the ICU, they would tie everything on the patient's bed into a small bundle and come and throw it into that very drum. Once in two-three hours a woman in a green-coloured dress would come and take away the bundles from the drum. The jeans clad youth was spitting on one such bundle.

'He is chewing pan masala and spitting his slimy saliva non-stop. Shouldn't he think how someone would be able to put their hands into that drum to clear it? They have kept this place as clean as a private hospital. One can't believe that this is a government hospital. He doesn't have the brains to think he is behaving like this in such a place. And he is wearing jeans as well!' Murugan felt so enraged that he really wanted to beat that youth to death.

'Our people will never change.' Arunmozhi said bitterly.

11

'She walked away from us saying she didn't want us, and look how she has now made us buy scent for her with our own hands, Muruga!'

'I was willing to forget all that she did, forget the statement that she gave, and was ready to spend as many lakhs as is needed to save her. But I can't do anything, my money has become worthless.' Murugan's body shook as he cried.

'You didn't talk to her for six years. Never asked her "Have you eaten?" Never enquired "Are you alright?" Never assured her "Don't worry, I'm here to take care." If we had given them three-four lakh rupees in one go, he would have bought two or three autos and had a business. They wouldn't have fought because they didn't have money. You shut me up every time I tried to talk about her. You didn't ask me for even a word about her. So I kept silent. Now my girl is about to die any minute.' Amaravathi hit herself repeatedly on her face.

'Did I want her to die?'

'You and your father kept away saying he was a loafer, an auto-driver guy, an uncultured guy, wasn't that enough to kill her?'

'Why didn't she listen to us?'

'When Yaman was standing at the doorway how could she listen to us?'

'Please keep quiet. Why are you creating such a ruckus when nothing has happened yet?' Latchumi asked.

'It was that roadside loafer who set fire to my daughter. And she saved him in her statement as if he were a good man!'

'It is that statement of hers that it happened by itself that makes me feel like dying. Such a shame for us!' Murugan expressed his anger.

Two-three girls came out of the hall and stood outside the door for a short while talking to each other. One of them said, 'We'll go down and come back.'

'Come back quickly or they won't let you inside.' A woman said. Two of them started walking down the stairs. One came and sat down on the step below where Amaravathi was sitting.

'God, why am I the unfortunate one to buy scent to

cover the stink of my own girl?' Amaravathi cried. The chubby woman who was sitting on the step below asked, 'Your daughter?' Amaravathi did not reply. Latchumi replied instead, 'Yes, my akka's daughter.'

'Did she immolate herself?'

'Yes.'

'An educated girl?'

'She studied Engineering.'

'More than uneducated girls, it is educated worldly-wise girls who die like this. Did he set her on fire?'

'Yes.'

'Why did you give your girl to such a dog? What work does he do?'

'He drives an auto.'

'How did you give a girl who studied Engineering to him?'

'He wouldn't get home the money he earned from driving the auto either. He would spend it on booze. If she asked why are you behaving like this, that was it. Only beating and kicks. Only punches.'

'If they couldn't get along, why didn't you say, "Get lost you bastard," and get her away?'

'He would go mad if she wasn't around. We had taken and kept her in our house in Mayavaram for a week saying we won't send her to him. He got drunk and was lying in the street in front. It became so ugly. "He can't live without me. If I stay here, he will bring you so much shame. I have got trapped with a mental case. I must go, there is no other way. I don't want you to suffer such shame because of me." She said and went back.'

'Is that guy completely bad-natured?'

'When in a good mood, he would wash her clothes himself. He would iron her clothes, make the food. If he had money in hand, he would celebrate her birthday, their wedding day. He would buy her expensive sarees, take her to every temple, and take her to different restaurants. He would go mad if he ran out of money. He would beat her up then. That is why it was my akka who would buy all their grocery, rice, lentils, oil, for so many years now. It was my akka who gave her money for treatment if she or her children fell ill. But whatever she gave worked only for that much time. Afterwards, he would beat her up saying "What has your amma given us?" A swine of a guy.' Latchumi gritted her teeth.

'Where is he?'

'He is standing inside, that dog. We came out because he was standing there. He won't stand in front of us, and we won't stand in front of him. Who can look at the face of that sinful beggar? If you look at his face you will be haunted by all the world's sins. I may even look at my sworn life-long enemy, but I won't look at him. Murdering bastard. He can't speak even one polite word.' Latchumi burst out.

'He sounds like a guy who doesn't know how to live happily.'

'If only he had been civil and well-behaved, my maama would have bought him a hundred autos. My akka kept giving him ten thousand and twenty thousand to help him. But he is the kind of guy to fall further and further however much you try to lift him. He could sleep only if he had spent all the money he had in hand. He had no money, no education, no comforts, and wasn't of a high caste. That is why he tortured her, because he was afraid she would desert him and run away. And now, he has burnt her, setting her on fire. He can't earn a paisa but he talks like a minister. He would beat his own appa and amma. "Why did you give birth to me?", he would ask. My husband and I told her so often to just tell him to get lost and come away, that we could file a case in the court and get a divorce. "Yes, Chitti, we can go to court, we can go to the police. But he would shame us everywhere. He will abuse us in the filthiest terms. He can't be controlled if he is drunk; he will only listen to us when he is sober. Once he is drunk, he won't listen to anybody. We will be the ones who will be shamed in the court and in front of the police. He is a psycho, he can't be changed. Either he should die or I should die. Only then will this be resolved." She has said this to me so often.' Tears flowed from Latchumi's eyes.

'One should be blessed to live happily in this world, otherwise you can't.'

'Let my girl die. Instead of dying every day, let her just go forever now. She is cursed, that is why she is dying at this young age itself. He killed my daughter out of his fear that she would leave him. Can a four-anna thread give him the right to kill her?' Amaravathi began to lament.

'File a case and have him thrown inside.' The woman said. Neither Latchumi nor Amaravathi opened their mouths in reply.

Three women who came up from downstairs said to the

woman sitting on the step below, 'What Kalyani, have you started a story session where you found a place to sit?'

'We are just talking to each other; are we fighting?' Kalyani asked.

'Alright, come now. Let us go and see if they allow us inside.' In reply Kalyani said, 'Right, I am coming.' She stood up and went with them.

In a short while, people started coming out one by one. Ravi, his appa, amma, and akka came out in that order. Both of Revathi's children came out with Ravi's akka and went directly to the staircase leading down to the fourth floor and stood on the first step.

Both the children looked at Amaravathi but did not go to her. She too didn't call them to come to her. Natesan looked at the children but did not call or speak to them. Murugan looked at the children once and then didn't look at them again. He was in a state of uncontrollable anger.

When she saw Ravi, his appa, his amma, and his akka, Amaravathi became so enraged that she felt as if her head would burst. She became even angrier when she saw Revathi's children. 'Born to a thieving bastard, they will be like him only! Dogs who ate with the money I gave them. What accursed people my daughter took care of! Faithless dogs! See if their eyes are even wet thinking about their mother lying there like that!' Amaravathi said this and carried on in anger, 'Come, let us go down. I can't stay in a place where stray dogs are standing around.'

'What do we do if they call us?' Latchumi asked.

'Why will they call? We have bought them the scent bottles, isn't it?'

'Why don't you go and ask the nurse what is happening?' Latchumi asked Murugan. Murugan didn't reply. He looked down.

'They have sent everyone out. How will they allow us inside now? They will only permit the attendant.' Arunmozhi said.

'Who is going to be the attendant today?' Latchumi's question angered Amaravathi. 'Why, are you going to be the attendant?' Amaravathi asked.

'I haven't seen her yet.'

'Idiot, just keep quiet. How much that female who gave birth to that filthy dog tortured my daughter! "Don't send her to work, she won't respect us once she goes to work. If a female goes to work, how will she respect her man?" She is the filthy female who taught him that. Let her die today!'

'What! Who is she to see our daughter when we are here?' Latchumi raised a counter-question.

'She is educated, rich, fair-skinned. If she goes to work, she will lose all respect for us. Isn't she the bitch that taught this to her filthy dog of a son day after day? It is because of that thieving filthy female that my daughter is lying there with her flesh cooked. She is the one who gave birth to Yama as her son. She should die. If her daughter had been lying like this with her flesh cooked, would she have come with powder on her face as if she were going to attend a wedding? Bitch! After all she is a bitch who sold lottery tickets! I am going down.' Amaravathi got up and began to go downstairs quickly. Latchumi, Murugan, and Natesan followed her down. When Arunmozhi began to go down last,

Ravi asked her, 'Which one of you is going to stay tonight?' Without thinking, Amaravathi replied, 'Let your amma or your akka stay.'

'Please wait. I'll go and ask them.' Ravi went and talked to his akka. He came back and said, 'My akka will stay.'

'Come out, I want to talk to you.' Arunmozhi said.

'What is the matter?'

'Why, won't you come if I call you? After all you are a murderer!'

'I'll come.'

12

'Will someone immolate herself?'

'I didn't do it. I swear on my god Ayyappan.'

'Are you putting on an act because we have let you be outside?'

'I am not acting.'

'Are you then saying she didn't get burnt at all?'

'If she had poured kerosene she wouldn't have burnt so much. She poured the diesel used for autos.'

'Diesel?' Arunmozhi covered her mouth with both her hands. 'Where were you at that time?'

'At home only, watching TV.'

'What had you fought about?'

'No fight took place that day. Four days earlier, her amma gave us forty thousand to pay the dues of the auto. I took five hundred rupees from it at two pm for my booze. She was angry and said, "My amma gave me the money to pay the auto dues. I have to pay it on the thirtieth. Why did you take money from it to drink? If you continue like this, I will die." I said as a joke, "Okay, die." Only a short time later, everything was over.' Ravi's body shook with his weeping.

'"I don't want my appa or amma, I don't want my anna. I will only marry him." She said and stood there obstinately. She didn't even listen to me. Is that why you set her on fire?'

'If her amma hadn't given money, if I hadn't taken five hundred from it to booze since it was a Sunday, nothing would have happened. She couldn't bear the fact that I had taken from the money her amma gave her.'

'Did her amma give the money for the first time now? How would she get angry only now? You are a big actor.' Arunmozhi said with anger.

'Believe me or don't believe me. I didn't set her on fire.' Ravi said and turned his face away as if unwilling to talk any further.

'You murdered her, and you are shouting at me! She is lying there about to die, and here you are, blind drunk! Are you a man or a beast?'

'You don't know me. My dad made me study, but I couldn't. He had me admitted to ITI. I couldn't finish that either. I couldn't get. Even that certificate.'

'Didn't we tell you to get that certificate and we'd find you a job?'

'They said that I hadn't paid the fee of twenty thousand. They said I could get the certificate only if we paid the money.'

'Why didn't you ask us?'

'I felt ashamed.'

'But it is maami who has given you money for the last six years, who took care of all your hospital bills.'

'…'

'How many times I myself told you on the phone, "Don't hit her, don't hit her," did you listen?'

As if there was nothing more to talk about, he said emotionlessly, 'Everything is over, akka.'

'Why did you think of us as your enemies without any reason? Why did you behave like a savage? In all these years, not one of us created trouble for you. We didn't shame you by dragging you to the police station or the court. All of us left you alone for her sake. You did not know even that much civility. How badly you behaved till the end!'

'I got angrier and angrier the more you ignored us. I am not educated like her anna. Don't have a job. So, she was disappointed in me. I had neither the comforts nor the money.' Ravi had become angry. To control it, he shook his arms three-four times. He stroked his beard and ran his fingers through his hair. He didn't look at Arunmozhi, looking down instead, and spoke.

'Do you think I like being a loafer?'

'Who spent money on the wedding? Didn't the marriage take place openly? She didn't come home for seven-eight months, but she was as before after that. Whenever I came, I talked to her. I kept in touch with her over the phone in any case. Who gave the house rent or the house-rent advance when you shifted home?' Arunmozhi asked and looked around. She was worried that Latchumi or Amaravathi may see her talking to Ravi.

'Whatever they did, whatever they gave, they gave to her as the auto driver's wife. Whenever you all talked of her, instead of saying Revathi didn't you say the auto driver's wife came, the auto driver's wife said, I met the auto driver's wife?' Ravi asked angrily.

'Who said that to you?'

'I know everything akka.' He said arrogantly.

'You should be in jail.' Arunmozhi said enraged.

'In all the years since our marriage neither Revathi's mother or her father have talked to me. They talked to me only here in the hospital. If they had done so earlier, she would not have immolated herself.'

'What? You are speaking again and again as if she immolated herself! Having killed her you are talking law like a seasoned criminal!' Arunmozhi's voice was louder and angrier.

'I agree I am a loafer. I am only an auto driver. I am a drunkard. I do get into fights often and end up in the police station. Like you all say I am a dog that cannot earn my food. In all these years, have I talked to any of you myself? Have I stood in front of you? All of you are highly educated. You are all in high positions. All of you are wealthy. You have everything but you don't have a large heart.'

'What are you saying?'

'Why couldn't you talk to me, why couldn't you allow me into that house? Why couldn't you talk to my children? This was her biggest regret. This is why I would abuse you all. So, she and I would fight every day. I am an unworthy guy, I won't say no. An unworthy guy would behave like an unworthy guy. But shouldn't worthies behave like worthies?'

'Did you behave well enough for us to talk to you? You fooled her by tattooing her name all over your body. You were a loafer then, but shouldn't you have become better after marriage? You fought at the auto stand all the time, she would tell me every time that you had been hauled off to the police station. If she asked you why you fought or why you were at the police station you would get drunk and come and hit her.'

'I am the one who fights. I am the one who goes to the police station. How does it matter to you?' The way he asked this seemed to convey that he thought whatever he said or did was right. It didn't seem as if he felt guilty at all about having set Revathi on fire. He seemed to be not at all afraid of any blame or sin under any circumstances. Arunmozhi wondered how such men existed, and asked, 'Isn't it shameful for us?'

'Thinking of shame, afraid of shame, you killed her.'

'What are you saying? The whole world knows you are the one who set her on fire. It is because we wanted her to live that we left you alone all these years. It was because of that we got her married to you.'

'I only hit her body every day. You punched her heart.'

'You speak as if you are a really good person. Why didn't you allow her to work? If she had gone to work, you would have had money, and if you had money, you would not have quarrelled. Your whole life would have been different.' When Arunmozhi said that her phone rang. It was Murugan. She picked up the phone and said, 'I'm coming.' Then, she looked around to see if anyone was searching for her.

'My mom said, the girl looks beautiful, don't send her to work. You will have new problems, new issues on the streets, at the auto stand.'

'How many times I told you to leave this town and come to Madras. Why didn't you come? Everything would have changed for the better if you had come.'

'I haven't been outside this town often. I cannot go to any city for the sake of money,'

'What is the compulsion to stay in this town?'

'Nothing.'

'Why should you stay in this town for nothing? To kill her?'

'I don't know.'

'If you speak dialogues like this, what else can you do but die without food?'

'It's okay. I can't leave this town. If I can earn money only by leaving this town, I don't want that money.'

'Stay wherever you want, wherever you wish. Why did you set her on fire? Tell me that.' Arunmozhi spoke angrily.

'When I got money driving my auto, I would be happy. I have struggled without money.'

'What am I asking, and what are you saying in reply?'

'I didn't burn Revathi, you burnt her.' He said it like an accusation.

'Hey, are you an idiot? Can't you speak honestly even for a minute?' Arunmozhi shouted, forgetting where she was standing.

'In all these years you have spoken to me for this length

of time only today. That too only because you are afraid Revathi is dying. You avoided me thinking I was a loafer, a vagabond, a depraved dog, an alcoholic pig, a beggar, an auto driver, that is what killed Revathi.'

'You are telling a lie.'

'I didn't have money, you had it. So, however much you shamed her, Revathi came to you. Your money shamed her. She won't have that shame now. She won't cry and weep, plead and cajole people for two thousand three thousand any longer. "Didn't you marry that auto guy not listening to any of us? So, suffer. You deserve this, you deserve even more." No one can say that any more. She will no longer be called auto guy's wife; she will no longer be shamed for it.'

'You talk so much about what is right and wrong, why did you pursue her when her status was so much higher than yours? You should have tried to earn money that would allow her to live according to her status, no? You should have worked for it, no? You won't leave the town. You won't let her go to work. You won't earn much money. And what you earned, you would drink away, and then come and talk about how we wronged you! You will set a girl on fire and blame others for it. You have a fully criminal brain. You are a talented loafer, someone who has used his experience of going all the time to the police station to talk like a pucca criminal!' As she was finishing, her cellphone rang. It was Murugan who was calling. She didn't answer the call but looked around. She felt relieved slightly that she couldn't see Murugan, Natesan, or Amaravathi.

'Didn't you shame her every day asking why she married an auto guy? Now, she will no longer feel that shame. It was that shame that burnt her. And who gave her that sense of shame?'

'If you had been alright, why would we have spoken like that?' Arunmozhi asked enraged.

'Someone is born lame. Someone loses his sight. Someone is dark. Someone is fair. Someone studies well. Someone can't study. What can one do? In the same way, I am quick to speak. I am quick-tempered. What can I do?' When Ravi asked this, Arunmozhi, wanting to shut him up, said distilling all her bitterness into words, 'Thieves know the law through and through. There is a law for each thief.'

'My dad wasn't wealthy, had no comforts. I wasn't educated. What can I do about it? I won't make my son an auto driver, I won't give my daughter in marriage to an auto driver, she would say this every day. That is not possible now. I don't have money. So, my son will have to become an auto driver. My daughter will end up with an auto driver, as his wife. It will embarrass you all. Only people like you, educated and employed, should remain alive, all else should die.'

Arunmozhi was astonished. How was he able to speak fluently like a lawyer, adding argument upon argument without a pause or hesitation? It seemed as if he had been given a speech to shut the mouth of anyone who questioned him about Revathi's immolation and had memorised it and was reciting it. She thought that he wasn't an ordinary man. But she didn't want to let him off easily and asked him to prick his conscience, 'If Revathi had been your daughter, would you give her in marriage to someone like you?'

'I won't.'

'Why not?'

'She would be my daughter.'

'One law for your daughter and another for somebody else's? Now you know your worth? We knew your worth and still got her married to you, didn't we?'

'For six years, she said, "Be good, be good," I didn't listen to her. I didn't feel like listening to her. What does it matter if I turn good now? For three days now, Revathi's appa has been going here and there with ten lakhs in his bag. If he had given that earlier, I would have bought ten autos and run them. I would also have become an owner. I wouldn't have been struggling to pay my dues. We wouldn't have quarrelled. We wouldn't have had money difficulties.' For a short while, he stood quietly looking somewhere into the distance. Then he spoke in a broken voice, 'I wanted to dress well, be happy, eat well. This was the reason she and I would quarrel. If just like me, you guys had also had no money, she wouldn't have immolated herself.'

'You speak so much like a good man, why are you standing here drunk at this time?'

'The amma who gave birth to me is going to die, akka.' Ravi began to cry. He wept uncontrollably.

'Your daughter is a five-year-old child. And what do you tell her about falling in love? Did you not say, "My daughter is very pretty, if anyone looks at her I will cut him up".'

'Yes, I said. I will say it tomorrow also. I will say it every day.'

'Your daughter is gold, and someone else's daughter is brass?'

'No.'

'Should we have cut you up like you are saying? Was

it wrong to have given you our daughter instead of cutting you up? Didn't you feel like showing to the world that you could live well?'

'I felt so. But I didn't have the money.'

Arunmozhi's phone rang. She picked up and spoke, 'I am standing here itself. I am talking to someone. I will come in a minute.' She disconnected the phone.

'They are phoning you constantly. They will begin to search for you. You should go, akka.' Ravi said.

'Behave well at least from now. Even now, she is the one who is protecting you, forgetting all the torture you inflicted on her. However, we can file a case against you any time we want. We don't know how she is. As soon as we know, we will ruin you. Beware.' She threatened him.

Suddenly, as if he was enraged, Ravi shouted, 'What will I achieve by being good, by being sane from now on? My own goddess is going to die.' He began to cry again. His phone rang. He picked it up and spoke, 'I am standing to the north. I am standing to the north of the emergency block, on the way to the Orthopedics building. Come.'

In a short while, Ravi's appa, amma, and Revathi's children came there. As soon as she saw Arunmozhi, Revathi's daughter started crying. Unable to bear the child's tears, Arunmozhi spoke to Ravi with a rage she had never felt before, 'You killed her. Now kill her children as well. They shouldn't stay alive with a murderer.' She hugged the two children and cried. She didn't see Amaravathi and Latchumi who were at a distance coming towards them.

13

'Why were you talking to that dog?' Latchumi screamed like a maddened animal.

'How dare you stand around with the murderer who set fire to my daughter?' Amaravathi glared at her.

'Can't you see where he has made us stand today? Bastard! How can you even look at his face?' Murugan clenched his teeth.

'He brought me shame for six years. He hit my girl and tortured her. Finally, he killed her.' Natesan moaned softly as if he was talking to someone else.

Arunmozhi did not open her mouth.

'The suffering he inflicted on me and my daughter cannot be put into words.' Amaravathi began to cry loudly oblivious of the fact that she was standing on the road.

'If you had a sense of shame, you wouldn't have talked to him.' Latchumi.

'What did he say, the loafer?' Murugan asked.

Arunmozhi stood there without showing any emotions. Everyone was more interested in abusing Ravi than in worrying about what was happening to Revathi. They had lost their sense of balance and were taking out the frustrations of six years in the harsh words that they were pouring out. While the others were saying this and that, Arunmozhi's mind was debating on whether what Ravi had said was right or wrong. She was surprised that he had talked so knowledgably. He knew how to win an argument against an opponent. She thought that Revathi must have fallen for his clever talk. She remembered what Revathi had said once, 'He is like an animal only when he is drunk. Otherwise, he does everything you tell him. You can't understand him.'

After Revathi's marriage, neither Natesan nor Murugan had gone even once to Ravi's house. They hadn't talked to any of Ravi's relatives, let alone Ravi. Even if they saw him on the way somewhere, they would avoid him like a snake. In the same way, no one related to Ravi had ever talked to anyone related to Revathi. It was only a year after Revathi's wedding that Murugan's marriage took place. Revathi attended it alone. Neither Natesan nor Murugan would speak a word to her, whether they saw her at home or they saw her outside. They would pass by her muttering, 'Dishonouring bitch.' Since news started coming within three-four months of marriage about fights, that he had hit her, kicked her, their bitterness against Revathi had increased rather than lessened. If there had been no problems, Natesan's as well as Murugan's mind may have changed. But Ravi had never created the circumstances for such a change. He continued to do things that would increase their hatred.

Was Ravi right in saying that if they had given five-ten lakhs, no fights would have taken place? Why didn't Revathi, who asked for five thousand ten thousand to pay auto dues, ask for one or two lakhs instead? Everyone knew that Amaravathi was giving money to Revathi, was helping her. Nobody had stopped her saying, 'Don't help her, don't give money to her.' Natesan and Murugan didn't help directly but stayed away from all this. She herself had talked to Revathi when she came home, when she met her, even on the phone, but why didn't it strike her even once to ask Revathi whether she needed money? She should have asked. She felt that not asking Revathi if she needed money was a terrible mistake. When she thought that she began to cry. Natesan and Murugan had a change of heart when they saw her crying.

Not knowing why she was crying, Natesan consoled her, 'We are not angry with you, amma. We are upset that he killed our daughter.'

'Alright, quiet.' Murugan said only this.

'Having seen her lying there completely burnt, how did you still have the heart to talk to him?' Amaravathi asked. 'It was wrong of me.' Arunmozhi replied honestly.

'How he used to abuse you and Murugan! "They too fell in love and married each other, how are they better than us?" How he talked about you two!'

Amaravathi's words embarrassed Arunmozhi and made her hang her head in shame. She knew only now that Ravi had talked like this about them, abused them. If she hadn't had education, belonged to the right caste, had the right job, would she have been able to marry Murugan? If she had been lower than Murugan in education, caste, and job, if she had had nothing, would she and Ravi have been the same? She felt angry when the thought struck her. She wanted to cry in a secluded place. She covered her face with her hanky and sobbed.

'Did we wish him ill? We wanted him to do well. That is why we tolerated everything. How often did he pour kuzhambu on her face? How often did he throw idlis on her face? I bore everything.'

'Keep quiet. It was to die at his hands that she was obstinate that she wanted only him.' Murugan said.

'He remained a good for nothing guy!' Amaravathi lamented.

'A loafer will always remain a loafer. Why do you keep talking about it?' Murugan shouted.

'We've let him go without filing a case. He may make fun of us saying they can't do anything to me. Eater of shit!' Latchumi said sharply. Natesan's face changed when he heard this. He snapped, 'Won't shit stink anyway?'

'He will get arrogant and say that she died by herself. Just see.' Latchumi said angrily.

'When has shit not smelled? Come, let us go.' Natesan said, and as if he didn't want to prolong this conversation he walked away immediately. The others followed him.

They crossed the emergency block, reached the road to the main gate and stood there wondering what to do next. They didn't talk to each other. They didn't look at each other. Murugan looked at the poles of the street lamps on both sides of the road leading to the main gate and wondered how long they could keep standing there at that spot. He asked, 'Shall we go home? Should I call for the car?'

'You all go. I will stay here.' Amaravathi said.

'What are you saying, Amma?' Murugan asked angrily.

'If I go home, I will be on tenterhooks worrying what's happening here. I don't feel as bad when I stay here.'

'You can't do anything even if you stay here. You have to sit here doing nothing.'

'Just listen to me, Thambi. I can't move from this place

even for a minute. When I sit here, when I look at the building, my heart feels comforted, as if she was here with me.'

'How will you stay here alone?'

'I'll go sit on the staircase.'

'There is no breeze there. The mosquitoes will eat you up.'

'Can't you see people sitting here and there? Go to the main gate and look around. Thousands of people are sleeping on the platform or sitting there.'

'Do you know what you are saying, Amma?'

'I'll stay with her, Murugan. You three go and come.' Latchumi said.

'Are you in your senses, Chitti? Do you know it is ten pm now?' Murugan shouted at her.

'Leave me alone, Thambi. It is enough for me to sit here looking at the building.'

Murugan hit himself on his head in anger. He said, 'Let us stay in a room somewhere. Let's go.' He rang up the driver Kumar and spoke, 'Get the car. Yes, we are standing in front of the emergency block.'

The car arrived. Arunmozhi got in first. Though Latchumi and Natesan hesitated a bit, they too got in. Murugan forced Amaravathi to get in, and then got in last.

'Home?' Kumar asked.

'Yes.' Murugan replied.

14

When they reached Tavalakuppam, Arunmozhi's phone rang. She picked it up: 'What? Is that so? Why suddenly? You don't know? Didn't you ask? We need to come immediately? Okay.'

'What happened?' Murugan asked urgently.

'Something has happened to my daughter.' Amaravathi panicked.

'Who talked?' Natesan asked.

'He only. They asked for some signature, he says.' As soon as they heard her, Natesan and Amaravathi started trembling. Their throats dried up and their bodies felt hot. They began to perspire despite the AC. Natesan who couldn't speak properly asked, 'What else did he say?'

'He asked whether to sign or not.'

'Turn the car around, turn back.' Amaravathi screamed.

'Call the doctor and ask him.' Arunmozhi said.

'Perhaps it is over.' Latchumi said.

'Keep quiet, Chitti.' Murugan glared.

'Call the doctor.' Amaravathi pleaded.

'Go fast.' Natesan told Kumar.

Murugan called Dhanikachalam. 'Vanakkam, sir. Murugan speaking. Please don't mind that I am calling so late, it is ten thirty now. I believe they asked for a signature. Should we sign or not? Okay sir. They asked to buy scent bottles in the evening. That is why we are scared. Okay, thank you sir.'

Before he could disconnect, Amaravathi, Arunmozhi, and Natesan asked in one voice, 'What did he say?'

'They ask for signatures when they want to administer a new medicine.'

'Do we have to sign?'

'He said we should sign immediately.'

'Tell us the truth, Thambi.' Amaravathi wept loudly.

'Go a bit faster, appa.' Murugan said to Kumar.

'Find out where that dog is, Murugan.' Latchumi said.

'You ask.' Murugan told Arunmozhi. Arunmozhi called immediately. 'Where are you? Come down immediately. We have reached Gorimedu.'

'Go at a greater speed, Kumar.' Natesan's voice quavered.

The car arrived and stopped in front of the emergency block. All five got down. Arunmozhi called Ravi as soon as she got down, 'Where are you? We are standing in front of the emergency block.' Ravi who was standing in a corner smoking a cigarette, threw down the half-smoked cigarette and ran to them.

'What happened?'

'The nurse called and asked us to sign. I asked for what and she said for a medicine. So, I asked you.'

'Did you see the doctor?'

'The doctor also told me to sign.'

'Have you signed?'

'No.'

'Run, run. First go and sign.' Arunmozhi hurried him. The other four were standing to a side. Seeing Ravi hesitating, Arunmozhi asked, 'What?'

'Will Revathi die, akka?' Ravi started crying. Arunmozhi also couldn't control her tears. But she also got angry.

'Are you drunk?'

'Even her death hasn't set you right. Get lost.' Arunmozhi said with a bitter heart and wiped her tears with her saree.

'You come with me, akka.'

Without telling anyone, without asking anyone, Arunmozhi began to walk with Ravi. The guards stopped them.

'The nurse called for a signature, sir. I need to go upstairs.' Ravi said.

'You are drunk. We can't let any drunk into the building.'

'I have to sign. I have a pass, see.'

'She can go in, not you.'

'Only he can sign.' Arunmozhi said.

'If I allow people who have been drinking, that too at night, the doctors will yell at us, amma.' The guard explained politely.

'My wife is about to die, and they are calling me to sign something. How is it your law not to permit me in these circumstances?' Ravi glared at the guard.

'Let me talk, will you remain quiet for a while?' Arunmozhi said to Ravi. She then pleaded with the guard. 'He is the patient's husband. He is the one who has to sign. If you have any doubts, please ask the doctor or nurse on the fifth floor.' Amaravathi, Latchumi, and Natesan, who were standing at a distance, thought some quarrel had broken out and walked towards them. Not bothering about them, Arunmozhi said to the guard, 'He came down only to ask me whether to sign or not. I'll bring him down as soon as he signs.'

'Okay, take him up. He is standing here drunk even as his wife is dying.' The guard said.

This made Ravi angry. 'You are no one to say that.' He glared at the guard.

'Whatever. We see thousands of people every day.' The guard said dismissively.

'What are you doing? Is this the time to talk like this and build up a quarrel?' Only when Arunmozhi asked him that did Ravi shut his mouth.

'Come,' said Arunmozhi and walked ahead. Ravi began to walk in too.

'Please allow us also to go in, sir. We will come back in five minutes.' Murugan pleaded.

'Come back quickly,' said the guard baldly. Murugan, Natesan, all four ran inside.

When they reached the fifth floor, it was Arunmozhi who knocked on the door. The guard opened the door only after she had knocked three-four times. When he saw Ravi, the guard didn't say a word. He opened the door fully and said, 'Come.' The others entered the hall along with Ravi. The guard did not say anything.

The guard knocked on the ICU door. The nurse who opened asked, 'What?'

'You asked me to call the patient Revathi's husband. He's come to sign.'

'Take him to the doctor's room.'

The guard and Ravi went inside the doctor's room. Arunmozhi went in with them.

Amaravathi spoke to the nurse who was about to shut the ICU door.

'Is my daughter sleeping or is she awake?'

'She is sleeping.'

'Can we see her?'

'Not now.'

'Please allow me in for a short while.' Amaravathi pleaded.

'This is not like other wards. This is for serious cases. If we let anyone inside any time, the patients will get infections.'

'Why did they ask for a signature at this time?' Murugan asked.

'You should ask the doctor.'

'Please see if my daughter is awake or asleep, amma. If she is awake, will you please tell her amma, "Your amma, appa, anna, are all here?"' Seeing Amaravathi in tears, the nurse replied, 'I will.' She shut the door.

'Don't talk on the phone. Will you be talking all night?' The guard asked the attendants and glared at them all. Some people were lying down, some others were sitting. Amaravathi, Natesan, and Latchumi were standing in a corner their eyes glued to the doctor's office. Murugan was standing next to the ICU door.

Ravi and Arunmozhi came out of the doctor's room. Ravi went immediately to the western corner of the hall and stood with his akka. As soon as Ravi started walking away, Amaravathi and Natesan surrounded Arunmozhi and asked her, 'What happened? What happened?'

'Did you ask what the signature was for?' Murugan asked.

'They are going to change the medicine. That's why.'

'Okay, come. Let's go and see the doctor.'

'I saw him just now.'

'I want to talk to him.' Murugan said and entered the doctor's room quickly. Arunmozhi entered along with him.

'Sir, I am the anna of the patient named Revathi.' Murugan told the doctor.

'Yes, tell me.'

'You have taken a signature. I want to know what the problem is.'

'It's late now. Come in the morning.'

'Any problem, sir?'

'Come in the morning.'

'In the evening, they asked us to buy scent bottles. We don't know why, sir.'

'Is that so? I came for night duty. I don't know what happened during the day.'

'Have they screened her off, sir?' When Arunmozhi asked this, the doctor's face grew stern.

'Who told you that?'

'No one sir. I am asking on my own.'

'Did any nurse tell you this?'

'I swear no one told me. I asked by myself because I had my suspicions.' Her eyes filled with tears. 'If the doctors or nurses don't tell us anything clearly, what can we do?' Murugan asked.

'Let's see.' The doctor said and got up and went into the ICU, as if not to give any opportunity for any more questions.

Murugan and Arunmozhi stood there. They stood looking at each other. The doctor's silence had filled them with horror. Tears brimmed their eyes. They came out of the doctor's room.

'What did the doctor say?' Amaravathi asked. Neither Murugan nor Arunmozhi opened their mouths.

'What happened? What did he say?' Natesan asked.

'Come in the morning, we can talk then, that's all he said.' Murugan spoke as if he was answering a stranger.

Seeing the three, Natesan, Murugan, and Amaravathi, talking to each other, a woman who was sitting nearby leaning on a wall told the woman sitting next to her as if secretively, 'It must be over. That is why they are calling and talking to them at this time.' The woman did not want others to hear but in the silence of the hall Murugan and Arunmozhi could hear her clearly.

'Please go out. It's time.' The guard said but he didn't compel them to leave. Arunmozhi, Amaravathi, and the others came out one by one. Ravi came out last and sat on the staircase.

When they reached the ground floor, Arunmozhi approached the guard and said, 'Many thanks, sir.' The guard acknowledged it with a shake of his head and said, 'An ambulance is arriving. Please don't stand in the way.'

An ambulance arrived and stopped. They took the patient down from the ambulance. It wasn't crowded like the morning. Only Latchumi ran to see whether the patient was a male or a female. The other four showed no emotions and walked away from the building standing towards the south at a little distance. Latchumi who had seen the patient joined them and said, 'Heart attack, they say.' No one gave any reply to it. Each one was standing looking in a different direction as if they wanted to see who would keep quiet for the longest time. There were no people walking about. There were no cars or bikes. They were surrounded by patches of darkness and light. A cool breeze was blowing.

'You go home.' Amaravathi said to Natesan.

'Who is going to steal the house?' Amaravathi did not reply to Natesan's question. Instead she said to Murugan, 'Tell the driver to get the car, Thambi.'

'What will you do?' Natesan asked.

'We'll see. You should go now.' Amaravathi said strictly as if she had come to some decision.

'You go too.' Latchumi told Arunmozhi who replied shortly, 'I'm not going.'

'Go, please.' Amaravathi said to Natesan. Natesan became angry with Amaravathi but didn't show it to her. Instead, he showed it to Murugan. 'Get the car.' Murugan called the driver. The car arrived in five minutes. Natesan got into the car and said as if giving an order, 'You must call every ten minutes and tell me what is happening.'

'Okay.' Murugan replied.

'Let's go, appa.' Natesan said to Kumar.

15

Natesan called Murugan. 'What happened? Why haven't you called at all? Why are you talking strangely? I am thinking of starting from here at five. Did that woman who was the attendant come back after cleaning? Don't know? You will know only when she comes out of the hall? Okay, are you sitting on the staircase? When that woman comes out ask her everything and let me know.' He kept the phone on the table. He sat on the chair. He couldn't do any work since he kept thinking about Revathi. He couldn't stop thinking about her even for a moment.

Naming her 'Revathi' after the star she was born under, going to the Vaideeswaran Temple to shave off her birth hair, going to admit her in pre-KG, going to Cluny School, Neyveli, for her admission, going to Anna University for her admission, going to fetch her for her holidays, celebrating her coming-of-age ritual in a big marriage hall, every event came to his memory one by one. The old memories brought tears to his eyes. So, he spoke to himself as if he was speaking to someone, 'Do children kill their parents? Or do parents kill their children?' He looked around at the house. It was filled with emptiness. The emptiness seemed to reinforce the bad times.

'There was no point in letting them be. Should have brought her back forcing a divorce.' He said.

He looked at the clock. For no reason at all, he went to the kitchen and returned immediately. He opened the door. He walked around the hall three-four times. As if he suddenly remembered something, he rang up Arunmozhi and spoke, 'Has that woman gone in and come out? She hasn't come out yet? As soon as she comes out ask her how Revathi is and let me know. You should talk immediately, understand? If she has a phone, call her and find out and let me know. Okay. Bye.' He kept the phone down. What to do next? He switched on the TV. In the Flash News they were showing again and again that eight members of the same family had died on the spot in an accident on their way back from Tirupati.

'People are dying wherever you see.' He said. He lowered the volume of the TV. Then, he walked around in the house. The phone rang. He picked it up anxiously. 'What happened, amma? You couldn't get her number? Did you ask him? Is that so? He has switched it off? Is he not there? When has he ever let us be in peace? You find out everything from that woman as soon as she comes out. Okay, bye.' Having spoked to Arunmozhi, he kept the phone down. He got up and went to brush his teeth. He seemed to do it out of force of habit.

'Kumar, come here at exactly six. Don't be late. I am ready already. You come.' He put the phone down. He checked the time, it was five. He looked at the TV screen. The news was about a husband and wife, along with their two-year-old child, being killed in an accident, hit by a truck. Seeing it, he spoke, 'About half the people die in accidents. The other half die by immolating themselves.' After a while he castigated the TV guys saying, 'They only show death all the time.' He picked up the phone and called Murugan. Before he could say 'Hello', Murugan cut the phone. He called Arunmozhi next. He could see her cut the call after two-three rings. It was just a moment. Why didn't either of them take his call? Was Revathi dead? His body began to tremble terribly. To stop it, he sat down on the chair. His body shook even more after sitting down. He picked up the phone to try again. His hand shook so much, the phone fell down. He thought it was an ill omen. His body trembled even more. He picked up the phone and called Murugan. He didn't pick up the phone. He then called Arunmozhi. She didn't pick up either. Tears began to flow down his face. They obscured the whole house. He got up with difficulty, tottered to the bed, and fell on it. His body seemed to be on fire. More than when he was standing, more than when he was sitting on the chair, he felt much greater fear when he was lying down. He feared that if he remained in bed, he would suffer a heart attack and die. His abdomen felt as if a ball of fire had been kept inside. He breathed through his nose as well as his mouth. Panic, anxiety, palpitation, trembling, didn't seem to go down. He got up and walked to the door with his body shaking.

There was movement on the road. Men and women, out for their morning walk were walking briskly. Worried that there may be someone known to them among the morning walkers and that they may know of her immolation and ask about it, he came back in. Even though the lights were on, he felt as if the house was sunk in darkness. As if he had just remembered to do so, he went to have a bath. After his bath, he wore his pants and shirt. He checked the time. Five thirty. He picked up the phone to call Murugan. The very next moment he decided against it and put the phone down. His heart fluttered as if he had got caught committing a murder. His body trembled. His mouth was dry. He couldn't sit. He went out again. The girl across the street stopped drawing the kolam and asked, 'How is it now, sir?'

'Anything can happen any minute.'

'It was in his heart to set fire to her. His heart must be made of stone! Even to think of what he did is such a horror, sir.' She said. At that time, the headmaster of Kavanoor school, Rajamanickam, came by. He saw Natesan and spoke, 'I heard what happened, sir. How is it?'

'Still the same, sir.'

'It will become alright. Please don't worry.'

'Thanks.'

'If I don't go walking even one day I feel as if I have lost something. May I go, sir?'

'Yes, sir.'

As if his life would stop if he didn't walk fast, Rajamanickam took off at great speed.

The woman opposite who was drawing the kolam, finished her kolam and went inside. Natesan looked to see if the car was coming. He couldn't see it. He checked the time. Six. He called Kumar. Kumar didn't answer the call. Natesan was enraged. He called Kumar again. Kumar picked up the phone.

'It is time. I have been waiting for an hour. Where ... you are waiting at the petrol bunk? Couldn't you have filled petrol on the way? Is that so? Okay, okay. Come a bit quickly.' He put the phone down.

Natesan, who was sitting on the chair, had a terrible headache. When he thought of relaxing with his head on the table, his eyes fell on the book that was about the Vallalar's norms for life—he remembered another book, *Idarkalaiyum Thiruppathikangal.* He had bought it when he had gone for a Mutrothal at the Chidambaram Natarajar temple. He had read that book two-three times in the first week after he had bought it. People would read the particular pathikangal that they needed—the unmarried who were praying for marriage, the childless who wanted to be blessed with a child, the sick who wanted to be cured, those whose minds were disturbed for mental peace. The belief was that if you read those specific pathikangal your prayers would be answered. He began to search for the book.

All unnecessary objects struck his eye. All that should have been chucked into the garbage was kept safely at home. But only the book he wanted he couldn't see. There was no chance for the book to get lost or stolen. He thought that no thief in the world would enter any house to steal a book and continued to search for the book. Natesan became angry and bitter with the house and with Amaravathi. Since he couldn't find the book anywhere, he got tired and sat down on a chair.

'She is a girl without any luck.' He said, and picked up Vallalar's book that showed the norms of life. Below that book was the book he had searched for. When he saw the book, his heart, and his body, both felt a welcome coolness. He now believed that nothing could happen to Revathi. 'I am really a madcap,' he said and picked up the book.

In the Devara Thirumurais all pathikangal are filled with grace. They cut away turmoil and give peace. Saivism gives significance to thirty-six philosophical concepts. Having read that the Thiruppathikangal were also anthologised accordingly, he began to turn the pages of the book to spot the pathigam for praying for a cure to illness, and the line 'Seivinai vanthu emai theendappera Thiruneelakandam' ('our past deeds will not touch us, this I swear on Thiruneelakandam') struck his eyes. He began to read the pathikam for the cure of illnesses. When he read the line 'thayum ili, thanthaiyum ili, thaan thaniyan kaan edi' ('without a mother, without a father, a loner, how is he a god'), he was confused whether this was the pathikam he had to read. He went on to read another verse, 'thunjalum thunjal illatha pozhtheenum, nencham nainthu ninaimin, naalthorum vanchakam atra adi vazhtha' ('whether asleep or awake, if your heart melts thinking every day of the deception-less god'), the words began to look merely like black dots. He took the book and entered the poojai room. There were five or six pictures of gods there. He kept repeating, 'My daughter should come back alive.' He prostrated himself before the gods. He lay like that for a little while. The images of gods that occupied his mind faded away in stages and Revathi's image slowly replaced them. Beginning with how she looked when Amaravathi's mother came and placed her on his lap just a little while after she was born, when she walked for the first time, when she began to play, when she was admitted in school, how she was when she went to Chennai to study, when you leaf through a photo album, the way you see photographs in chronological sequence, the same way her form and his memories took life and she grew up in his mind.

He stood up and folded his hands in obeisance once again. He took the thiruneeru and, differently from his usual practice, smeared it all over his forehead. The distance between the house Revathi lived in and his house could not have been even one kilometre. Why had it never struck him to go there even once in those six years? Even though she shifted houses many times she always shifted within Burma Nagar into neighbouring houses. How was one kilometre an unwalkable distance? A thousand questions were raised within his heart but he had answers to none of them.

He started locking all the doors of the house one by one, beginning with the door to the garden. He locked the main door. He locked the gate. He stood on the street and looked to see if the car was in sight. The car was nowhere in sight. He called Murugan. Murugan picked up the phone.

'What happened? Has that woman come out? What did she say? She never went into the ICU? Shouldn't she have asked why they didn't call her? Oh, she asked and they said they would call later? How surprising! This is why we should have sent one of our people as the attendant. We made a big mistake, Thambi. Has that woman come out? When? About ten minutes ago? Okay, who talked to her? Not you? So, Arunmozhi talked? If Arunmozhi is next to you, give her the phone. She isn't close to you? I'll start in five minutes. Ask Arunmozhi to call me.'

He couldn't stand since hearing from Murugan that they had not called Revathi's attendant into the ICU. His legs felt like they had turned into rubber. His throat dried up. His body felt like it was on fire. His heart was beating much, much, faster than normal. He perspired profusely. It seemed as if insects were flying in his eyes. Unable to stand by himself, he held on to the gate.

He called but Kumar did not pick up the phone.

The woman next door was coming out and seeing Natesan she came to him and asked, 'What happened, sir?'

'It is the same.'

'We couldn't see her even though we were there yesterday. We were so sad. Even though we had travelled so much we couldn't have the good fortune to see her. Will she survive, sir?'

'Can't say.'

'Aiyo, so sad.' The woman melted in sympathy and asked, 'Did you come alone or has madam also come?'

'I came alone.'

'Why do our female children do like this? Yesterday, in Ulundhurpettai it seems a girl also immolated herself like Revathi. She didn't just immolate herself, she hugged her two children tightly and both died on the spot. Only that girl has been taken to Vizhupuram Hospital. They said in the news yesterday. I think that every day, if we take the whole country, at least ten-twenty people immolate themselves.'

'Could be.'

'We can't keep them at home. And if get them married they act like this. One has to live in fear every day. Shall I get you some tea, sir?'

'No need, amma. The car is coming, and I will leave immediately.'

'Wait a second. I will call my sir.' The woman went into the house.

The car arrived. Natesan got in. The car left.

'There were lorries and buses queued up in the bunk, sir. That's why I am late.' Natesan wasn't interested in listening to Kumar's explanation and said with irritation, 'Press on the accelerator, go fast.'

A street dog howled loudly.

16

Natesan couldn't sit straight. So, he leaned back and closed his eyes. He was scared to open his eyes and look around. It was as if he thought that a big accident would occur if he opened his eyes. The way he was leaning made him look like a corpse that had been lain there. Kumar who saw this in the rear-view mirror said, 'Nothing will happen, don't be afraid, sir.' He didn't hear what he said.

It was when the car had crossed Neyveli that the phone rang. He picked it up and spoke in a lifeless voice, 'Yes, Murugan. What happened? I am on my way and have crossed Neyveli. What are you saying? I should come later? What is the point saying it now? Okay. Did you talk to that woman again? Did you go and ask the nurse why she didn't call the attendant? What did she say in reply? She told you to see the doctor? I should return home? What are you saying? You think Revathi has died? Oh, god! They may say any time? Aiyo, god! They always say after eight o'clock? Oh, Siva! You might have to call the police? Okay, I will go back. Tell that woman to speak to me. Shall we assume it is over? Pazhani andava.' Even while he was saying that the phone slipped from his hand and fell. Without his saying so, Kumar drove to the side of the road and stopped the car.

'Should we go home, sir?' Kumar asked.

Since he couldn't speak, he gestured to Kumar to wait.

Kumar picked up the phone and gave it to him. He called Murugan. It was busy. He called Arunmozhi. It was busy. He called Amaravathi. She didn't pick up. Arunmozhi called. He picked up the phone and spoke.

'What, amma? Last evening itself, they had drawn the curtains around her bed? Did the other attendants say this? Everybody is saying it must have got over last night itself? Oh god! What is this? They didn't allow anyone near Revathi's bed? Only the nurse and doctor haven't opened their mouths yet? They will only say after eight? Only if we get the police, they will release the body? Okay, call me. I will be here only. My phone is switched on.' His body felt cold like never before.

'Just lie down on the seat, sir.' Kumar said. Natesan lay down on the seat like a child. Kumar started the car.

He stopped in front of the house and took the keys from Natesan and opened the door. He held Natesan in his arms and helped him into the house and to his bed.

'I will be in the car, sir.' Kumar said and went out.

PART FOUR

1

'Yes, Thambi. Is it over? When did she take her last breath? Don't know? Is this why they took the signature last night itself? I'll go to the station immediately. They'll release the body only in the presence of the police. I'll get them along with me. We have to come before four? What am I going to do for so long? I will come immediately. Why should I see whether that dog turns up or not? I'll take all the expenses and get the police along. My daughter is gone. Am I going to wait for that dog to go get the police himself? We called her "amma, amma", and he has made us call her a "body". You don't cry, appa. Why am I going to cry? My daughter's life is over. It is because I wanted her to stay alive that I acted all these years as if I had no eyes, as if I had no tongue. You disconnect now, I am leaving.' He kept the phone down and at the same speed locked the door. He came to the car and said agitatedly, 'Let's go, Kumar. We have to go to the police station.'

'You got the news, sir.'

'It is over, Kumar. They said just now.' Natesan cried.

'Sit down sir. Let's go.' Kumar started the car. When Natesan was about to climb in, Thamotharan from the house opposite came to talk to him.

'What happened, sir?'

'It's over. I got the call just now. I am going to call the police.'

'Will the body come here or go to the boy's house?'

'I'll get her body here.'

'Will that boy agree to it?'

'Who is going to ask that bastard? Do I need the permission of stray dogs to cremate my own daughter? I don't have time now. I need to go to the police station. I'll come.' He said to Thamotharan and got into the car quickly.

'Go straight to the police station.'

He called the Mangalampettai Inspector. The phone was switched off. He wondered whom to call, whom to catch.

The car arrived at the police station and stopped in front. He got out of the car and went in quickly. Two policemen were sitting inside. He went to them and said, 'Vanakkam, sir. My daughter named Revathi was burnt in a fire. She died this morning at JIPMER. They say the body will be released only if the police are there. They won't release the body after four o'clock. It would be good if someone comes with me sir.' Natesan spoke fast but with respect.

'Is that so? When did it happen?' Special Sub-Inspector Ramalingam asked.

'On the twenty-fourth, sir.'

'Please stay outside. We will send someone when the SI and the Inspector arrive.'

'It will get late, sir.'

'But you are telling us just now. Can we start immediately? Everyone has gone to Palakkarai where the strikers are blockading the road.'

Natesan didn't know what to say. He said very politely and in a mild voice, 'They say we cannot receive the body if we go late.'

'We are only two of us here, as you can see. The SI in charge of Law and Order has to come. It can be done only when he comes. I don't know if the FIR has been filed or not. If it hasn't been done, the FIR has to be filed. Wait a little while. Alright, did the police come to the hospital to do an enquiry?'

'Two people came, sir.'

'Do you know their names?'

'One was called Ganesan. The person who looked like a young boy was called Anantha Kumar.'

'Is that so? Neither of them has come today. I don't know if they are on leave or what. Perhaps they have gone to the street blockade site. We will know the status of your case only if the two arrive.'

'Do you know their phone numbers sir? If you give me, I will try to talk to them.'

'Don't be in a rush.' Ramalingam said and turned to Special Sub-Inspector Kuppusami and asked, 'Where have Ganesan and Anandha Kumar gone?'

'I think to the place where they are blockading the road.' Kuppusami said, writing something.

'A girl child going to Pre-KG fell off an auto and was hit by a bus and died this morning. That is why the blockade of the road. They have gone to clear the blockade. They will be back. Please wait for a while.'

'Please call and find out, sir. Mangalampettai Inspector is

quite close to me. He is the one who helped me that day. He sent two policemen.' Natesan spoke as politely as possible. He seemed to think that if the police came immediately all his worries would be over.

'We don't know how long this blockade will last. Then at eleven we have an anti-drugs rally. It is a procession by school children. The procession will go all around the town. They will come back only after everything is over. You go and have your tiffin and come back later. When you come, bring along four people to act as witnesses.' Ramalingam said patiently.

'Please have some consideration, sir. Expenses is not an issue, sir.' Natesan said. The phone in the Inspector's room rang at that time. Ramalingam got up quickly and went into the Inspector's room and spoke on the phone. 'Vanakkam. Virudhachalam Police Station. Ayya, yes ayya. A street blockade ayya. Everyone has gone there ayya. I'll tell them ayya.' He spoke very politely and then came and sat down in his chair as before. He seemed to be thinking of something. He then asked as if he had just become aware of his surroundings, 'How are you related to the girl who was immolated?'

'Appa, sir.'

As if there was no other question to be asked, he said dismissively, 'Wait outside please,' and went out with his cellphone in hand. Natesan stood there waiting. He looked at Kuppusami. He was writing something without a pause.

'Sir.' Natesan called him.

'Please wait outside.' Kuppusami said without looking up at him or pausing in his writing. Natesan looked around to see if anyone else was there. In the jail inside the police station, there were some young men sitting in their underwear. Their faces did not show any feeling or worry that they were in a police station. They were sitting happily as if they were in a movie theatre. When he saw that he went out as if he shouldn't remain inside. Kumar, who was standing outside the police station, asked, 'What happened, sir?'

'They say the SI has to come. The Inspector has to come.' Natesan said angrily as if reporting something distasteful.

'Ask their rates sir. That's the only way to get the job done.'

'I said I will pay for their expenses.'

'Aiyo, sir. You don't know how a station works. Did you tell them how much?'

'No.'

'You should say that.'

'How can I ask the police how much they want?'

'Sir, it is a problem here only if you don't ask. If you ask, there will be no problem at all.' Kumar laughed softly.

'Will you go and ask? Tell them I will pay whatever they want. Don't lower it by even one rupee. We want the police to come. That's all.'

'Okay, I'll come.' Kumar said and went into the police station. He returned as quickly and said, 'He said he would let us know when the SI comes.'

'They said they need four people as witnesses, Kumar.'

'I have the people. Should I ask them to come, sir? Our boys will be at the stand.'

'Drivers?'

'Yes, sir.'

'No need, Kumar. I'll arrange it.' Natesan called three-four people. To each of them, he said, 'I need you to sign something. Can you come to the police station for a short while? Then, come immediately please.' It seemed from his expression that all the people he had asked to come and sign as witnesses had agreed. 'Shall we go and see the SI?' He asked.

'Sit in the car for a while, sir. You are highly agitated. Something may happen to you.'

'My daughter herself is gone. I am old man, what will I accomplish by living any longer?' Natesan's eyes filled with tears. Seeing his face, and his tears, Kumar said, 'It will be a huge problem if we get caught in traffic, sir. However, let's try. Please sit down.' He got into the car.

They couldn't cross the office of the District Revenue Officer. Buses, cars, autos, and bikes had backed up from Palakkarai to the Office of the District Revenue Officer. 'We can't go any further, sir.' Kumar said.

Natesan felt as if his head would burst. He felt uncontrollable anger when he saw the traffic jam that extended for a furlong.

'Chee, what country is this? At the drop of a hat, they stop buses, they blockade roads. How do they turn a single person's loss into the loss of a thousand ten thousand people? Why do they admit a toddler in school?' Natesan lamented in his anger. 'Drive the car, Kumar. Let us go and stand at the side.'

Within a minute after they stopped, there were cars,

autos, bikes, and buses lined up behind the car for about two-three hundred meters. Natesan was astonished. His anger increased at the same time. Unable to show his anger, he said pathetically, 'Can we turn back?'

'Sit back, let me try.' Kumar said and tried to move the car. He couldn't move the car even five-ten feet either in front or behind. The number of vehicles was increasing moment by moment. Natesan was surprised that there were so many vehicles in this town. How to escape from this jam was a bigger worry now than Revathi's death.

'There is traffic in all four directions. The whole town has got jammed.' Kumar said.

'It was a mistake to send a toddler to school. A bigger mistake was to send that toddler to school by auto. Nobody asks the parents why they sent such a small child to school. They don't ask the school either. They are blockading the road because the driver ran the bus over the child and killed her. The death of a child is so difficult to bear. But how is it right to think that thousands of people who had nothing to do with this should die?' He burst out in anger. Kumar did not reply to it but only smiled slightly. Then, he said, 'They are blockading Palakkarai road because they know it will cause a massive traffic jam.'

'Are they doing it because of the sorrow of losing a child, or are they doing it to see their faces on TV?' Kumar did not reply to this but said instead, 'I'll go and check the situation, sir.' He started walking.

Kumar was a big strength to Natesan when he was nearby. Natesan felt lost when Kumar walked away. He looked at the vehicles standing in front and behind. The noise of the horns gave him a headache. What could he do? Nothing could be done. He leaned his head back in his seat.

'It is a problem when you don't have them, and children are a problem when you have them.' He said to himself despondently. He wasn't so disturbed when Amaravathi's appa and amma died, or even when his own appa and amma died, or when his thambi died. The deaths of friends, relatives, and acquaintances had registered only as news in his mind. Whenever relatives died or acquaintances died, he would say, 'We all are going to die one day.' He couldn't say that now.

In a few moments of the horns of the various vehicles together reaching a crescendo, the vehicles started moving slowly. He checked the time. He realised that they had been standing there for more than an hour in front of the office of the District Revenue Officer.

Kumar came running and saying, 'Sit back, sir,' started the car.

'Shall we go and see the SI?'

'If we go and see him now, he will get irritated, sir. Let us go back to the police station.' Natesan did not oppose this.

When the car arrived at the police station, Natesan got down. Kumar parked the car at one side and went directly into the station. He came back at once. 'What happened, Kumar?' Natesan asked.

'No one has come yet, sir.'

Natesan got a call. 'Yes, Raja. I am standing in front of the station only. Come quickly. Oh, you came once before? Okay, come now.' He kept the phone down. He looked around to see if the Inspector was coming. A quarter of an hour passed by. The Inspector arrived in a Tata Sumo. In another five minutes, the Sub-Inspector arrived on a bike. Four other policemen followed them one after another on bikes. Kumar stopped Natesan who was about to follow them in immediately, saying, 'Go in after five-ten minutes sir. If you go immediately, they will take out all the tension they have been under today on you. Also stand to a side sir. If they see you standing in the way, they will call you in and yell at you.' He didn't speak a word in reply. He was struck that Kumar knew all the characteristics of policemen. He went and stood near the car. He rang the Mangalampettai Inspector. His face lost all life when he realised the phone was switched off. The phone rang. He picked it up and spoke.

'Yes, she died this morning only. We'll take the body today itself. Can't keep it. I will let you know when we leave JIPMER.' He said to someone.

'Go in, sir.' Kumar said.

'Will you also come?'

'You should go alone. Go straight to the Inspector's room. That's how the work will be done. First room.'

Natesan went hesitantly and stood in front of the Inspector's room. 'Vanakkam, sir.'

'What?' The Inspector growled.

'My daughter immolated herself. She died this morning. They said only when the police come, they can release the body. I have been waiting since the morning.'

'Who are you?'

'Father of the girl who immolated herself, sir.'

'Where do you stay?'

'Periyar Nagar South, sir.'

'What do you do?'

'I am the HM of the Mangalampettai Higher Secondary School, sir.'

The Inspector looked Natesan up and down as if he was researching him. Then he asked, 'Are you an HM?' He said indifferently.

'Yes, sir.'

The Inspector rang the calling bell on his desk. The policeman who was standing guard with a rifle in hand came to the door of the Inspector's room and stood at attention after saying 'Ayya!'

'Who all are there?'

'Everyone is there. They are getting ready to go to the Anti-Drug rally, Ayya.'

'If Law and Order Selvam is there, ask him to come.'

'Ayya.' He went to the Sub-Inspector's room and came back with Selvam.

'He is saying something. Check what it is. And then among the two people injured in the accident on Karkudal Road last night, one has died at Cuddalore Hospital. Who is going to receive the body?'

'Don't know. I will check, sir.'

'I'll check the rally and come. Ready the papers. If the DSP calls tell him that I have gone to oversee the arrangements for the rally. I'll come back and question the three thieving dogs in the lockup. When the Crime SI comes ask him to talk to me. Tell all the available policemen to go ahead.'

'Sir.'

'Tell the driver to bring the car.'

'Sir,' said Selvam and came out of the Inspector's room and stood there. He said, 'All of you go to the rally. Ayya has started.' Seven-eight policemen ran out immediately. They mounted their bikes and sped away. When the Inspector came out and was about to get into the Tata Sumo, a man and a woman came crying and paid their respect to him. 'What?' He asked angrily.

'A guy has forced my daughter who is studying in Plus One to run away with him, ayya.' The woman cried.

'You don't know how to raise a daughter. Instead, you raise a hue and cry here. Come back at five o'clock and give a written complaint. Or go to the women's police station. Coming and standing in front when I am about to leave!' He shouted at her and then told the driver, 'Go.' The car started.

As soon as the car left, Selvam went back to his room and sat down.

Not knowing what to do, that man and woman continued standing outside the police station and began to cry. Natesan's heart was wrung looking at the way they were standing, the way they were crying.

'They will make them run away with them now, and then they will set them on fire and burn them.' He murmured to himself.

Natesan didn't know what to do next. He wondered why they found it such a problem to send just one policeman with him. Even though he was confused, he thought let what happens happen and went and stood humbly in front of Sub-Inspector Selvam's room. Selvam was talking to someone on the cellphone. 'Nowadays the cellphone is staple for everyone. I doubt if the world can carry on without it now. We can count the number of people in the world who don't have cellphones. Now a lot of crime happens only on the cellphone. Yes, yes. Taking photos of girls walking on the road, of women bathing at home, of women walking anywhere, and uploading it all on the net and making money. Everything is technology, sir. It is a huge problem to deal with. Let us see, sir.'

It is only after he had finished the phone conversation that Selvam noticed Natesan standing outside the room. As if seeing him for the first time, he asked, 'What do you want?'

'My daughter was immolated and died sir. The body is in JIPMER.' Before Natesan could finish, Selvam said, 'Please come in.'

Natesan entered the room.

'Is there anyone there?' Selvam asked.

A policewoman named Sumathi appeared outside the door and she said a polite, 'Ayya.'

'Who are all there?'

'Ramalingam ayya, and Kuppusami ayya are there. All others have gone for the arrangements for the Anti-Drug rally, Ayya.'

'Ask Ramalingam to come.'

'Ayya,' Sumathi said and went straight to Ramalingam to say, 'Ayya is calling.' Ramalingam got up immediately and coming to Selvam's room and standing outside the door, said 'Ayya.'

'Do you know about the case he is talking about?'

'He came and told me in the morning.'

'Has the FIR been filed?'

'I don't know. I will check.'

'Has someone gone for the body of the person who died in the Karkudal roads accident?'

'They have gone.'

'Who went to take the statements for this case?'

'Head Constable Ganesan, and Anantha Kumar.'

'Where are they two?'

'Don't know, Ayya.'

'Shouldn't they be the ones to go?'

'They can go, but if the Ayya instructs, some others can go.'

'Ready the papers. Phone the two of them and ask them to report to the station.'

'Ayya.' Ramalingam returned to this room and sat on his chair.

Selvam leaned back fully on his chair and stretched his arms. He yawned. As if he remembered Natesan only then, asked as if he was talking about ordinary matters, 'When did the event happen?'

'Twenty-fourth, sir.'

'How did it happen?'

'I don't know, sir.'

'Really?' Selvam's manner made it clear that he did not believe Natesan. Who would speak the truth in a police station?

'Yes, sir.'

'Where did the girl stay?'

'Burma Nagar, sir.'

'Where do you stay?'

'Periyar Nagar South.'

'Who are you to the girl who was immolated?'

'Her appa.'

'What do you do?'

'HM, sir. At the Mangalampettai Higher Secondary School.'

Selvam looked Natesan up and down. Whatever struck him, he called out to someone, 'Hey.' The policewoman Sumathi stood outside the door and said, 'Ayya.'

'Bring a chair.'

Sumathi brought a plastic chair, placed it in the room, and left.

'Please sit down.'

Natesan shrank into the chair.

'Don't you really know how the event happened?'

'We got the call at four o'clock. That is when we came to know about it.'

'What does your son-in-law do?'

'He drives an auto.'

'Your daughter?'

'B.E. Computer Science. She was a Merit student at Anna University.' Natesan's eyes filled with tears.

'Was it a love marriage?'

'...'

'Did the marriage take place, or did they elope?' Selvam jeered.

'I only had them married. It took place in Sabitha Kalyana Mandapam.'

'Do you have any suspicions about your daughter's immolation?'

'...'

'If you are suspicious, give it to us in writing. We can file a case and ask for remand immediately.'

'I gave in writing that it had happened on its own to the policemen who came to take our statements.'

'Why did you do that?' Selvam asked surprised.

'Such a deep wound in my heart.'

Seeing Natesan's face, and the way he was sitting and talking, Selvam said, 'You can change it even now. You have to decide whether you want a case or not. Did the two quarrel often?'

'He would get drunk every day and hit her, sir.'

'How do you know?'

'My daughter used to tell my wife over the phone. So, I know, though my wife would only tell me one in a hundred of what she knew. She would hide half the things thinking I would get angry. People in the street, people I met on the way, would also tell me.'

'Didn't you go and tick him off?'

'I didn't talk a word to him in these six years. Whatever conversation they had was only with my wife.'

'Is this daughter your only child?'

'I have a son, sir.'

'What does he do?'

'He works as a Team Leader in TCS in Madras.'

'Is he married?'

'Yes, sir.'

'What does that girl do?'

'She is also working as Team Leader in TCS.'

'Who among you would talk to your daughter often?'

'My wife only, sir. My daughter-in-law would also speak to her now and then.'

'Where are your wife and daughter-in-law now?'

'At the hospital, sir.'

'In Pondicherry?'

'Yes, sir.'

'I have to talk to them.' Selvam said and asked considerately and politely, 'Have you ever come to the station before this?'

'No, sir.' Natesan's eyes filled up with tears. 'Not wanting to face the ignominy of going to the police station and court was the only reason I had them married, sir. I let her remain with him for all these years. The place I didn't want to visit, for which I bore everything, I have finally come to that place.' Hearing the sound of crying, Ramalingam, Kuppusami, Sumathi, all of them came and stood outside Selvam's room and looked at Natesan. They then returned to their places. Natesan didn't notice anything and continued crying.

'Hey.' Selvam called out.

Ramalingam came and stood at the door.

'Isn't there anyone else?'

'Sumathi is around, sir.'

'Tell her to come.'

Ramalingam went away. Sumathi came and stood outside the door and said, 'Ayya.'

'Get some water.'

Sumathi brought the water and kept it on the table.

'Not for me. Give it there.' He pointed to Natesan.

'No need, sir.'

'It's okay. Drink.'

Sumathi handed him the water. Natesan drank.

'Call Ramalingam.'

'Ayya,' said Sumathi and she took the tumbler and went out.

'A girl educated in Anna University falls in love with and marries an auto driver. This is what everyone calls fate.' Selvam smiled. He asked Ramalingam who was standing at the door, 'Do you know the guy he is talking about?'

'His name is Ravi. You know him too, Ayya. The three people you caught and sat inside the lockup last week for fighting at the auto stand, he is one of them. The one with the beard.'

'Oh, that dog?' Selvam laughed sarcastically. He then asked, 'What happened to the papers?'

'I am getting them ready.'

'Do it quickly. We don't have time.'

'Ayya.' Ramalingam said and left.

The phone rang. Picking up the cellphone, Selvam said to Natesan, 'You too should go, and give your statement in writing.' He began to speak on the phone.

2

Natesan sat down on the bench in front of Kuppusami and Ramalingam.

'I had asked you to get four people to sign as witnesses. Have they come?' Ramalingam asked.

'They have come. They are standing outside, sir.'

'Ask them to come in.'

Natesan got up and went out quickly. Only Aravindan had come from amongst the people he had called. When he realised that the other three weren't there it seemed as if his head would burst in his sudden anger. He rang up Raja immediately and spoke, 'What happened, Thambi? I asked you to come then itself and you haven't come yet! Are you coming or not? Should I call someone else? What did you say? You are at the teashop? Okay, come immediately.' Rasa came running from the teashop in front.

'Did Satish come?' Natesan asked Aravindan.

'He is standing next to the Iluppai tree, sir.'

'Call him, call him.' Natesan shouted.

Aravindan ran towards the tree. Throwing down the cigarette he was smoking, Satish came running. 'I had asked a teacher, Devaraj, to come. Did he come?'

'He came sir. He was standing here only. I don't know where he went.' Aravindan said evasively.

Natesan called Devaraj. There was no answer. 'He can't stand in one place for even five minutes. He keeps running. What kind of a man is he? Even the one who rules the land will not run like this.' Natesan said frustratedly. He rang

Devaraj again. When the phone was picked up, he said, 'Sir, they are calling for signatures. If you have some other work, do it, and I will call someone else. Are you coming? Okay, please do come, but you must come immediately. We don't have time.' Natesan spoke in a rush. Within three to four minutes, Devaraj came on his bike from Periyar Nagar side.

'I will also sign, sir.' Kumar said.

'It won't be a problem for you?'

'How can you ask this, sir? I am also a man like the others' Kumar got angry.

'Very good. Come. We don't have time.' When they were entering the station, Murugan called. Natesan picked up the phone and began to talk immediately, 'What, Thambi? I am at the station only. They just asked for witnesses to sign. They are not delaying. It will get over now. I'll come now. Bye. I will call you later.' He finished the call quickly and walked in.

When he saw Natesan and the others, Ramalingam asked, 'So, you have come?'

'It is getting late, sir.' Natesan said softly.

'First you give us in writing on a white sheet.' Ramalingam began to search in the files on his table and in the drawers for a blank sheet. He couldn't find any.

'Do you have white paper?' He asked Kuppusami who was sitting next to him.

'No, appa.'

'I had kept more than ten sheets here. Who knows where it is lost?' Ramalingam began to search again in between files.

Natesan lost patience. He asked politely, 'Can I buy the paper?'

'Why should you take the trouble?' Ramalingam seemed to think for a minute then, as if doing a great favour, he said, 'Okay, go buy it.'

'Go buy a quire of paper.' Natesan gave money to Aravindan and hurried him away. He took off and returned almost immediately with the paper. Ramalingam took the quire of paper and gave a sheet to Natesan and said, 'Please write.' He took the paper and sat down on the bench. He tried to write. His hand shook. The pen slipped from his hand and fell. His eyes filled with tears. He looked down. The phone rang. He picked it up, 'Yes, Thambi? Yes, I am at the station. They asked me only now to write the application. What should I write? That we have our suspicions? Or that we have none? So, you feel we should say goodbye to the whole thing now? They say we can change our position even now. Why don't you ask Amma and let me know? No need? He has turned us into helpless females! Okay, I'll come. Am I saying no? Okay, appa, put off the phone.' He asked Ramalingam in a pathetic voice, 'What should I write, sir?'

'Write your address. State the relationship between the girl who died of immolation and you. Writer whether the incident took place on its own, whether someone abetted it, did someone else light the fire, and whether you have any suspicions about the event, and if so, write it clearly. If you have no suspicions, write that and give us.' Ramalingam said.

Natesan started to write. He couldn't hold the pen, which shook. The letters wouldn't be formed properly. Not only were they in lines and circles they also ran into each other. Everyone there looked at Natesan. He didn't look at anyone. Tears streamed down his face.

'Sit for a while. You can write later.' Kuppusami said.

'May I write, sir?' Aravindan asked. Natesan did not reply. He sat quietly for a while. He rested his head on the table to control the trembling of his body.

'I, Natesan, s/o Kasipillai, resident of Cuddalore District, Virudhachalam Taluk, Virudhachalam Town, Periyar Nagar South, 414, Kurinji Street, state that my daughter Revathi, resident of Cuddalore District, Virudhachalam Town, Burma Nagar, Rojappoo Street, was hurt badly in a fire accident that took place on 24.06.16 when she was cooking. She was taken to the Government Hospital at Virudhachalam, where she received first aid. She was then taken to JIPMER, Pondicherry, for further treatment. The treatment was not successful, and she died today, 28.06.16, in the morning at 8.05 am. I state humbly that neither my family nor I have any suspicions about her death.

Yours truthfully,

K. Natesan.'

When he signed the statement, he forgot that he was in a police station, that there were people all around, and he broke down and cried convulsively as if he had fallen into a fire.

Ramalingam read what Natesan had written. He screwed up his face immediately. 'This doesn't have any information about when they were married, whether they have any children, the name of the husband.' Natesan was furious and snatched the paper from his hands forgetting that he was a policeman.

'PS:

My daughter Revathi was married to a man named Ravi six years ago. My daughter has two children. My daughter's marriage took place in Sabitha Marriage Mandapam in Virudhachalam.'

Natesan began to shake with tears. 'Bloody criminal,' he said again and again.

Ramalingam, who took the paper, said, 'You cannot write this as PS sir,' and returned it. Kuppusami, who was watching all this, said. 'It's okay, Ramalingam. It is an issue only if there is a case. This is not a case. Just end the matter.' He took the paper from Natesan's hands and gave it to Ramalingam.

'He has made me write with my own hand that it happened by itself! What sin did I commit, oh god!' Natesan cried loudly again.

Ramalingam picked up a small thick notebook and said, 'The witnesses should sign one after another. First, write the name, then the address, and then sign. Write your mobile number as well.'

Aravindan signed first. Then, Raja, Satish, and Devaraj, wrote their address and signed, one after another. Kumar asked then, 'Are four people enough? Can one more person sign?'

'If there is, he could sign. Nothing wrong in it.' Ramalingam said as if he was helping them out. Kumar took the notebook immediately, wrote his address and signed. Ramalingam looked at the notebook and then took out a thick notebook that looked like a billbook and said, 'Sign here like you did in the other notebook. The order should not change. Once you have signed, you have to give your fingerprints below.' The five did accordingly and returned the notebook to him.

Ramalingam began to search for something in the files on the table and in the drawers. However much he searched, he couldn't find it.

'What are you searching for?' Kuppusami asked.

'I can't find the carbon paper. Whatever you keep here gets lost. I can see only the small carbon sheet. I want a big one.'

'Don't say that paper got lost in the police station, that carbon paper got lost in the police station. People who are watching us will laugh.' Kuppusami said and began to search on his table and in the drawers. He couldn't find any.

Natesan asked, 'Can I buy it, sir?'

'Don't think this is a badly run station because we don't have white paper or carbon paper. I don't know where I kept them. I was on leave for two days. So, the confusion.' Ramalingam began to search for the carbon paper again.

'It's okay, sir. I will buy it.' Natesan said.

'Okay, send thambi to buy it.' Ramalingam said.

Aravindan ran to the petty shop in front of the police station to buy carbon paper. Ramalingam began to search for something else. Natesan looked at his watch. He could see that time was going fast.

'Sir, it is getting late.' He said politely.

'Wait a bit. I am searching for the form I have to fill for JIPMER.' He began to search through all the files on his table.

'Come here, sir.' Kumar called Natesan. They went out to where the car was parked.

'Have you given the money or not?' Kumar asked authoritatively.

'Not yet. How can I give money inside the police station?' Natesan asked like a small child.

'What, sir?! Spending so much time! Just throw the money. If they don't receive the cash, they will spend all day searching for something or the other.' Kumar said with controlled anger.

'I am ready to give whatever they ask for. I never said I don't have money. Is money more important to me than my daughter?'

'What's the use saying this again and again. The money in your pocket should go into their pockets. Only then will the work be done. You wait here, sir. I'll go in.' Kumar went quickly into the police station and came back almost immediately with Ramalingam. When they reached the car, he asked, 'How much do we give for station expenses, sir?'

'It's your wish. Give what you want to.' Ramalingam said, his voice sounding considerate, the way it had never done before.

'Would five thousand do, sir?'

'Yes, we have expenses in the station.'

'Give him the money, sir.' When Kumar said this to Natesan, he handed over the money to Ramalingam.

'Give one thousand more.' Kumar said in an authoritative tone.

Natesan gave the money.

'Please keep this thousand for yourself. Please depute someone soon, we can't be late. We have to receive the body and cremate it today itself, sir.' Kumar ordered Ramalingam.

'You go eat and come back. The papers will be ready.' Ramalingam said considerately, and went into the police station.

'Couldn't they have asked this earlier?' Natesan said in frustration.

'They won't ask. We are the ones who have to ask.' Kumar laughed.

'I kept quiet thinking it could go wrong if we ask or offer the money ourselves. Not bad, you concluded the matter in a jiffy.'

'We could have given in the station itself. But recently they have installed cameras within the station. That is why I brought him outside. Just see, the papers will be ready in ten minutes.' He said confidently.

'If I had come earlier to this place, my daughter would be alive now.'

'You can't say that sir. Our time on earth is limited. Your daughter's time was up. That's all.' Kumar spoke with the firmness of an astrologer.

3

Kathiravan, the Secretary of the Tamil Nadu Progressive Party, who was travelling on his bike, saw Natesan and turned back. He stopped next to Natesan and asked, 'What are you doing here, sir?'

'My daughter died, thambi.'

'When sir?'

'This morning.'

'How?'

'…'

'The girl Revathi on the poster, is that her?'

'There are posters?'

'The people from the auto union are pasting posters on the Periyar Nagar bus stand just now. I didn't know it was your daughter. Where is the body?'

'At JIPMER. They say they will release the body only if the police are there. I have been waiting here since morning.'

'You should have sent word to me, sir. Come, let us see.' Kathiravan took Natesan along into the police station.

'Hello, Councillor. You aren't seen this side at all!' Ramalingam said with a false smile.

'I am here only. How can I stay away from the station? If we were the ruling party, I would have had to come every day. But we aren't even the opposition!' He laughed and then asked, 'Who is inside?'

'Law and Order.'

'I'll go see him.' Kathiravan entered Selvam's room. Sumathi came and placed a chair without being asked.

Selvam smiled at him and said, 'Well, Kathiravan, it has been a week since I saw you last.'

'Where can I go without seeing Ayya?' Kathiravan replied.

'Bring another.' Selvam told Sumathi. The chair came in a short while. Kathiravan forced Natesan to sit down. Then he spoke to Selvam, 'I studied under sir only. If today I know something it is because of sir. He is not the kind of man to come to places like this. Does Ayya know about his case?'

'I enquired.'

'If Ayya takes interest and sends someone fast, it would be good.'

'Why do you have to say so much? Just a word would do.'

'He didn't say anything to me. I was on the road and saw sir standing here and turned around. Other than studies, he won't speak about anything unless we broach the topic.'

'Sumathi!'

'Ayya.' Sumathi stood at the door.

'Call Ramalingam.'

Ramalingam came and stood at the door.

'What happened to the papers?'

'They are getting ready, Ayya.'

'For how many hours?'

'The FIR was registered only now.'

'What, you are registering three days after the incident? How did you send men to take statements without registering the FIR?'

Ramalingam didn't speak. Selvam's expression changed. He looked at Ramalingam as if he wanted to burn him.

'How many hours does it take to register an FIR? Having given a daughter to death how many hours will a man give duty at the station?'

'It is ready. I was waiting for Inspector Ayya to arrive.'

'What does this have to do with the Inspector? First, get the pad.'

'Ayya,' said Ramalingam and went to his room and giving him the FIR form and the application written by Natesan told Kuppusami, 'Write this immediately.'

'Tell me the FIR number.'

'You wrote the FIR for the Karkudal accident this morning, didn't you? Write the next number.'

Kuppusami began to write. Ramalingam began to search for something in the files on his table. 'I don't know where the form for JIPMER went!'

Natesan and Kathiravan came out of Selvam's room. Sitting down on the bench in front of Ramalingam's table, Kathiravan asked, 'What are you searching for, sir?'

'I can't find the form for JIPMER. They won't accept the form for our GH.' Ramalingam said and continued searching. Kathiravan also began to search in the files on the table. He picked up a paper and showing it to Ramalingam, said, 'Here it is, see?'

'You are the councillor!' Ramalingam said with a laugh and taking the paper began to fill in details about Revathi one by one asking Natesan for each detail.

The Secretary of Tamil People's Party, Arul, entered the room. Ramalingam and Kuppusami said simultaneously in one voice, 'Come in, Councillor.' Seeing Natesan there, Arul looked shocked and asked, 'What are you doing here, sir?'

'My daughter died.'

'Is that so?' Arul asked. Then he asked Ramalingam, 'What's happened to sir's matter?'

'It is ready. We can send in five minutes.'

'Sir, come with me for a minute.' He took Natesan to Selvam's room.

'Oh, have you also come for sir?' Selvam asked and smiled.

'He is my sir. A tiger in Maths. A teacher who would never take leave.'

'Really?' Selvam asked in surprise.

'Thambi is exaggerating, sir.' Natesan said in a subdued voice.

'Sumathi!' Selvam called. Sumathi came running from the next room.

'Ask Ramalingam to come.'

Sumathi went and Ramalingam came. As he entered, he said, 'It is ready sir. We can send it.'

'Who is going with the copy of the FIR?'

'Ganesan and Anandha Kumar went to take the statements. But they are nor here now.'

'Who else is available?'

'Abdulla.'

'Write his name down. Ask Abdulla to come.'

'Ayya.'

Ramalingam left. Abdulla came and standing at attention at the door, said, 'Ayya!'

'You come to Pondy with me. I need to examine the party.'

'Ayya.'

'Get the FIR copy.'

'Ayya.' Abdulla went to Ramalingam. He brought the pad and kept it on Selvam's table. Selvam signed it. Abdulla took the pad out.

'Should we do anything for the station expenses, sir?' Arul asked.

'What are you asking? You are speaking to us. Kathiravan

has spoken to us. Kathivaran himself sat there and wrote the FIR.' Selvam smiled. He remained silent for some time. Then he said slowly, 'I also studied in a Government School. It is because there were four good teachers that I am sitting in this place.' When he was speaking, Kathiravan entered with a pad in hand.

'What Councillor? You are bringing the pad?' He asked snidely.

'My teacher, sir.'

Selvam took the pad and signed, and called loudly, 'Abdulla.' Abdulla came running.

'Can't you bring the pad?' Selvam asked and threw the pad down in anger. Abdulla, who became afraid, didn't say anything and picked up the pad and left.

'Has the Inspector arrived?' Arul asked.

'Don't know.'

'I'll go and check, sir.' Arul said and went to the Inspector's room. Natesan also went out.

'Abdulla.' Selvam called. Abdulla came at once.

'Speak to the party and arrange for a car. It should be AC. Take the pad. Everything should be in order. If we go there and then find that something is wrong in one place or the other, we won't be able to receive the body. Then we will have to go tomorrow also. You should read the paper twice. Quickly. It is already one o'clock.'

'Ayya.' Abdulla said and went straight to Natesan and said, 'Sir, arrange for an AC car. We can leave as soon as it arrives.'

Natesan called Kumar, 'Kumar, get an AC car. Quickly.' Kumar rang up and called for an AC car.

As if it struck him just then, Kuppusami asked, 'Have we received intimation from Pondicherry police?'

'No, we haven't heard from them.' Ramalingam shouted not caring this was the station.

'It was wrong to ready the papers without intimation from them. We need to write the time, date, bed number as per their intimation. We can send our men only two hours after we have received the intimation.' When Kuppusami said this, Ramalingam's face changed abruptly. Natesan, who was listening to them, felt as if his heart would stop beating. He was so angry that his body seemed to be burning. His eyes brimmed over with tears. 'It is better to die,' he said and sat down on the bench.

'What should we do, sir?' Kumar asked.

'Who is there at the hospital?' Kuppusami asked.

'The girl's brother.' Kumar said.

'Call him at once and let him know. There is a police booth close to the emergency block, to the south. Ask him to go there and inform them of the girl's death. They will intimate us immediately. Quick.' Kuppusami said.

'Call him quickly. It is only after we get the intimation from there, and we reflect the information in our papers can we leave. Otherwise, we cannot proceed. If we do, there will be a legal tangle. The Pondicherry police will ask how we came without information. They won't release the body.' Ramalingam spoke in a rush.

Aravindan said angrily, 'How can they speak like this after taking our money?'

'Keep quiet now. Don't spoil things when they are about to be concluded.' Rasa cautioned him.

Kumar asked Natesan, 'Give me your son's number, sir.' He took Murugan's number and called him and told him about the issue and said, 'Quick, quick. You must run. We can leave only when we get the phone call from there.'

Only ten minutes must have passed. The police station received a call from Pondicherry police. It was Sumathi who picked up the call. 'Which ward? Which bed? Name of the patient, admission number, ward, date, time, time of death, date, the name of the doctor who signed the death certificate,' she asked for and wrote down each detail. Ramalingam took the paper from her immediately and began to read out the details and Kuppusami began to write them down fast.

4

Natesan got a call. He went out since he didn't want to talk in the police station. 'Yes, Thambi. It is done. Why would I delay matters? Have they taken the body to the mortuary? Siva! Alright.' He disconnected the call. At that moment, Head Constable Ganesan and Anandha Kumar arrived on their bikes. Seeing Natesan, Anandha Kumar stood respectfully to a side and asked, 'What happened, sir?'

'It ended in the morning, thambi.'

'Please come with me for a minute.' Anandha Kumar said and walked ten long steps to the east. Natesan followed him. He took out his purse from his pant pocket and took out a thousand rupee note and proffered it to Natesan.

'What is this for, thambi?'

'When we came for taking the statements, you gave money to the Head. This was given to me as my share. It was wrong to have taken the money after seeing the girl. Now, the girl has expired. I can't keep this money.'

'No, no.' Natesan was adamant in not taking the money.

'Buy her a garland with this money. Or use it for the "mortuary materials" they will ask you to buy to conduct the post-mortem.' He tried to force the money into Natesan's hands.

'No, keep it.'

'It was wrong of you to let him go. You should have had him arrested. He has killed a girl. He has sent two children to the streets. You let him go because you were ashamed to go to the police station and court. Is your honour and respect more important than three lives? Our honour is what we think it to be.

'Your daughter has died. Now she has no problems. Those children will have all their problems from now. They will fall in love in their arrogance. They will give birth to children and die. The children will have to cry all the time saying, 'My amma is dead, my amma is dead.' They should die yearning for her. Is this a problem that can be resolved through crying? Do something for me, sir. It is good for the children to be brought up by the mother's family only. If you can, please raise those children. Don't make them orphans by saying when my daughter herself is gone what do I have to do with them.' Natesan did not give any reply to Anandha Kumar.

'Do you know where I was since early in the morning? Some woman left a three-hour-old newborn baby girl in front of our GH. I am coming here after the baby was taken into the Government's Cradle Scheme for abandoned babies. Why, sir, are these women like that?'

'I don't have your maturity.' Natesan couldn't help breaking into tears as he said this. He began to cry without caring that he was on the road. His mind and body had shaken off all sense of shame.

'You should go. If someone sees, they will think wrongly.' Anandha Kumar said this and keeping the thousand rupee note in Natesan's shirt pocket, he went quickly into the police station.

Natesan walked to the entrance of the police station. Selvam and Abdulla came out at the same time. They both got into the car that Kumar showed them. Natesan ran inside quickly and said to Arul and Kathiravan, 'I'm going thambi,' and came out. Kathiravan accompanied him and told Kumar, 'Go fast thambi. Don't stop the car on the way. It is already late.'

Natesan said, 'I will go now,' to Raja, Aravindan, Devaraj, and Satish. All four said in one voice, 'Go quickly. Go and bring the body.'

Kathiravan and Arul said in one voice to Selvam, 'The body has to be received today itself, sir.'

Selvam said, 'It is such a wonder to see both Councillors speaking together,' and laughed.

'Even if we belong to different parties, we studied with the same teacher, sir,' Arul said. Kathiravan only smiled.

'Drive, appa,' Selvam told the driver. Kumar's car began to run behind Selvam's.

5

When they had crossed Kullanchavadhi and reached Thambipettai, four-five policemen stopped the cars. Selvam's car took off after pausing for a moment. Kumar got down from the car. The policeman who approached him said, 'Bring your RC Book, permit, and license and show them to the Inspector.' He then gestured with his hand to stop a lorry. Kumar stood there as if he had nothing that the policeman had asked for.

'Why are you standing, thambi? Go fast and show the documents.' Natesan urged Kumar. Kumar went to the Inspector and said, 'Sir, the Virudhachalam SI was in the car in the front, and we are going with him. We have to receive a body in JIPMER, we are going with the police for that only. I haven't brought anything in the rush.' The Inspector looked him up and down and went to the car. He asked Natesan, 'Are you going to receive a dead body?'

'Yes, sir.' Natesan got down from the car.

'Who is it?'

'My daughter, sir.'

'Okay, please sit.' The Inspector said, and then to Kumar, 'Hey, drive the car.'

'Do we have to see Ayya, sir?'

'You don't need to do any shit. If you go later than four o'clock, they won't release the body. Run.' The Inspector said.

'Thanks, sir.' Kumar said and started the car.

When they reached Cuddalore, Natesan received a call from Murugan. Natesan picked up the phone and began speaking, 'We have reached Cuddalore. I will be at the hospital in half an hour. What, that dog is saying he will take the body? You should have said no. Why did you say yes? Why didn't you ask me? What, Amma said she doesn't need to come to our house as a corpse? Why do you have to do what she says? My daughter's corpse, shouldn't I take it to our house and then to the cremation ground from home? Should I have to take it from a strange guy's house? She is not fortunate even in her death. We seem to stand aside till the end saying honour, honour, Thambi.' He was weeping when he kept the phone down. He couldn't sit and lay down in the back seat and closed his eyes.

Selvam's car went straight to the building where they did postmortems. Kumar's car was right behind the other car.

'Sir, we have arrived.' Kumar said. Natesan got down from the car. He seemed to have no energy to do even that. As soon as they got down from the car, Selvam and Abdulla went to the doctor's room in the postmortem building.

When they saw Natesan, Amaravathi, Murugan, Latchumi, Arunmozhi, all of them came to him. Latchumi cried on seeing Natesan. Murugan and Arunmozhi cried too. But Natesan did not weep.

'Why did you say the body could be taken to his house?' He asked Murugan loudly.

'I'll tell you later.' Murugan replied as if he didn't want to talk further on this.

'I will not lay my daughter down as a corpse in my house.' Amaravathi said.

'Come there,' Murugan took Amaravathi and stood at a distance.

Selvam, who came out of the postmortem building, asked Natesan, 'Please ask your wife to come here. I want to ask her a few questions.'

'Thambi, bring Amma here.'

Murugan and Amaravathi came.

'Come with me for a bit, amma.' Selvam walked with her separately. Stopping in the shade of a beech tree, he asked her, 'How did it happen, amma?'

'...'

'Normally, no SI will come to the hospital with the FIR to conduct an enquiry. I have come. There is a reason. I have my suspicions about this death. Mangalampettai SI also talked to me. If you speak the truth, we can file a case.'

'I gave him the girl. I gave twenty sovereigns. I fed them for six years. I paid the auto dues. I gave the house rent. I gave the advance money every time they shifted house. And finally, sir, I gave the statement, "My daughter died in an accident, no one is the cause for her death"!' Amaravathi spoke every word clearly and slowly. Then, suddenly, she cried aloud. She showed no hesitation or embarrassment in crying in front of a stranger. Selvam stood quietly, waiting for her to finish crying.

'Do you think she didn't die by herself?'

'He only killed her. He is that kind of a man. Did she do it to herself? I don't know. But my daughter is dead. I didn't see anything with my own eyes.'

'It is enough if you say even now. We can file a case. We can catch and throw him inside. We have the opportunity still. Let him stay inside for ten days at least.'

'Instead of going to police and court, it is better that my daughter's corpse goes to the cremation ground without any problems, sir.' Amaravathi spoke decisively.

'I don't understand.'

'If we file a case against him, he will go inside immediately. He won't let us receive the corpse. He won't let us cremate it. He will drink and come and shout, "Only I can receive the corpse, only I will burn it." He will create a ruckus. In his support, two loafers will come and stand in the street. For how many days will my daughter's corpse lie here? My daughter's corpse should not stink. Instead of his going to jail, I'd rather my daughter's corpse goes to the cremation ground in a proper manner. My daughter's corpse should go to the cremation ground without anyone lamenting, "How she is torturing us even after her death".' Tears poured from Amaravathi's eyes. She could not stand straight. She looked as if she was going to faint any time.

Selvam did not speak anything for some time. He looked at Amaravathi in astonishment. As if he was very tired, he said, 'I will write it happened by itself,' and took out the white sheet he had kept in his diary and said, 'Please sign at the bottom of this paper.' Amaravathi drew a line in the name of her signature.

'You can go, amma.'

Amaravathi folded her hands.

'Please, don't do that.' Selvam said and called Natesan to sign as witness. Natesan signed and said, 'I'll come and see you in the station tomorrow morning, sir. It is too crowded here.'

'Why do you want to see me in the station?'

'Just like that, sir.'

'You are standing here having lost your daughter, the apple of your eye. On top of it, you are giving a false statement so that you will be spared a court case. How can I take money from you? What a good decision you have made.'

'If my daughter were alive, and I had to go from police to court time and again, I wouldn't mind. When my daughter herself isn't there, what will I gain by filing a case? It is only for the reason that I shouldn't step into a station, shouldn't step into a court, that I had left my daughter in that house for six years. Even now, I am letting go for the same reason. Who will tell the world that a piece of shit is related to them?' Angry words and tears were pouring out of Natesan. Just then Abdulla came out of the postmortem building and said, 'The doctor's here.' Selvam started walking towards the doctor's room with Abdulla.

'Have you given the news to all those we need to?' Natesan asked Murugan.

'We didn't know whether we could receive the body or not till one o'clock. We didn't know whether the police would come or not. Even if we could take the body, we didn't know whether we could cremate it today. People have been sitting here unable to receive the body for two-three days because the police hasn't come. So, I decided to let people know only after you came. Only after I knew that you had started with the police did I talk to that dog about where to take the body. I told him that we want to cremate tonight itself.'

'Can we take the body today and cremate it as well?'

'I have told him. He is making preparations.'

'We could have taken the body home and taken it from there.'

'He is already drunk. He put on an act in the morning, rolling around screaming and crying "My wife is dead. How will I live now?" He rolled on the ground saying, "I am going to die, I am going to die," the actor. One couldn't talk to him. He keeps repeating whatever he says. He acts as if he is blabbering. No one who sees the way he acts will believe he was the one to burn her. What would he say if we insisted that we were taking the body to our house? What accounts do we have to settle after she is dead? She should burn peacefully in the cremation fire. She is already burnt.' Murugan let go of all his sense of shame and began to cry convulsively. Natesan too felt like crying, seeing Murugan weep like this.

'Who all do we have to inform?' Arunmozhi asked.

'We didn't tell many people about her marriage itself. Why should we inform them of her death?' Natesan asked. She didn't open her mouth.

A khaki-clad man who came out of the postmortem building asked, 'Who are the relatives of the body called Revathi?' Immediately, Murugan, Natesan, and all, ran.

'Go to the medical shop and ask for mortuary stuff. They'll give you. Buy it and get it here.' He said and went back.

Murugan went with Kumar to the main gate.

Natesan sat under a huge rain tree. Latchumi and Amaravathi who accompanied him sat down next to him. Only Arunmozhi kept standing. A car came and parked in front of them. Seven-eight of Arunmozhi's colleagues from office got down from the car and walked towards them. Arunmozhi went to them. All of them began to talk to her. Then, they stood around Natesan and Amaravathi, and began to ask many questions.

A little away to the west from where Natesan was, there were four groups of people sitting. There was a crowd standing outside the postmortem building. Policemen were busy going in and out.

'Why are they sitting in so many groups?' Natesan asked.

'They are waiting to receive their corpses.' Latchumi replied.

'All these groups?'

'Each one is waiting for its own corpse.'

'Siva!'

'Seven corpses have left here since morning.' When Latchumi was saying this, a man who came out of the postmortem room announced, 'Those who have come for Kattunemili Lalitha, come now.' Immediately, a crowd of seven-eight people ran to the postmortem building. Some workers brought the corpse out. A mortuary van came and stopped. They placed the body in the van. The van began to move the next moment. Four-five people ran weeping to a car and climbed in. The car started immediately. It looked like a scene from a movie. Only after watching that scene did Natesan ask, 'Have you arranged for a van to take the body?'

'We have arranged it. It is that black van standing to the west.' Arunmozhi pointed to the mortuary van. A car arrived at that moment. Seven-eight friends of Murugan got out of the car. They came to speak about Revathi's immolation to Arunmozhi, Natesan, and Amaravathi.

'We could have taken the body to our home. I am not able to spend ten minutes by myself even with my daughter's corpse. I don't know why Murugan took such a hasty decision.' Natesan showed his anger at Murugan. Latchumi, who was standing close said, 'Don't scold him. From the moment they said "Call the attendant" in the morning, he has been running here and there, to see the nurse, to see the doctor, he just ran everywhere. When they said, "Revathi is dead" the way he hit himself, the way he cried, all the people in the hospital gathered to see him. Each one of them exclaimed, "What an anna!"' Her eyes filled with tears when she recounted this. Wiping her eyes with her saree, she said, 'He is the one who brought the body out of the ICU, brought it into the lift, and then placed the corpse on the stretcher and pushed it to the mortuary. The hospital people just came along.'

'Where was that dog then?'

'His sister and he were with us only.'

'Why didn't you allow them to push the body?'

'That loafer came running to the body. He created a scene. He shouted, "amma, amma". He fell and rolled on the ground. Murugan didn't give way to anything. He said, "Don't come near." When he still came near, Murugan pushed him away. Once, Murugan even hit him three or four times. Even then he didn't go away. Even I couldn't believe that Murugan had so much love for Revathi. He must have bottled it up in his heart. She would have been so happy if she had known when alive that Murugan would cry so much, would be so shaken. Though she had education, though she had money, though she had loving relatives, she went away without enjoying anything. She was so unfortunate. If she had been fortunate, would she have suffered such a death at this age?' Latchumi cried silently.

'Where was your akka then?'

'She fell in a faint when she heard Revathi was dead. What a job it was to lift her and take her for treatment, get her the medicines and then the injection. I thought that she was going too. It was such a situation. On one side, the corpse had to be brought out, on the other we had to look after the unconscious woman. In all this someone had to control that loafer who was jumping at the body and crying. I didn't know whom to cry for. Almost went mad running hither and thither.'

Selvam and Abdulla came out. Selvam called Natesan.

'All the work is over. The body will come out in ten minutes. Receive it and see to all that has to be done. I'll go straight to Chidambaram and release the car. Please give him five hundred.' Natesan took out a thousand rupees and gave it to Abdulla. Then he said, 'You haven't eaten anything. I feel sorry for that.'

'If we had stopped to eat somewhere, we couldn't have brought the body out today. That is why I asked for a car as well. If we had come a little later, all of you would have been dying here today and tomorrow. What does it matter if we don't have one meal?'

'I'll give the lunch money to the driver, sir.' Natesan called the driver.

'No. I will eat at home. Don't give any money.' Selvam said firmly. He got into the car and said, 'I'll come.' The car started. Natesan folded his hands in the direction the car went.

6

Natesan came to the front of the postmortem building. He climbed the stairs and walked a bit ahead. In the west was a sign for the doctor's room. Some doctors and three-four policemen were sitting in the room. To the east, a door was open. One could see three-four men in khaki doing something inside. He opened the door slightly and looked inside. There was a row of stone slabs with corpses on them. There must have been more than thirty corpses there.

He asked a man inside, 'Which is Revathi's body?'

'The one lying on this stone slab. It is going out soon.'

'Can I see?'

'Go ahead.'

Natesan went inside. Revathi's body was lying stiff like

a goat that had been skinned completely. Here and there was some blood seepage. Fluid was dripping at places. There was not a thread of cloth on the body. His limbs shook uncontrollably. 'Amma,' he said and hitting himself on the face began to cry loudly.

'Go out. That is why we don't allow anyone inside.' A man glared at Natesan. Another man near him opened a quarter bottle of brandy and poured it into his own mouth. After finishing the drink, he came to Natesan and escorted him out.

Seeing Natesan coming out crying, not only Amaravathi and Latchumi, even Arunmozhi's friends who had come from Chennai, and Murugan's friends came running. Even Ravi and his sister who were standing apart at a distance and Ravi's friends who were with them came running and surrounded Natesan. Natesan saw Ravi. So much anger and rage burst forth from somewhere within him. He shouted loudly at Ravi.

'Is this how I gave my daughter to you, you beggar? You dastardly fellow. Go inside and see my girl. She is lying there like cooked meat. Don't stand in front of me. She protected you when she was alive, she has protected you even in her death. Go. There is no one now left to protect you. Go. Get lost. I will kill you, rascal. You don't know how sickening you are. You are a filthy dog. I should have finished you off a long time ago. I let you be. Now, my daughter is gone. What do I have to do with you? I am suffering the horror of seeing my daughter dead and you alive! God, what sin did I commit?' He hit himself again and again on his face.

A crying Ravi tried to enter the postmortem room. The man there said, 'No one can come inside. You will upset us.' And he shut the door.

Murugan arrived by car and, taking the mortuary materials, ran to the doctor's room. He gave the bag of materials. As soon as they said, 'Please wait outside,' he came out. Seeing everyone standing around Natesan and that Natesan was crying, he came running to them and asked, 'What happened?'

'He went inside and saw the body. He has been crying ever since.' Arunmozhi said.

'Why did you send him inside?'

'He went by himself.'

'Take him away,' Murugan said and only then he noticed that his friends had come. Tears came to his eyes when he saw them. He hugged each one of them and cried.

'Relatives of the body called Revathi, come.' When the man who came out of the postmortem room announced this, not only Murugan and Natesan, not only Amaravathi and Latchumi, but also Arunmozhi's friends, Murugan's friends, Ravi, his akka, and his friends, all went in a crowd to the door of the postmortem building.

'Who is receiving the body?'

'I am.' Murugan went to the front.

'Sign here.'

Murugan signed on three papers. The worker took two and gave one to Murugan. Then, he said, 'Give us something.'

'How much?'

'We are always with corpses. Live with them. Give us what you wish.' The man said smiling.

Murugan gave him a thousand. Two-three of Murugan's friends gave one hundred each, competing to show their generosity. The man took all with a smile and folded his hands to all of them. He said, 'Wait. I will get the body.'

They brought the corpse out. The more than thirty people who were there tried to see the corpse at the same time. A man in the crowd said, 'Check if a different body has been brought outside by mistake.' Latchumi and Arunmozhi checked to see if it was Revathi's body. Other than the face, the rest of the body was tightly wrapped in white cloth. It was Revathi's corpse.

'Bring the van.' Murugan shouted. The mortuary van came and halted. When they were lifting the corpse into the van, Amaravathi said, 'Don't lift her, don't lift her. I want to see her.'

'No need, Amma.' Murugan stopped her.

'Don't go near, Akka.' Latchumi held Amaravathi and dragged her back.

'Leave her alone.' Arunmozhi said authoritatively.

Amaravathi came to the corpse. 'Everybody please stand apart. Let her look.' Arunmozhi said. Amaravathi lovingly caressed the corpse from the face to the feet as if she was caressing a newborn baby. She pressed her face to the face of the corpse.

'Are you asleep amma? Sleep. You'll have no more problems now. You won't cry wondering whether you made a mistake. No dog can hit you now. You need no longer run to the house opposite or the neighbouring house to hide, afraid of his beatings. You don't need to hide anything in your heart, hoping your amma doesn't find out. You don't need to plead to anyone, "Please don't tell Amma."'

'Enough. Come, Amma. Get up, Amma.' Murugan said.

'Now, no dog will hawk and spit on your face. No bad words spoken by any loafer will fall on your ears. From now, it is only sleep for my daughter. Her tongue won't speak. Her body will not move. Her shadow won't fall on the ground. When you went to school, I would wait for you to come back in the evening. When you went to college, I would wait for you to come during the holidays. Where have you gone now, amma? From the time I heard you were dead I have stopped worrying. I have stopped crying as well.'

'Come away, Akka. Let the corpse go.' Latchumi pulled Amaravathi by her hand.

'You made me wait for your death. You made me say with my own mouth that it would be good if your life ebbed away. You are not dead, my golden one. It is only when I, your mother, die that you will die. Till I am alive you will live in my heart, amma. My daughter, sleep well.'

'Amma.' Murugan shouted.

'Let her cry.' Arunmozhi said.

'Now, my mind is not agitated like the ocean. It is not burning like fire. You are asleep, isn't it? That is why my mind has calmed down. My body has cooled. I am not doing anything. I am incapable of doing anything.'

'It is five o'clock already and we are still here. Don't we have to take the body and cremate it?' Anbu, who had come with Ravi, said.

'Who are you, you bastard? All bastards should keep their

mouths shut. We are the relatives of the corpse. Stray dogs should not speak. Let her cry. We cannot come to that house to cry.' Arunmozhi said enraged.

'Hey, none of you should speak.' Ravi said loudly.

'You made me sit for four days for your death. You didn't die, amma. It is your fear that is dead. From now you won't feel hunger. You won't feel thirst. Sleep, amma. Sleep peacefully. Now what can affect you, my princess? Sleep, precious. There is a place for everything. But there is no place for you to stand apart in this world, on this earth. You didn't see the state your appa and anna were in these four days. Thambi, your thangai has fallen asleep. God, no mother should meet this fate of seeing her daughter in this state.'

'Come, amma.' Murugan held Amaravathi and lifted her and took her to the car and made her sit inside. They lifted the corpse into the mortuary van. The van started. Kumar's car followed the mortuary van. Next was Ravi's car. The one following was the car with Murugan's friends. Finally, the car with Arunmozhi's friends followed. The funeral procession had started. When they passed the emergency block, Amaravathi turned around to look.

She could see a girl who had been immolated being brought down from an ambulance which had just arrived and being placed on a stretcher and pushed inside.

THE END

smooth [illegible] We are the [illegible] for [illegible] that [illegible]

[illegible] Aryan [illegible]

[illegible]

place [illegible] and [illegible] on this [illegible] earth [illegible]

[illegible]

[illegible] passed [illegible]

[illegible]

ACKNOWLEDGEMENTS

I must thank Mini Krishnan, CS Lakshmi, and Abhirami Sriram for encouraging me to translate the book, and Imayam for trusting me with it. Both Mini and Lakshmi ensured that I got off to a good start! Imayam suggested that we change the title of the book in translation and participated fully in the process. Many thanks.

As usual, I must thank my first reader N Kamala, whose criticism is always of immense help, and then thank Shubha and Julius who still found a way of supplying cups of tea even if they were in a foreign land by simply hosting us there.

Thanks are also due to my sister Anu who is my constant sounding board.

ABOUT THE AUTHOR AND THE TRANSLATOR

Imayam is a major contemporary writer in Tamil. He has published seven novels, seven short story collections and a novella so far. Among the various awards he has won are the Sahitya Akademi award (2020) for his novel *Selladha Panam*, and the Kuvempu Rashtriya Puraskar National Award (2022).

GJV Prasad, poet and translator, was Professor of English at Jawaharlal Nehru University.

